THE LUCKY LIST

A ST. PATRICK'S DAY ROM COM

MYA MORE

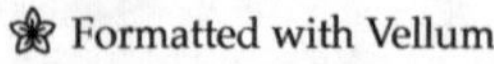 Formatted with Vellum

To all the moms who feel alone, feel like they're doing this wrong, feel like they're not enough. You're not alone. None of us know what we're doing all of the time. And you are enough. You are an amazing mom, even if your walls are covered in crayons, your floors are littered with Band-Aid wrappers and Hot Wheels, and every surface of your kitchen is covered in a sticky substance you're pretty sure is syrup.

This hot firefighter's for you. May his ladder bring you to new heights.

CONTENT WARNINGS

Mention of a miscarriage & infertility (side character)
Impact play (light BDSM)
Poop and fart humor… a lot of it.

You know your limits and triggers. Your mental health is important.

Any scenes with kink depicted in this book are for entertainment purposes and are not intended to be educational or accurate depictions of a BDSM/kink lifestyle. Please do your research before engaging in similar acts to make sure you are your partner(s) are informed and safe.

DICKTIONARY 🌶

For anyone wondering where the steamy scenes take place—whether you're eager to dive right in or prefer to skip them altogether—you'll find them in the following chapters:

🌶 Chapter 10
🌶 Chapter 12
🌶 Chapter 14
🌶 Chapter 18
🌶 Chapter 20
🌶 Chapter 21
🌶 Epilogue
🌶 Bonus scene (download)

PLAYLIST ♬

Lucky - Britney Spears
Miss Independent - Kelly Clarkson
Wood - Taylor Swift
Firefighter - StoryBots
Camera - Ed Sheeran
DAISIES - Justin Bieber
Lucky Girl - Carlina
Pokémon Theme - Pokémon
ME! (feat. Brendon Urie of Panic! At The Disco) - Taylor Swift
Get Lucky (feat. Pharrell Williams and Nile Rodgers)
Lucky - Jason Mraz, Colbie Caillat
Here Come the Grannies! - Bluey, Joff Bush
Certain Things (feat. Chasing Grace) - James Arthur
Like I'm Gonna Lose You (feat. John Legend) - Meghan Trainor)
Irish Blessing - The Harmonic Circle
When You Have to Go Potty, Stop and Go Right Away! - Daniel
Tiger's Neighborhood
Lucky Star - Madonna
Fireman - Lil Wayne
Irish Blessing - Sarah Holthusen
Curious George Theme Song - Dr. John

Brave - Sara Bareilles
Slow Hands - Niall Horan
Lucky - Jonas Brothers
Bluey Theme Tune Extended - Bluey
Irish Celebration - Macklemore & Ryan Lewis
Would That I - Hozier
I Love Lucy - Dutch Melrose, benny mayne
PAW Patrol Opening Theme - PAW Patrol
Scars to Your Beautiful - Alessia Cara
Mom Life - Heather Evans
Lucy - Claire Rosinkranz
Four Times Table - Numberblocks
Lucky - Pinto Picasso
We Will Rock You - Remastered - Queen
The Poop Song - Teddy Casey

CHAPTER 1

LUCY

"Boys have a penis, and girls have a… a buh-gi-nuh." Micah splashes a gallon of bathwater over the side of the tub as his little brother Levi chants "PEE-NIS" on repeat. "And there's a hole in your penis, and that's where the peepee comes out."

"Pee pee! PEE-NIS!" Levi hits the S hard as he grabs an empty shampoo bottle and fills it with water, then pretends to pee with it, spraying me in the process.

I reach for another towel in the closet and come up empty. Why are there never any clean towels? Where do they all keep going?

They're probably in the hamper. I really need to do another load of laundry.

It's just another Saturday night in our house, except now with more colorful language since my oldest has decided to give my youngest a biology lesson. "Boys, it's okay to talk about this stuff at home—"

"About penises and baginas?"

"Right. That. But you do not talk about that stuff at school. Understand?" I attempt to wrangle Levi so I can rub some shampoo in his hair.

"Okay, Mommy," Micah says.

"PEE-NIS!" Levi squeals.

I'm so screwed.

If I get another call from Levi's preschool, I will lose my mind. Levi keeps getting in trouble for using inappropriate language. Apparently, he's the only one in the class with an older brother to teach him these words. Thankfully, Micah's teacher is my friend Bella. She's much more understanding about things like this.

Levi's preschool is not as understanding.

These are the parts of motherhood I wish someone had prepared me for.

Levi splashes me with water from his empty-bottle-turned-squirt-gun, and I shake my head, clearing my intrusive thoughts. I love my kids, but I'm exhausted.

"Okay, you two are turning into prunes, so let's finish up and get our jammies on." I soap up the washcloth and hand it to Micah, and he does the quickest full body scrub known to man.

"I think you missed a couple spots there, buddy." I turn to Levi, handing him another soaped-up cloth. "Your turn. Wash your body."

"I can't. It's too hard. You do it, Mama."

And because I want to enjoy a glass of wine before I go to bed and we're already running behind schedule for their bedtime, I decide to pull out my go-to. "I bet you can't do it faster than your brother."

Levi sizes up Micah, takes the rag, and proceeds to do an even worse job than his older brother.

Whatever. Good enough.

"I win!" Micah declares.

"Nuh-uh!"

"Yes-huh. You didn't clean your penis and testicles," Micah says.

"TESS-TICK-UH-BULLS!" Levi shouts as he haphazardly

rubs the washcloth all over his privates. "Look at my pee-nis, Mama. It's floppy. I make it dance!" He then proceeds to wiggle his hips side to side, causing his penis to indeed dance. Micah decides he wants to try the penis dance too, and pretty soon they're shaking their penises in unison. I drop my head to hide my smile. It's really hard not to laugh at their potty humor, but I need to be the adult here.

"Okay, that's quite enough."

"Swipe the card, Mama!" Micah whines.

I groan. When do boys learn how to successfully wipe their own asses?

In my early days of parenting and potty training, in an effort to teach them about said wiping, I likened washing their cracks to swiping a credit card through a slot. It helped in bath time and potty training, but now I regret it.

In unison, they turn around, holding their cheeks open as they bend over.

"Look at my booty, Mama!" Levi squeals as both he and Micah break out into giggles.

Did I think this is how I was going to be spending my Saturday nights as an adult? Double-fisting washcloths while two little boys bend over—asses way too close to my face for comfort—so I can swipe their cheeks in a synchronized ballet of private part washing after I've already watched a pas de deux of penises?

No. No, I did not.

But I wouldn't trade my boys for anything in the world. I just wish they would learn how to wipe their butts. And pee in the toilet. And stop talking about farts in public.

Once I get my feral monsters toweled off, teeth brushed, and in pajamas, it only takes four books, five rounds of snuggles and scratches, and three songs to get them tucked in. The moments when they're finally calm, drifting off as they cuddle up to me, make everything worth it, and I know I'll miss these days when they're older. Hell, I already miss the ones that have passed.

Their mere existence is a blessing of me making my own luck, and I love them, but being a single mom to two rambunctious young boys has drained my energy, my sanity, and my bank account. And I'm low-key mad that no one told me to invest in Pokémon and Band-Aids when I found out I was having a boy. If I had, I'd be rich by now instead of living off a meager teacher's salary.

But that's my luck, or rather my lack of. If the word "unlucky" had a picture next to it in the dictionary, it would just be my face. I can't catch a break in any area of my life. Growing up in a volatile household, I learned early on that I could only depend on myself. I've dated a few men, and each one was great...until they weren't. The last one was particularly awful, making me question my self-worth.

Sure, I have a great job that I love, but every year I get stuck with the most difficult students. And it seems like other teachers have their shit together way more than I do.

And I have friends I love, but I'm way too independent to ever let myself depend on them. What if they see how chaotic my life and brain really are and leave me too?

Even my body has felt unlucky at times. Endometriosis affects one in ten women, and I'm one of them. The one thing I ever knew with any certainty was that I wanted to be a mom, and I was determined not to let luck fuck me over on that front.

Once I pour myself a glass of chardonnay, I settle onto the couch and pull up the group chat, overwhelmed with how behind I am. Our bedtime routine takes thirty minutes most nights, which means I've missed countless messages and dozens of long voice memos. I'm about to close it, resigned to catch up with the girls later, when my name in a text catches my attention.

Bella: LUCY! Where are you? We found you a piece of Grade A man meat! Do you copy?

Raven: Bella, you're at a ten, I'm gonna need you to take it down to a two.

Bella: 😙

Summer: [photo of a guy who resembles a younger Ben Affleck]

Bella: He kinda looks like Ben Affleck back in the early 2000s when he was cute.

Raven: Why are we shopping for men for our friend?

Summer: Wouldn't it be cool if we could actually shop for men? Make a list and find someone that has everything you want?

Bella: Ooh I love lists!

Raven: I'm pretty sure you can. That's what dating apps are for.

Raven: Summer, I've seen how picky you are when we go shopping, are you sure you wanna put a guy through all that?

Summer: Every house I sell goes through a thorough inspection. I don't want to let any clients end up with a dud of a house. There's nothing wrong with having high expectations. I want to know what I'm getting into before I commit to a thirty-year mortgage. I think it's only fair that I do the same with men.

Bella: So you don't end up with a dud?

Then there's a four-minute voice memo where Summer lists all the parts of a house inspection and compares each to her requirements in a guy. I listen to it at 2x speed to try to get caught up. It's very thorough.

Raven: Sounds romantic.

Bella: It is! She wants someone to check all her boxes before he checks her box.

Raven: …

Bella: Her lady box. You know. Her vagina.

Raven: 🙂

Me: I've had enough vagina tonight.

Raven: Ummm, I'm gonna need you to elaborate.

Me: Enough vagina talk. Not actual vagina.

Bella: Is Micah still talking about BAGINAS?

Me: Yes. Thanks for that.

Summer: What is happening now?

Bella: During story time yesterday, one of the kids gave us a full lesson on private parts before I could stop him. It was worse than the fart that stopped class for thirty minutes last fall! Micah was particularly fascinated by the topic though.

Me: I could hear your entire class laughing during fart-pocalypse.

Summer: But did you hear the fart?

Me: No, just the fallout.

Raven: I don't know how you two do it. I love my kids, and all of yours, but that's my limit. There's no way I could put up with a bunch of tiny humans all day at work.

Summer: Can we circle back to the meaty man?

Bella: Yes!

Me: Can we not? I love you guys, but I have terrible luck when it comes to dating.

Summer: That's why we are intervening!

Bella: We know what you like. We'll find you a good one.

Raven: She likes firefighters, that's all she talks about ever since that calendar came out.

Bella: I'm pretty partial to Mr. December.

Raven: We know.

Summer: Which firefighter are you partial to, Lucy?

Raven: To which are you partial?

Bella: Nobody cares about grammar in DMs, Raven.

Raven: Sorry, old habits die hard when you stare at newspaper copy all day.

Bella: Hey ladies, what's black and white and read all over?

Raven: That joke only works when you say it out loud because read is a homophone for red.

Bella: I wasn't gonna say a newspaper.

Summer: What were you going to say?

Bella: A sunburnt penguin.

Raven: 😐

Bella: That killed with the kindergartners.

Summer: Can we get back to Lucy's date?

Bella: Thanks for wrangling the kittens, mom!

Summer: I got you.

Raven: Kittens?

Bella: Kittens are hard to wrangle because they do what they want and wander all over. Just like this convo.

Raven: Ah.

Me: I'm not going on a date. When would I even have time?

Bella: We'll help.

Summer: He's a man in uniform!

Raven: What kind of uniform?

Me: Is he a firefighter?

Summer: …

Raven: 😖

Summer: He's my cousin's best friend's older brother…in-law.

Bella: Come again, now?

Raven: I couldn't follow that if I tried.

Me: So you don't know him personally?

Summer: Not technically, but he's cute. I sent a picture earlier. Scroll up.

Me: Oh yeah. I saw it.

Summer: So, what do you think? Can I set it up?

Me: Summer, are you sure you don't want to date him?

Summer: He's not my type.

Raven: Yeah, her type is her best friend's brother. 😅

Summer: Oh my God, Raven. That was one time!

Bella: What was one time?

Me: You don't know this story?

Bella: What story? Tell me the story!
Summer: I kissed Raven's brother RJ in tenth grade. It was during a game of truth or dare.
Raven: He still asks about you.
Me: He does not!
Bella: Wait, there's more to this story, right?
Summer: You're lying. He definitely does not ask about me.
Raven: Yes, he does. He wants to know if you still have your braces.
Bella: Why would he care about that?
Summer: OMG HE DOES NOT 🪨
Me: Shut up!

I giggle, kicking my feet as I take another sip of my wine, thankful to have distracted them from setting me up.

Bella: What am I missing?
Me: I can't believe you've never heard this story!
Bella: We weren't all the same year back in school.
Me: Yeah, but I know we've talked about this at an after-hours PTO meeting at the bar.
Bella: If I was drunk at one of those, I wouldn't remember anything.
Bella: Can someone just tell me!
Raven: Someone dared Summer to kiss my brother.
Bella: Who dared her?
Me: Raven did!
Bella: 😶
Raven: I knew she had a crush on him. I also knew he was a disgusting creature, and I figured if she kissed him, she'd get over her crush and move on.
Bella: I appreciate the logic. Very on brand for you.
Me: Oh she got over him alright!
Bella: Was he a bad kisser?
Raven: You could say that.

Summer: It wasn't his fault!
Bella: WHAT HAPPENED?
Me: They got stuck together!
Bella: NOOOOOOOOOO
Raven: Yes. My idiot brother came in all hot and mashed his face into hers and their braces got caught.
Summer: He's not an idiot. He was sweet.
Raven: He drooled all over you.
Summer: Because we were stuck together!
Bella: This is amazing!
Summer: He was really sweet about everything, but I was mortified because it was my first kiss.
Bella: It was not!
Me: Wait. Really? I didn't know that part.
Raven: It was his first kiss too.
Bella: SHUT UP! THAT'S SO ROMANTIC!!!
Summer: It was the opposite of romantic.
Me: Sounds like he has my bad luck.
Bella: Is he single?
Raven: Tired of Hardy already?
Bella: Not for me, for Summer.
Summer: Nope. We're shopping for Lucy's man meat. I am off the meat market.
Raven: Eww. Please don't use the term meat when referring to my brother.
Summer: So should I set up the date, Lucy?
Me: With brace face?
Raven: Hehe, now that nickname I like.
Summer: No, with your hottie in the uniform.
Me: What kind of uniform?
Bella: Does it matter? It'll look good on your bedroom floor.

Me: And you promise he's not a creep?
Summer: I don't think he is.
Raven: That does not inspire confidence.

Summer: But he's so cute! He looks like Ben Affleck!
Me: He is cute. And I do love a good butt chin.
Raven: You mean cleft chin.
Summer: Then it's settled?
Raven: You could just play it safe with coffee.
Me: Raven, you have the most sense out of all of us. Why are you encouraging this?
Raven: Honestly, I don't know.
Bella: I'll watch your class.
Summer: I'll set it up.
Me: Oh my God, you guys placed a bet, didn't you?

I sigh and take another gulp of wine. Our group is known to do this. Last Christmas the three of us placed bets on Bella and Hardy falling in love. Our DM has gone suspiciously quiet, and I know I'm not getting anything else out of them, so I finish my wine, resigned to my fate.

Me: Fine, set it up.
Summer: Yay! You should make a list!
Me: What kind of list?
Raven: How about a list of desirable traits you're looking for in a man in case this one doesn't work out?
Bella: Boring! Make a sex list!

I think over their suggestions. Bella is the only one I've shared much about my past with, all the shitty men that have let me down. I've been called fat, boring in bed, forgettable. I sure know how to pick 'em, huh?

But the thought of making a list is pretty tempting. I rip a slip of paper out of one of the half-colored-in notebooks the boys have destroyed and start jotting down some ideas. If I'm going to jump back into the dating world, I might as well be clear about what I want, even if I'm the only one who will ever see this.

Lucy's Get Lucky List

1. Be less boring in bed
2. Role-play
3. Have multiple orgasms
4. Tie someone up
5. Sit on someone's face
6. Spankings?
7. Hook up with a guy with an accent. Mr. March? I wish!

CHAPTER 2
MIKE

A call comes into dispatch for medical up at the school. It's never the kind of call you want to get, but at least it's not life-threatening, so there's comfort in that.

When we pull up on the scene, Principal Adams directs us to the playground. It's one of those rare fifty-degree days in Chestnut Mountain where you forget you're in the middle of February. Much different from the mild temperatures of Ireland.

I spot Bella, and she waves me over. She's sitting on the ground in the empty playground next to a little boy clutching his arm against his chest. "Hey, Mike."

"Who's your friend?" I ask as I squat beside them.

"This is Micah."

"Hey, Micah, I'm Mike. It's nice to meet you."

Micah doesn't move, just pulls his arm tighter against his body.

I look at Bella. "Is he shy?"

Bella leans closer to me, lowering her voice. "He's not a big fan of men."

I nod at her, letting her know I've got this. "Do you want to check out my ambulance over there?"

Micah's eyes flick over to the rig briefly before settling on the ground in front of him again, a small sniffle causing a tremor in his body.

"Hey, Bella, do you know someone who'd like to push the buttons? Maybe turn on the lights and the siren?"

Micah straightens and raises his good arm like he's in class waiting to be called on.

"No fair. Hardy said I'm not allowed to touch any of the buttons."

"Hardy's back at the station. I won't tell him if you won't."

Bella laughs and looks over at Micah. "First one there gets to toot the horn."

"Actually, let's walk over there. Don't need anyone else getting hurt now," I say, looking between them.

Bella winks as she pretends to be at the starting line of a race. "Ready, set, go!"

Micah walks over to the rig, right as Bella pretends to trip and then dramatically falls to the ground. "Save yourselves! Go without me!"

I open the door to the cab, and my partner Rudy shows Micah all the buttons, pointing out what each one does. After several minutes of pressing every button he can, he reluctantly lets me look at his arm.

Bella brushes herself off and joins us.

"Have his parents been contacted?"

"His mom teaches with me, but she's off today. I'll let her know. How bad is it? She's kind of preoccupied right now, and I don't want to freak her out if it isn't a big deal."

"It's well and truly banjaxed."

"What?"

"Broken. I'd like to take him to the hospital to get it checked out. It's probably a minor fracture, but they'll be more equipped to handle it just in case it's not."

"Shoot. Okay, I'll call her." She pulls out her phone and

dials. And waits. And dials again. "Crap. She's not answering."

The principal walks up and pats Bella on the back. She's an older woman with grey hair and a smile that could light up a room. She looks like trouble. My kind of people. "Bella, I can watch your class the rest of the day and take your kids home. Why don't you go with Micah until Lucy can get there?"

"Can Miss Carlisle sit with me?" Micah asks hesitantly as I help him into the back of the ambulance.

I shrug and look at her. "It's grand by me, but if you come with us, I can't promise ya a lift back now."

She waves me off. "It's okay. We'll figure something out. Oddly enough, Micah's mom is usually the one giving me rides. Let's get this kid to the hospital."

We load up the rig and head toward Denver. Micah is very quiet during the ride, but he takes everything in, looking at all the equipment as I pull out a SAM splint and start forming it to stabilize his arm.

The vehicle jolts, bumping us around a wee bit, and Micah lets out a yowl when his arm knocks against the side of the stretcher. Big tears spill down his face as he starts hiccupping in breaths.

Bella squeezes his good hand and wipes his face with her sleeve. "It's okay, buddy. I know it hurts, but you're being so brave. We're almost there." She looks at me on the last part, and I nod.

I hold out a stethoscope, gesturing for Micah to take it while I reach behind me for a sterile glove. Once she distracts him, letting him listen to her heartbeat, I blow up two gloves and tie them off, drawing a silly face on one of them with a marker.

"Here you go." I hold out the blank glove, and he takes it, then I show off the one I made with the face.

His responding giggle comforts me more than it should.

There's something about this kid that draws me in. I like to help people, and I've got a knack for especially difficult cases.

"That looks like Squirtle!" he squeals, looking at my glove balloon.

I twist it back toward me, and feckin' hell, the kid's right. "Don't tell me you're a Pokémon fan?"

Micah nods.

"Should I draw his signature shades?"

Micah shakes his head, and I hand him the marker as Bella holds the balloon in place for him to draw on one-handed. He draws a decent-looking Pokémon himself.

"Is that Binacle?"

"It's hard because he's 'posed to have two heads, but I can't draw both or the rock."

"True. But you could flip it over and pretend that's the other head."

His eyes get big, and I watch as Bella flips over the glove for him to continue while I slip his arm into a sling.

"How do you know so much about a kid's show?" Bella asks.

"My Da needed to get in shape, but he's proper stubborn, that one. Had to trick him with Pokémon Go to get him out of the house and walking 'round town."

"Who's your favorite Pokémon?" Micah asks.

"I like Charizard because he breathes fire and I'm also a firefighter."

"That's my mom's favorite!" Micah squeals like the news is surprising.

Bella nods. "It is. I've gotten into many heated discussions with her about Pokémon characters. My favorite is Jigglypuff."

I laugh. "That tracks for you."

"Right? Who doesn't love a little jiggly ball of fun, and just when you think he's all sweet and innocent, he unleashes the ultimate power!" She lets out an overly dramatic evil laugh, and Micah giggles at her antics.

"Isn't Jigglypuff's power that he puts people to sleep with his singing?" Micah asks.

"Well, I never said I was a good singer." She winks at Micah right as we pull up to the hospital.

As the ambulance slows, I hop out of my seat, ready to transport him inside. Rudy opens the door for us, and we wheel the stretcher into the ER.

Once we get them checked in and transferred to a triage room, I'm about to hand off the paperwork to a nurse when a small voice stops me.

"Can you stay with us?" Micah asks.

Bella looks at me, shocked. I'm at a loss for words. Rudy just shrugs.

"I'd love to, buddy. Lemme check in with dispatch. If they say it's fine, we'll stay. But if another call comes in, we'll have to head out."

"Okay." He looks defeated, and it breaks me a little.

I gesture for Rudy to join me in the hall. "You okay hanging out here for a bit if they give us the go-ahead?"

"That's cool. There's a nurse who works here that I talk to sometimes," Rudy says.

"Thanks, man."

I radio dispatch and get the green light to stay, so I walk over to the nurse's station. "I'm gonna hang around with the patient in room twelve. He's not a big fan of fellas and we kinda bonded, so I'd like to stay until his mom gets here. There's someone that can stay with him if we get called out."

"Sounds good, sugar," she says, barely looking up at me.

"Say, you have anything to occupy kids? Some coloring books? LEGO?" I lean over the counter, trying to get her attention.

She looks up from her charting. "Sure do. I'm kinda busy here, though. It's over at the charge nurses' station. Just tell 'em Doris sent you."

"Thanks, doll." I wink and flash her my biggest smile.

She playfully rolls her eyes. "Oh, you're a heartbreaker, I can tell. Just don't get tangled up with any of my nurses like your partner there."

"Yes, ma'am."

As luck would have it, I find a Pokémon coloring book and a pack of mostly unbroken crayons and return to Micah's room. "Look what I found!" I pull back the curtain and notice Micah curled up on his side, quietly crying as Bella soothes him.

They startle at the sound of me, and then Micah perks up. "I thought you left."

Were those tears for me? Why does that make my heart ache?

"Aye, no, lad. Just went to grab you something," I say, holding up the coloring book.

"Does it have Binacle?"

Together we search for his favorite Pokémon, and I hold the book in place so he can color one-handed.

Micah continues wincing as we work, the occasional tear splashing onto the page. I can tell the lad's in pain and I know he needs some relief, but there's not much they can do for him until his mom gets here.

A nurse walks in, pulling out the rolling stool as she wheels over to the side of the bed. "Hey, Micah, how's your arm feeling?" she asks.

He lets out a stuttered breath. "It hurts."

The nurse nods in understanding, turning to Bella. "Are you the parent?"

Bella stands from her chair. "I'm his teacher. His mom is on her way."

The nurse slides over to the computer and taps on the keyboard, most likely confirming the information. "Micah, can you tell me what happened?"

"I jumped off the big slide on the playground and landed on my arm."

"Oof, that'll do it. The doctor will be in shortly. He'll probably order some X-rays." She turns to Bella. "Let us know when mom gets here."

Bella nods and the nurse leaves the room.

Micah lies back on the bed, silent tears streaming down his face. I've only just met him, but it breaks my heart to see him in so much pain. I lean over, getting closer to the bed.

"I think you're really brave, Micah. I know it hurts, but they're going to fix you up good as new."

He sniffles as his eyes connect with mine. They're a deep shade of green, but the redness makes the color in them even more striking.

When he doesn't say anything, I continue. "You know who else is a little guy but is really brave?"

He shakes his head.

"Pikachu."

A tiny smile lights up one side of his face. "He *is* brave."

"And so are you. Maybe I should call you Mikachu, since you're so brave."

He nods as he wipes a tear from his cheek, pinching his eyes shut as he lies still on the bed. "And you talk like the guy on my favorite cereal. The one with the marshmallows." His words are choppy like it hurts to get them out. The adrenaline has probably worn off; the pain in his arm must be hitting him hard.

"I'm happy to be your lucky charm."

He smiles weakly as he wipes a tear from his cheek and pinches his eyes shut.

If there was something I could do to help him, I'd be moving mountains. I hate seeing kids in pain. I just pray his mother can get here soon.

CHAPTER 3

LUCY

I do not do stuff like this. I never miss school and certainly not for something as frivolous as this. But I had a dentist's appointment scheduled this morning, so I already had a sub.

When I arrive at the agreed-upon meeting place, Chestnut Roasters, I order a coffee and pick out a table, then nervously look around waiting for my date.

A few minutes later, a very attractive man walks in. When he sees me, I wave, and he heads in my direction. He looks like the 2015 version of Ben Affleck had a baby with 1997 Matt Damon.

He takes a seat, and he seems nice enough, but several minutes in, I already know that I've got to figure out a way to get out of this catastrophe of a date. My friends mean well, but they set me up with the weirdest man on the planet. I get why they picked him, though—on paper he looks great. Hell, in person, he looks fantastic.

Even though he agreed to a coffee date, he admits he doesn't drink coffee. I take another big sip of mine, unbothered by his confession. He had ample opportunity to suggest other options for our date.

He then proceeds to tell me that he has a severe allergy to shellfish and then stares at me for several seconds when I don't give him the reaction he so obviously wants. I can't believe I'm entertaining this, but I take the bait. "What does a shellfish allergy have to do with coffee?"

"You don't know? That's surprising. I thought you were a teacher."

I blink several times. "I teach second grade. You do know that teachers don't know everything, right? We have special-ized areas we focus on, and we're humans like everyone else. Being a teacher doesn't make me smarter than the general population, it just means I enjoy shaping young minds and teaching them about a particular topic I've studied at length."

"Sorry, I didn't mean to offend you." He smiles like he's placating me.

Worried I'm overthinking things—with my luck and history of shitty exes, I probably am—I return a polite smile and gesture for him to continue. "You were saying?"

"I can't have coffee because of my allergy. Well, I can have some coffee, but I can't get it from any old place."

"And why's that?"

"Cockroaches."

I nearly spit in his face, but I cover my mouth in the nick of time as coffee shoots all over my hand.

"Jesus! Are you trying to kill me?" he shouts as he stands and backs away from the table.

Fuck my luck. Even though he hasn't fully explained the connection, I apparently did try to kill the man. "I'm so sorry!" I run over to the counter and grab a bunch of napkins to clean up the table then settle back in my seat.

I smile awkwardly as I wipe up the mess. "So, cock-roaches?"

He examines me for a moment, then reluctantly sits. "Yeah. It's been proven that low-quality coffee can be cross-contami-nated with ground-up cockroaches. And if you have an allergy like mine, you'd know that cockroaches contain the same protein as shellfish."

"I did not know that," I say as I take another sip of my coffee. I remind myself to fact-check him after this date is over.

"Do you want to head over to Pine Dining and grab lunch?"

I've nearly murdered this man with coffee. What's a little lunch?

When we get to the restaurant, he orders the most expensive thing on the menu, and when the bill comes, he does the "pat my pockets" dance, claiming he forgot his wallet.

"I'll Venmo you," he says as he takes a bite of a forty-two-dollar steak that I definitely can't afford on my teacher's salary.

A coffee date was supposed to be safe. With two wild little boys, it's hard to find a sitter, so I figured a date while they were in school was best. I don't have to pick up Levi until two, so I have plenty of time. But this is a disaster. Good on paper is terrible in person.

Once we finish, I'm ready for this date to be over, ready to head back to my car and drive away as fast as I can. We're walking down Main Street toward our vehicles when a small dog runs toward us, leash trailing behind it and its owner running to catch up. I instantly recognize the woman as Susy, the owner of Peak Sweets.

Before I get a chance to process what's happening, not-Ben Affleck grabs me by the arms, using me as a human shield.

I break from his hold and drop down to scoop up the adorable brown fluffball running toward me. An out-of-breath Susy offers me a smile as she approaches. "I'm so sorry, Lucy! Webster hates walking on a leash and runs off every chance he gets." She looks over my shoulder at my date, still cowering behind me. "It's okay, he doesn't bite."

He takes a step back. "I don't like dogs."

If everything else wasn't enough, that definitely seals it. I could never trust anyone who doesn't like dogs. "It's okay, I love Webster. Is he hanging out with you at the shop today?"

"Yup. His separation anxiety is getting worse, and I hate leaving him alone in his kennel. If I don't use it, he'll chew up the house, but when I put him in it, he whines like he's in doggy jail. One of the firefighters said I could drop him at the station and they'd keep him company during the day, but I just hate being away from him."

A throat clears behind me. "I'm pretty sure you can't have a dog in an establishment that serves food," my date says pointing to her shop.

Susy's eyes narrow. "He's a service dog."

"Do you have any documentation for that?"

I totally spaced out for a good portion of our date, and now I'm trying to remember what he said he did.

"What are you, the dog police?" Susy asks.

"No, just a concerned citizen. I'm Doug."

Doug. That's his name. He never formally introduced himself, and the girls never told me, but I recognized him from his picture.

"Well, the boys and I would be happy to watch Webster if you don't want him to be alone," I offer.

"I appreciate that," Susy says, before giving my date a suspicious look. "Is he giving you any trouble?"

"Nope." I don't offer more, not wanting the Chestnut Mountain rumor mill to start ramping up any more than it's going to. It's inevitable since we've been seen together in two local businesses today.

I hand Webster back to Susy and say goodbye as we continue our walk to our cars.

Doug's clammy hand grabs mine. "This is the first real date I've ever been on."

I would be flattered at that… if this man wasn't over thirty. Even though he's attractive, he spent our entire meal talking about the different kinds of worms he likes, and when I asked him if he fished, he said no and looked at me like it was a ridiculous question.

"Oh?" I ask, unsure of how else to respond.

"Clearly it's not yours."

I stop walking and yank my hand from his. "What's that supposed to mean?"

He turns back to me, floundering. "Because you said you have kids. Clearly, you've been on dates before."

"You don't know that for sure." I mean, I have, but I'm not about to share any more of my backstory with this infuriatingly odd man.

"So, you only do hookups?"

"I didn't say that."

"If you don't date and don't hook up, did you conceive your kids through Immaculate Conception or something?" His face is smug, like he thinks he's caught me in a trap.

"I don't think that's any of your business." Crossing my arms over my chest, I glower at him.

"I'd like to make it my business," he says, wiggling his eyebrows in a way he probably thinks looks sexy, but it actually makes him look like a deranged clown.

Fuck, now I'm picturing Ben Affleck dressed as a sad clown doing a dance with his eyebrows. I need to get out of here.

"This was… well, it was." I don't know what else to say so I awkwardly turn and shuffle quickly toward my car, determined to leave bug-obsessed wannabe Ben Affleck behind.

When I get the car door open, I notice my cell on the floorboard where it must've fallen out of my purse earlier.

I grab it and throw my bag in the passenger seat. There are dozens of missed calls, but the only texts are from Bella, and they just say, "Call me!!!"

My phone connects to my car, and I dial Bella immediately, already heading toward Levi's preschool.

"Okay, so don't panic," Bella's voice says, filling my car speakers.

My heart stops. "I wasn't, but now I am. What's going on? Is everything okay?"

"I'm at the hospital with Micah—"

"What!"

"He's okay, but Mike thinks he might have a broken arm."

"What? Who's Mike?" I press harder on the accelerator, trying to get to Levi's school faster.

"Hardy's coworker, Mike. Mr. March in the calendar. The one with the Irish accent."

I know exactly who she's talking about.

"He was the one that found Isaac during the school fire, remember?"

"I remember, but why does he think Micah's arm is broken?"

"He fell at recess. Or jumped? Anyway, I had to call 911, and he's who they sent out. I know Micah doesn't like men, but he was the closest."

"And he didn't freak out?"

"He was a little unsure at first, but Mike's been really good with him."

"I'm getting Levi now, then I'll head to the hospital. What happened?"

"Everyone was playing, and the recess monitor was distracted by two kids fighting over a pack of Gushers. Apparently, some of the first-grade boys challenged the kindergarten boys to a contest to see who could jump off the highest playground item. Micah ran to the top of the blue slide and jumped off it."

"Oh my God, the really big one that we wish they would tear down for that very reason?"

"That's the one. Anyway, he landed on his arm. The monitor sent some kids to come get me after it happened, and I've been with him ever since. He's doing really well. You'd be proud."

"Okay. That's good." My mind is racing a mile a minute.

I've got to get Levi and make it to the hospital and figure out how I'm going to occupy him while we wait on Micah to get checked out.

A horn honks behind me, and I notice a plain white car with a police light pulling up on my bumper.

"Fuck, I'm getting pulled over."

"Oh shit! I'll let you go. Don't worry, I can hold things down here. Do what you need to do. Just be safe."

"I'll call you back." We hang up, and I pull to the side of the road. Could this day get any worse?

Leaning over to root around in my glovebox and purse, I'm distracted as I fish out everything I need to give the officer, when a tap on my window startles me.

"Oh my God, Doug! You scared me." I roll down the window as he crosses his arms over his chest.

"License and registration."

I blink at him in confusion. Is he pranking me?

He thrusts his hips out slightly, and the sun gleams off the badge clipped to his belt. He definitely wasn't wearing that earlier.

"Are you a cop?"

He frowns at me. "State trooper."

Man in uniform. My mom group DMs make a lot more sense now. State trooper is technically a uniform, even if he isn't currently wearing it. I really should have gotten more details from Summer. Or paid attention to him when he talked about what he did. I at least should have said goodbye. His interaction with Susy is starting to make more sense now.

"I'm sorry to ditch you like that back there, but I got a call from my friend that my kid got hurt at school and I've got to grab his brother and head to the hospital." I try to look sweet, but my heart is racing, and I feel like my face is twitching.

His answering scowl isn't reassuring. "License and registration, ma'am."

"It's okay. We just shared a meal. You can call me Lucy."

He doesn't even crack a smile.

Swallowing down my anxiety, I hand him the documents and twist my hands in my lap.

"Stay here while I run this." He taps my car as he walks back to his.

Is this really happening?

When he returns, he issues me a ticket, pointing to where I need to sign.

"Guess I'm not getting reimbursed for that meal," I mutter to myself.

"What was that?"

"Thanks for the meal."

Once he releases me, I drive under the speed limit to Levi's school, cursing Doug the whole time.

This is why I don't do relationships. I have the worst luck with men.

I fear he may have ruined Ben Affleck for me. And butt chins. And coffee.

When I get to the hospital, I text Bella to let her know I'm here and hurry inside, nearly knocking over three people in my race to get to Micah. Levi fidgets in my arms, begging me to put him down, but I know it's faster to carry him so he doesn't wander off.

"Lucy!" Bella's voice calls out from behind me.

I race over to her, and she pulls me into a hug. "Where is he?"

"He's in the ER. I'll take you back," she says, just as Levi makes grabby hands for her, leaning away from me.

"Come here, big guy," she coos as she takes him and points over my shoulder to indicate where we're headed.

"Thanks." I turn around without looking and run smack

dab into a brick wall. Or cinderblock? It's hard to tell from the searing pain in my face, but I'd say the wall won. "Son of a—"

"Oh my God, Lucy, are you okay? You're bleeding."

"Mama, oh no!"

The last thing I remember is looking down at my bloody hands as everything fades to black.

CHAPTER 4

MIKE

Micah is putting the finishing touches on Bulbasaur and I'm coloring in Charizard's fire tail when I hear a commotion in the hallway.

"I'll be right back, lad. I'm going to check on that. Sit tight." I hustle over just in time to see a beautiful blonde woman walk face first into the wall. She looks vaguely familiar. Then I see Bella behind her, holding a small boy, and it clicks. This must be Micah's mom.

She rears back from the wall, blood pouring out of her nose. Bella shouts something, but I can't make it out as my brain shifts into emergency mode. The blonde looks disoriented, and I rush over right as her body goes limp. It's not the most graceful catch, but at least I prevent her from falling onto the floor.

"Mama!" the little boy wails as he reaches toward us, but Bella wraps a comforting arm around his torso and turns to shield him.

"Let's go check on your brother," she says as she takes the long way back to his room, looping around the back of the nurse's station.

I lift her as a nurse rushes over, motioning me into an empty room. I gently set her on the bed and check her vitals.

"What happened?" the nurse asks, all business.

"I heard noise in the hallway, came out to check, and I watched her walk into a wall. I think the sight of blood made her pass out."

The nurse pushes me out of the way as she checks her nose. "It doesn't look broken, but lemme order a scan and get transport up here." She slips out of the room, and I pull up the chair next to her. She's curled up on her side, and I place a hand on the bed to steady myself as I lean over her to reach the bed remote.

"Ohhhh," she groans, and I breathe a sigh of relief that she's alert. Fingers glide along my forearm. "Mmm, firefighter."

I chuckle when I realize she's tracing my tattoo. Her touch sets off a wave of warmth that radiates through my whole body. That's new. "It's a firefighter walking out of flames. I got it when I joined the Chestnut Mountain battalion a few years back."

My voice startles her. She retracts her hand, and I instantly miss her touch.

"Oh my God. You're... March... I'm so embarrassed." She shrinks back on the bed, tries to cover her face with her hands, and hisses when her fingers graze the skin. "My head."

"Took a nasty smack to the face, did ya?" I grin down at her.

"You look like that, and you have an accent. How is that fair?" The words spill out as her face scrunches up like she's mortified at the admission. And then tears well in her eyes, most likely due to the pain from contorting her face.

"Easy there, lass. They've ordered a scan for ya. Wanna make sure ya don't have a concussion. Should be wheeling you back in a few."

"Am I dreaming? Is this real?"

"Wanna touch my tattoo again and see for yourself?" I revel in the blush lighting up her cheeks. Her mention of March means she must be familiar with my calendar spread, and I delight in that fact more than I should.

She bolts upright on the bed. "Micah. Oh my God, I need to see Micah."

I place a hand on her shoulder. "He's fine, was coloring Bulbasaur when I left him. Bella went to sit with him."

Her eyes search mine like she's trying to process my words. "He doesn't like men."

"Seemed grand by me."

"This is the worst ending to a first date I've ever had."

I can't help teasing her. "Didn't realize this was a date, love. I would've worn my Mr. March outfit."

Blood rushes to her cheeks. "Oh. My. God."

"Ms. Lovejoy? I'm here to take you to radiology," the patient transporter says, pulling back the curtain.

She looks at me panicked. "I'll stay with the lad. Go get checked out."

Once she leaves the room, I head over to check on Micah, but his room is empty so they must have taken him back to get an X-ray. Hopefully, the two of them will be reunited in radiology.

I decide to take a walk down the hallway in search of my partner when I hear muffled moans coming from a storage closet.

Feckin' hell, is everyone getting laid except for me?

Good for Rudy.

After another stroll around the ER, I see them wheeling Micah back to his room, but as I get closer, I notice Micah's mom hustling over and I hesitate.

Fuck, she's beautiful. Even flustered, covered in dried blood, with the stress of the situation creasing her face, she's still captivating.

I watch as the doctor walks over and feel like I'm spying on a private family moment. Bella is still juggling the wee one, and I try to decide how I should play this.

Should I go over there and give her my number? Reach out to Bella or Hardy later to check up on her?

A hand claps my shoulder, and I glance behind me to see Rudy's self-satisfied look. "You ready to head out?"

No, I want to stay here with the woman who's captured my attention for the first time in years. But I nod and follow him down the hall back to our ambulance.

CHAPTER 5

LUCY

After the worst date of my life, a speeding ticket I cannot afford, and an embarrassing run-in with that hot fire-fighter that ended with no broken bones for me and a cast for Micah, I'm resigned to my fate. Lady Luck hates me. Every man in my life lets me down. First my dad, then my shitty ex, and especially Doug. Even Mr. March didn't stay true to his word. He said he'd watch Micah, but he was nowhere to be found once I got back from my scan.

I know two things with absolute certainty. One, men cannot be trusted. And two, I'm never leaving my house ever again. Or at least not tonight.

"Mama! I's got no Pull-Ups!"

But I have kids so that's not an option.

Fuck you, Lady Luck.

I walk into Levi's room where he's sitting bare-assed on the carpet. Knowing how poorly this kid wipes his own ass, I shudder and make a mental note to hit that spot with the Bissell tomorrow.

Yawning, I search through Levi's drawers trying to find him a Pull-Up. "Ugh, I'm so tired, buddy. I just want to go to bed. I feel so old. I used to have all this energy until I had you guys."

"You're not old, Mama."

"Thanks, buddy. But I definitely feel it. Look at all the wrinkles you guys have given me." I wave a hand in front of my eyes.

"Where?" He scoots his bare ass across the floor like a dog as he tries to get closer to examine my face.

I point to the lines on my forehead and the slight crow's feet around my eyes. "See?"

"Those aren't wrinkles." He furrows his brows in concentration as he looks up at me.

"Yes, they are."

"I have wrinkles on my tess-tick-uh-bulls. See?" Levi stands up and lifts his shirt as he wiggles his junk around, and Micah erupts into laughter in the doorway.

"Please put on some pants." I cover my face with my hands to hide my smile. Even when they are being ridiculous and gross, I love these boys so freaking much.

After searching through his dresser and coming up empty, I grab a pair of undies. "I guess we're going Pull-Up free tonight, buddy."

"But I need it," he whines.

Levi was potty-trained very early, much earlier than his brother, but he's still such a heavy sleeper that we've had to rely on a little help at night. How did I not realize we were out of Pull-Ups?

"Fu—" I catch myself. "Fudgsicles!" I groan when I search his closet for extra sheets and a waterproof mattress protector and come up empty. Clearly I'm doing laundry tomorrow too.

"I want a Fudgsicle!" Levi cries.

I really need to come up with alternative curses that don't involve food he likes to eat. "I'm sorry, buddy, it looks like we're gonna have to run to the store to get some Pull-Ups."

"And Fudgsicles!" he adds, pulling on the undies I hand him.

"I want a Fudgsicle too!" Micah calls from the doorway.

Pulling my phone out of my pocket, I look at the time. Shit, we've got fifteen minutes to get to the store before it closes. "Okay, both of you get shoes and coats on, we don't have much time." If I try to change them out of their pajamas, we'll never make it. It's late enough that we shouldn't see anyone we know anyway.

Minutes later, by some miracle, we park at Chestnut Mountain Market, and I hurry the boys inside. There isn't even time to corral them in a cart like I normally would. I nod at Ned as we tear through the store like a pack of rabid raccoons on trash night, running past the aisle of Valentine's Day items that are marked half off.

Damn, I could use some cheap chocolate, but if I stop near candy, we'll never get out of here. Luckily the baby section is near the freezers, so we can avoid the confectionary temptation.

"I'll get the diapers!" Micah shouts like the helpful oldest child he is, and I follow Levi as he runs to the ice cream cooler.

I'm not five steps behind the kid, but he's already opened the freezer door and has climbed halfway inside by the time I reach him.

"Whoa there, buddy, you can't climb in there like that," I say, hoisting him out of the freezer as I slide him onto my hip.

"Yes, I can, it was easy."

Oh, how I love kid logic. We have minutes till the store closes, and my patience is running thin. Micah would never question a rule like that. Levi thinks they're meant to be tested. Why is it always the second-born?

"Just because you can doesn't mean you should."

Then he asks me the question every parent hates most when trying to corral an unruly child.

"Why?" Levi fidgets in my arms as I grab the Fudgsicles.

Because you could get hurt. Because you could break something that I can't afford to fix. Because it's not safe. Because I don't want anyone to think I'm a shit parent because you won't behave in public. "Because I said so."

"But why?"

"Do you want the Fudgsicle or not?" I ask, setting him down.

"Got the diapers!" Micah exclaims as he walks up.

"I don't wear diapers!" Levi argues.

"They're Pull-Ups," I say, trying to quell their impending sibling fight.

"Look like diapers to me." Micah hands me the package. Thank goodness they're the right size, but they're pink and covered in princesses.

"Those are for girls!" Levi squeals.

"Are not!" Micah argues.

"Are too." Levi balls his fists and stomps his foot.

"Anyone can wear pink, just like anyone can wear blue. But if you don't want these characters, we can pick out different ones."

Micah shakes his head. "They only had these in his size."

"I don't want princess Pull-Ups!" Levi whines, and I know we have about thirty seconds before we are in full-blown meltdown territory.

"Let's go check to see if they have anything else." I scoop up Levi, and we walk down the aisle.

Micah was right; the only Pull-Ups close to Levi's size are the princess ones. He's pretty big for his age, and the smaller ones don't fit him. "Can we do these tonight, Levi? They're all out of everything else. Or you can wear underwear?"

Levi thrashes in my arms. "I don't want to wear underwear!" He's loud enough to make a scene if anyone is left in the store with us.

"Hold on, I have an idea." I hoist Levi higher on my hip and walk over to the adult diaper section. Quickly scanning the shelf, I spot a pair of extra-small adult diapers and praise the heavens when I see that it includes his weight in the range on the package. "How about these, buddy? No princesses, they're plain white, and they should fit you."

He takes the package out of my hand and inspects it closely. My back protests and I set him down on the ground as he hugs the package against his chest and yawns.

"Are those diapers for grown-ups?" Micah asks, looking at one of the packages on the shelf.

"No diapers, I want Pull-Ups!" Levi shouts as he throws the diapers on the floor.

I swing my head toward Micah as I mouth the word "Why?" at him. He shrugs his shoulders, giving me a sheepish look, and when I turn back to Levi, he's gone.

"Levi!" I shout as I take off down the aisle, rounding the endcap when I run smack into another fucking wall.

Except it's not a wall this time. It's the muscular backside of a tall man. I bounce off his butt like a kid in a bouncy castle and land on my ass on the floor. "Shit!"

"That's a bad word!" Levi scolds, and I realize this brick wall of a man is holding him. Relief washes over me—until the man turns around and I see who it is.

"Well, hello there, a chroí. We've got to stop meeting this way," Mr. March says in his irresistible accent.

I blink up at him like a fool. It takes several seconds for me to realize that he's holding out a hand to help me up. As soon as I slide my hand into his giant one, a rush of warmth lights up my insides, and I clench my thighs together to ease the ache building there. His eyes track the movement, widening slightly, then they move slowly up my body before locking with mine.

It almost feels like a scene out of a movie, where the two love interests meet and something passes over them, drawing them together like magnets.

Almost.

Except I feel like Mike and I are two Barbie dolls that Lady Luck keeps mashing together like a manic child, and instead of some magical, fairy-tale book romance, we're just awkwardly crashing and banging until we come out bruised and broken.

Okay, that might be a little dramatic.

But that's the kind of luck I have.

And I know this is true, because it's at that exact moment when Micah runs up to us shouting, "Mama, you forgot your diapers."

My eyes go comically wide, and I watch in horror as Mike's eyes roam back down to my crotch. Oh my God, is he trying to see if I'm wearing a diaper right now? I hold the box of fudge pops out in front of myself as if it will stop his leering. Except I realize that I'm now covering my crotch with something that looks like a giant turd, and I awkwardly hide it behind me. "It's not... I don't..." All words escape me as I shift nervously in front of him.

"Hey, you're the Pokémon guy!" Micah exclaims.

His eyes shift to Micah, and a smile lights up his face. "See any interesting Squirtles around here?" There's a small smirk on his face when he says this as his eyes drift back to the diapers I'm now clutching to my chest. "Or do you prefer a fire type?"

I'm not sure if he's making a joke about Pokémon or about him being a firefighter. Either way, mortification consumes me as I grab Levi out of his arms and speed-walk to the checkout with Micah struggling to keep up behind me.

"Mo-om! Mama, wait!"

I stomp to the counter and throw my items down with more force than I intend. I'm still pissed at Mike a little. He doesn't get to be all cute and charming.

Ignoring all of his attempts to get my attention, I hurry out of the store and pile the kids back into their car seats, convinced I'm going to die alone.

CHAPTER 6
MIKE

"**C**ome and get it!" I shout, leaning my head out of the kitchen. A moment later, a half dozen guys and gals barrel into the room, lining up to eat my latest lunch creation.

I'm still not sure how it happened, and I certainly didn't plan it, but being the firehouse's resident cook has brought me more joy than I expected.

It started out small a couple years ago, just a simple casserole dish that I threw a few extra ingredients in, trying to clean out the pantry. I didn't know what the fuck I was doing, and I was just praying I didn't kill anyone. But to my surprise everyone loved it, and I started getting requests.

That one dish turned into ten more, and before I knew it, I was cooking every night, sometimes on my off days. It felt good to be needed for once in my life, knowing that there were people who depended on me.

After I fix myself a plate, I squeeze in next to RJ and dig in. For once, there's not a word spoken at the table, no good-natured ribbing of the rookies, no jokes about riding the pole. Just utter silence as the entire table shovels food in their mouths like it's their last meal on Earth.

"Damn, that was good. What did you put in it this time?"

Hardy asks, pushing his empty plate away from him as he leans back in his chair. "I'm gonna have to put in an extra session in the gym, and I don't even care."

Blaze raises his hand. "I made the mystery basket for him tonight. I don't even know what all I threw in there. I let my nephew pick."

"Fucking delicious," Rudy adds, letting out a giant burp.

Melissa surprises us, letting out a long belch as she pats her stomach.

Someone else burps in response, and the table quickly erupts into grins as we all try to one up each other.

"Ladies, gents, and assorted degenerates, tonight's meal was a tasty chicken and sausage jambalaya that included tinned black beans, a Mexican rice packet that I doctored, a little juice from a tin of mandarin oranges, and venison kielbasa courtesy of the random cupboard shite Blaze's nephew threw in."

It sounds disgusting, but it turned out to be pretty good.

"What's your nephew's name? Flame?" Rudy asks.

Melissa laughs. "Do you have a niece named Ember?"

"You know my name isn't actually Blaze, right? It's important that you know that."

"Then you shouldn't have burned so much food your rookie year, *Blaze*." Rudy elbows Blaze in the side as he shovels another bite in his mouth.

"I'm glad it turned out okay." I look down at my plate, suddenly a little self-conscious. I'm not an expert chef, I just enjoy doing it, so I know I still have a lot to learn. "I read somewhere that I was supposed to tenderize the meat, but I'm not sure that mattered for this recipe."

"I'll tenderize your meat," Rudy says, and we all break out into laughter.

"If you go anywhere near my meat, I'll throat-punch you," Blaze says.

I laugh. "No one wants to touch your meat, you feckin' arsehole."

The conversation moves from food to teasing as it often does with this group, and I smile to myself. If I'm not spending time with my folks, this is where I feel most at home.

My parents and I emigrated from Ireland when I was sixteen. I was the only child born to Aidan and Ciara O'Connor, and I was determined to carry on the family name after my Ma wasn't able to conceive again after me.

But growing up with parents who had the ultimate love story added a lot of pressure on me to get it right. I'm not going to settle down and marry just anyone. I want to find the right woman. And while I've enjoyed the company of a lot of lassies in my day, not everyone has the patience to put up with my goofball ways.

"Can't you take anything seriously?"

"You'd be the perfect guy if you weren't so obnoxious."

"You're hot, but that's about all you have to offer."

I try not to let my exes' words get to me, but it's a punch to the gut every time I think I've found a good woman, only to let my true self out and find out that they only like the way I look.

Ma would constantly ask me when I was going to give her grandkids. And I felt like I was disappointing her when I couldn't give her an answer. I got so desperate at one point I donated to a sperm bank, thinking that if I couldn't find the right person to have a kid with, at least someone might want to have my kids. It was stupid, I know.

I want nothing more in the world than to have a family. A little brood running around that look like me, share my name, and could carry on the O'Connor legacy. It would make my Ma happy. It would make *me* happy.

But years of unsuccessful relationships have discouraged me. So, I spend hours in the gym as a distraction, and I've poured myself into work, determined to be the best, most dependable guy on the crew. And for the last few years, this cooking thing has become my latest obsession.

"Hey, are we out of coffee?" Rudy yells, pulling me out of my thoughts. I look around and realize I'm the last one at the table.

"There should be more in the cupboard," I say, rounding up all the discarded dishes at the table and depositing them in the sink.

"I can't find any," Rudy calls back, waving his hand up and down at the empty shelf where the coffee should be.

"Whose turn was it to stock the coffee?" Blaze asks.

"It was the rookie's turn," Hardy says. We all look at RJ, who throws up his hands in apology.

"I got it, I'm off shift anyway," I say, pulling on my jacket. None of these guys can leave because they're on duty.

"What would we do without you?" Hardy says quietly, before addressing the group. "We can always depend on Mike. Be more like Mike, you lazy fucking assholes."

"Yes, sir," a few guys reply, the rookies more enthusiastically than the others.

It's about a fifteen-minute walk to Chestnut Mountain Roasters. I should drive, but I want to burn off a little of that meal and some of my anxious energy.

When I approach the door to the coffee shop, I notice the back of a familiar head of blonde hair. I couldn't help but chuckle at the way she ran out of the market the other night. I was hoping to see her again.

Her delectably plump arse is against the door, pushing it open, hands full of coffees, so I pull it open for her.

All that force she was using to lean into the door propels her backward, and she falls arse-first toward the concrete.

"Oh shit!" she cries.

I catch her under the arms, but it jostles the cup holder in her hands, spilling coffee all over her.

"Fuck you, Lady Luck," she mumbles, and I can't stop my escaping chuckle.

My laughter causes her to look up at me. "You!"

"We've got to stop meeting like this." I wink at her as I set her on her feet.

Her entire face turns a shade of red I've only seen on one of our firetrucks, and I can't help but wonder if I could turn her entire body that color either with my words or my hands.

"I'm soaking wet," she moans.

I'd like to see you soaking wet for me.

Her eyes shoot up to mine as her mouth falls open. "What?"

Oh shit, did I say that out loud?

"Let me help you clean up." That's right, just move right past it. Don't make it any more awkward than it needs to be.

"No, it's fine. I don't need your help. I can take care of myself, I always do," she huffs as she drops her purse, all the contents spilling out. "Fuck."

"Here, lemme help." I bend down and start scooping things into her purse, but she snatches it from me, grabs the empty cups, and stands. "Let me at least replace your coffees."

"It's fine. I should cut back anyway."

"Surely those weren't all for you?"

Ire flashes in her eyes. "What if they were? I'm an over-worked teacher and a single mom to two little boys. I mainline coffee like it's my job."

I lift my hands in surrender as I flash her my killer smile. "That's fair."

"No. You don't get to be charming too," she blurts, and then her eyes go big, like she can't believe she just said that.

"So let me see if I'm understanding. You think I'm hot, you're mad for my accent, and find me charming, eh?" I say, laying the Irish lilt on extra thick.

"I didn't say you were hot," she scoffs.

"No, you just admitted you fancy my calendar spread." I'm

not sure why I'm still teasing her, but the thrill of it excites me more than anything has in quite a while.

She opens her mouth to respond, and I wait desperately for her to speak, hoping she'll prick me with her words. "It doesn't matter; you clearly can't follow through with your promises. I need to go," she says. Disappointment pokes me.

"Your coffee?" I call out, but she's already walking away quickly, still clutching the empty cups and holder as her round, perfect arse sways behind her. I can't follow through with my promises? What is she on about? Fuck, how did I screw this up already?

I stand there like a fool watching her for several minutes. What is it about this woman that draws me in so much? Something rustles at my feet. I bend down to pick up a folded piece of paper on the ground and read it.

"Holy feckin' Christ," I say in a whisper. She would die if she knew she dropped this, and I look up the street, but she's already disappeared.

I need to think carefully about how I play this. If I don't handle it just right, I might scare her away—but if I can pull this off, I can show her how committed I am to following through, and we may just have the best time of our lives.

Pocketing the paper, I head into the coffee shop so I can complete my initial task. But my mind is filled with dirty thoughts as I think about all the things I want to do to the naughty single mom.

CHAPTER 7

LUCY

Could I embarrass myself even further with that ridiculously hot man? Yes, of course I could. I was determined not to go back into the coffee shop, so I ended up bringing alternative beverages to today's playdate.

Since it's too cold to play outside, and none of us wanted to drag all the kids into Denver, we end up at Raven's house. It's the only one large enough to fit our gaggle of children.

"So how did the date go?" Summer asks.

We all stare at her in shocked amusement.

"What? What am I missing?" she asks.

"Read the room." Raven chuckles as she crosses her arms over her chest.

"Bad, I take it?"

Bella nods. "Bad doesn't even begin to cover it."

"Sorry. I've been locked up in the house dodging the flu from my kids," Summer says.

We all rear back, pushing our chairs away from the table like she has the plague. And considering how bad the flu has been this season, it's not an inaccurate assessment.

"Did you bring your sick kids to our playdate?" Raven asks. She's always been the no-nonsense one in our group, and

I'm thankful she's not afraid to say what I'm thinking but would never voice.

"I would never." Summer puts a hand to her chest as though she's offended by the accusation. "You think I'm going to risk all of us like that? I've had the flu shot and so have most of my kids, but you know how hard it is with Logan. Between his diabetes and egg allergy, it's nearly impossible to get him a flu shot. He's the one that got it, and I was able to isolate the other kids and Lysol the crap out of everything. We've been flu-free for over a week now, so we're all good."

"So calm your tits, ladies," Bella adds, gesturing for us to take our seats.

I place a hand on Summer's arm. "Sorry, we didn't mean to be assholes about it, but I've seen playgroups dissolve over less, and I would be devastated if I lost you all over something like that."

"We would never let that happen," Bella adds. "You all are stuck with my awkward ass. I don't think I could make new friends if I tried."

"Agreed. Why is making friends so fucking hard in your thirties?" I ask.

"I don't want to lose you all either. Though I could do with a little less swearing around the kids," Summer adds, looking between me and Bella.

"They can't hear us. I can barely hear myself over all that racket they're making," Raven says, taking a sip of her wine.

"Oh my God, why would you say that out loud? You'll jinx us," I whine.

"Please tell me you don't buy into that magic-is-real bullshit. Jinxes aren't real, they're just a tactic moms use to get their kids to shut up for five minutes," Raven says into the rim of her cup.

"I'm parenting wrong, because that is brilliant." I stuff a Goldfish cracker in my mouth.

"You just trick them into saying a common phrase, say it at

the same time as them, call jinx, and they can't speak again until you say their name. It buys me at least five minutes every time," Raven explains.

Bella nods. "I got Isaac to be quiet for two whole hours once."

"That doesn't count, he was probably an only child then. They'll be quiet for hours," Summer says.

"Accurate." Bella pops a couple fruit snacks in her mouth. "Loving this charchoochie spread by the way." She laughs. "Coochie spread. I love the way you spread your coochie on this plate."

Normally, I'd be laughing at Bella's typical perverted word vomit, but Levi takes that moment to run into the room.

"Coochie!" Levi parrots as he climbs on my lap, using me as a booster to grab the snacks he wants off the tray. I put on my sternest face because I'm the adult and this kid repeats every word he hears. If he sees me laugh at his antics, it will only encourage him to repeat it more. But fuck, do I want to laugh.

Bella gives me an apologetic look. "Charcuterie. Can you say char-coo-ter-ee, Levi?" Bella asks. I giggle at her attempted recovery.

"Cooter!" Levi says around a mouthful of fruit snacks.

Somehow this has gone from comically bad to worse, and we all trade glances, trying not to be the first to break into laughter.

"I was going to add more to the *charcuterie*," Raven says, emphasizing the *char*, and I give her an appreciative glance. "Like olives, pickles, and more for the adult palate, but I ran out of time so all you get are some dumped-out Lunchables, Goldfish, and gummies in cartoon shapes."

"Oh, I love a good pickle!" I shoot Bella a warning look. "But the presentation is so fancy," she adds.

Summer shrugs. "Tastes good to me."

"Love you, Mama," Levi says, giving me a big sticky kiss on the lips as he scampers off.

"Well, I'm definitely getting the flu now," I tease, winking at Summer.

"Oh my God, no one is getting the flu," she moans.

"Can we get back to Lucy's tragically bad date?" Raven gets us on track again.

"What was so bad about it?" Summer asks.

"Everything, but it's how it ended that was the worst."

"He gave her a speeding ticket," Raven says.

The shocked look on Summer's face is comical. "What?"

Bella leans forward, resting her arms on the table. "Yeah, she was on her way to the hospital because Micah broke his arm."

"I heard about that part," Summer says, taking a bite of cheese and crackers.

"But did they tell you about how I ran into a wall when I got there and the same hot firefighter that rescued my son had to rescue me?"

Summer smacks Raven and Bella's arms in unison. "They did not tell me that! What's with you two embarrassing your-selves in front of firefighters?"

"You've done it too." I laugh incredulously. "Do we need to talk about that kiss again?"

"That's different. RJ wasn't a firefighter then," Summer says, pouting.

"Well, I, for one, do not plan on embarrassing myself in front of a firefighter. Frankly, I do not see the appeal. But I'm happy for you two." Raven pops another gummy in her mouth.

"To be fair, I embarrassed myself in front of Hardy *and* Mike on Halloween," Bella says.

"That should make me feel better, but oddly, it does not," I say, taking a sip of my wine.

"Wait, was your boob out too?" Summer looks at me, horror-stricken.

I laugh and shake my head, thinking about how Bella met her now-boyfriend when she'd accidentally exposed herself to the guys. "No. I saw blood and passed out, and when I came to, I was in a hospital bed and his sexy forearm tattoo was in my face. I was confused and woozy and I think I referred to him as Mr. March before they took me back for scans."

"Oh my God, that's so embarrassing!" Summer clasps her hands over her mouth.

"Don't worry, I've embarrassed myself plenty since then."

Three sets of eyes stare at me expectantly.

"I literally ran into his ass in the grocery store a few days ago. Like turned a corner and bounced off it while I was chasing after Levi, and Micah walked up and handed me 'my adult diapers.' But they weren't for me, they were out of Levi's size, so we grabbed adult ones. Never did get a chance to explain that to Mr. March, though. Then today, he opened the door for me at Chestnut Mountain Roasters as I was pushing it open with my butt, and I fell and spilled all our coffees all over myself."

"Is that why you were late?" Raven asks.

Summer leans forward in her chair as if she's invested. "Is that why you brought wine instead?"

"Yup. There was no way I was going back in there after the scene I made."

"I'm sure it wasn't that bad," Bella says, tossing a cube of cheese into the air and then catching it.

"On to the reason why we're here." Summer turns to me. "I know you think you're unlucky in love, and I'll admit Doug was a truly terrible date, but we're going to change that."

"And what do you propose?" Raven asks skeptically.

Bella claps her hands excitedly. "I asked Lucy to make a list."

"The list of qualities you're looking for in a man that I suggested you make?" Raven asks.

"Even better. She made a sex list!" Bella says.

"Keep your voice down," Summer scolds.

I chuckle as I reach into my purse hanging off the back of my chair. A tiny prick of panic hits me when I can't find the paper, and I grab the purse, setting it on the table so I can dig through it. Oh my God, where is it? "Umm, guys…"

Summer looks wary. "What is it?"

"I can't find my list."

Bella takes my purse and dumps it out on the table. "Sorry, I feel like this will be faster than us watching you root around in that thing."

Taking a quick scan of the contents, my worst fears are confirmed. "It's not here."

Raven takes the empty purse, comically holding the sides open as she dumps out nothing but air and a few Cheez-It crumbs. "Let's not panic. I'm sure there's a logical explanation."

My head whips to her. "It didn't sprout legs and walk away!" Deep breaths. They're trying to help. This is not their fault.

"Let's retrace your steps. Where did you see it last?" Bella asks.

My breathing picks up as I try to piece together what could have happened. "I made it the night you suggested it, and I stuffed it in my purse so Micah wouldn't find it."

Bella nods. "Understandable. He's the strongest reader in my class."

"But it's not in your purse."

"I know that, Raven!" I snap. Bella rests a hand on my arm. "Sorry, I'm just freaking out."

"I would be too," Raven says. "But keep thinking. Would the boys have gone through your purse?"

"No. They haven't before, but there's a first time for—"

Holy fucking shit.

My hands start shaking and I clasp them together trying to control my nerves. "My purse fell when I dropped the coffees, and everything spilled out."

Summer's mouth drops open as if she's already figured out what I just did. "Hot Irish firefighter has your sex list!" She immediately scans the room for little ears.

Raven and Bella's mouths fall open, and I drop my head in my hands. "This is not happening."

Bella squeezes my arm tighter. "Please tell me you didn't put your name on it."

My head pops up. "Of course my name was on it," I say through gritted teeth. "I teach second grade and I tell my students to label everything, so yes, my name is at the top of that thing."

"What if *he* didn't find it?"

My eyes shoot to Raven's. "Why would you say that? Do you want my anxiety to spiral?"

"I was just going to suggest that it blew away and no one found it, but what if Ned found it?" Raven says.

"Oh my God, that man's a bigger gossip than my shitty neighbor Mrs. Johnson!" Bella cries, and then her eyes dart to mine. "Want me to suss him out? Feel around and see if he knows anything?"

"Dear God, no! If he didn't find it, you're just gonna give him ammunition to figure out what you're talking about."

Bella pats my arm. "You're right."

"I can't believe I'm saying this, but now I'm hoping Mike found it," I say.

"Maybe he'd help you complete the list," Summer says with a wink.

I fake a smile back and nod as they continue talking, but inwardly I'm a mess of nerves. I made that list in a wine-induced haze, but I'm pretty sure I mentioned wanting to fuck

Mr. March. I know I wrote something about an accent. Shit, what else did I put on there?

CHAPTER 8

MIKE

I'm a man on a mission. Carl at Meat Cute promised he could special order everything I need for tomorrow's crew meal. If you care about your food, you go to the butcher.

Ever since we started our own version of *Chopped*, the crew has tried to one-up each other suggesting some of the weirdest shite to challenge me.

Not everything I've created with their suggestions has been palatable, and if they give me a list of gross ingredients, I'll make a backup dish just in case. And because I love chaos, the rookies get served the gobshite meal, and everyone else gets the good one. Watching the rookies insist it's delicious while clearly suffering is feckin' hilarious. But they clean their plates because they know better than to complain.

One night after a particularly rank casserole made with chicken feet, cottage cheese, and caramelized carrots, I nearly lost it at the table. RJ kept pushing a talon around his plate, pretending to cough every time he turned his head so he could dry heave. Hardy gave me a knowing look, so I filled him in on the joke. Now he's my partner in crime, deliberately suggesting the foulest shite imaginable whenever the rookies get unruly. It's been a surprisingly effective way to keep them in line.

Carl is still helping several people in front of me when a tiny set of hands grabs both of my arse cheeks and squeezes.

"Tushy!" a small voice squeals.

I chuckle to myself, deciding to ignore it since it's probably just a toddler who's still learning about boundaries.

"Oh my God, Levi, no! We do not touch people's bottoms!"

Feckin' hell, I know that voice. When he squeezes again, I decide to have some fun.

I jump and spin, turning to face him as I puff out my chest and put my hands on my hips. "Who is touching my tushy! Don't you know it's bad luck to pinch someone before St. Patrick's Day!" I bellow in my best Papa Bear voice. It's not true, but I decide to have fun with the wee one.

The kid looks taken aback for a split second before he breaks into a fit of giggles. "You sound funny!"

"Levi, that's not nice!" Lucy scolds, grabbing his hand and pulling him back. "Say you're sorry."

She won't make eye contact, and something about that doesn't sit right with me.

"I sorry," Levi says.

"It's okay, pal. But you really shouldn't touch people's bottoms. What if they farted in your face?" I don't know why I'm egging him on, but there's something in his giggle that makes my heart feel at ease.

"Fart!"

"Not again. I just got him to stop saying that one," Lucy groans, dropping her head.

"Sorry, I was just trying to break the tension," I say.

"Fart, fart, fart!" Levi continues before breaking out his best impression of a fart by blowing his lips against his hand.

"It's fine."

Oh shite, I really fucked up.

Levi looks like he's about to make a run for it when she

scoops him up, placing him on her hip just as Micah pokes his head out from behind her.

"Hey there," I say, pretending to tip my hat to him.

"Hi." He takes a step out from behind his mom, still clutching her shirt.

"How's the arm?"

"It doesn't hurt anymore. Want to sign my cast?"

"Of course I do." I pat down my pockets in a big show. "But I don't have a pen."

His face drops, and he lets out a big sigh. "It's okay."

Like hell if I'm gonna let that go. "I know I have some at the firehouse. Whataya say we head over there, and I can sign your cast? And maybe you guys would like to sit in the big fire truck?"

Micah looks up at Lucy, tugging on her shirt. "Pleeeease, Mama, can we?"

"Fire truck. Fire truck!" Levi chants.

"I guess we're going to the firehouse," she says with only a hint of exasperation.

"There's two trucks and an ambulance. They can run around, push all the buttons, and it's fully enclosed and staffed, so they can't run off. And if they get hurt, you know you'll get the best EMT in town," I say, taking a step closer to her.

"Oh, is Hardy working today?" she quips, finally making eye contact with me, a hint of challenge in her emerald-green eyes. I like this fire in her.

I clutch my chest as I wince. "You wound me, Lucy."

"Oh no, he has an ouchie," Levi says, pointing at me. "Kiss it, Mama. Kiss his ouchie better."

"Yeah, Mama, kiss it better," I say.

Her eyes flick to my chest, then up to my lips, lingering briefly before she shakes her head quickly as if to snap herself out of what she's feeling. "Mr. Mike is a big boy, I'm sure he doesn't need kisses to feel better."

"Yes, he does. They always make boo-boos better," Levi insists.

I tilt my head at her, hoping she'll listen to her little instigator. "I do. I need it to feel better," I say, popping open a button with one hand and pulling the collar of my polo open to expose my pec.

"This is ridiculous," she grumbles.

"You have to ask him where it hurts," Levi adds.

I'm going to give this kid every piece of candy we have in the firehouse when this is over. I don't think I've ever had a better wingman.

"Fine. Where does it hurt?" She rolls her eyes as she hoists Levi higher on her hip.

"Here." I slowly trace the hard lines of my pec with a finger and revel in the way her eyes track the movement.

She exhales deeply as she slowly leans into my chest. When she's millimeters away, she mutters an almost inaudible "*so stupid*" and literally pecks me like a chicken, her nose poking me more than anything. I don't think she even puckered her lips.

"Not like that, Mama, like this." Levi leans over, puckers his lips, and plants one on my shirt. There's some sort of food residue still present on his face, and he smears it on the fabric. I chuckle as Lucy's eyes fixate on it.

"Oh jeez, I'm so sorry." Her eyes are still stuck on the stain.

I shrug, unbothered. "I have a Tide pen at the firehouse."

Her eyes flick up to mine, and I hold her stare, waiting for her to make the next move.

She glances around me instead. "Why is this taking so long?"

"Kiss his boo-boo, Mama," Levi whines as Micah pokes his head out from behind her again, suddenly interested in our conversation.

"I need a good kiss, you know, to make sure my boo-boo fully heals."

Her brows pinch, and she narrows her eyes at me. When she leans forward, she exhales slowly, deliberately, and the warmth of it tickles my skin.

Those emerald-green eyes stay locked on mine. Not flustered. Not shy. Challenging.

Something tightens low in my gut. The sudden, unmistakable awareness that this woman isn't playing along for her kids anymore. It feels like she's choosing this. Choosing me. Choosing to stand this close.

There's no room left in my head for restraint. No polite thought will survive this. All I can think about is putting her on her knees, forcing her to look me in the eyes while choking on my cock.

The second her plush pink lips caress my bare skin, I know I've fucked up. And now I have a boner in public. I move my hands in front of my crotch, willing my dick to deflate.

"Better?" she asks, a hint of snark in her tone as her eyes flick down to my pants.

"Loads," I rasp.

"Hey, Mike, I've got your special order," a voice calls from behind me, and I spin on my heel as I step up to the counter, thankful for the momentary reprieve so I can collect myself.

Carl rings me up, and I have him add Lucy's purchase to my tab. I'm almost out the door when I hear her protest. The way she objects tells me she's not used to anyone stepping in for her. That might be a problem. Or it might be exactly what she needs.

The store is empty now when she calls out, "Mike, you didn't have to do that. Let me pay you back."

"I'm headed to the firehouse. We'll have to square up over there. That is, if you don't have too many other things on your *list* for today," I say as I exit the store, not entirely confident she'll follow, but for once hopeful that she will.

CHAPTER 9
LUCY

*D*id he just imply what I think he did?

Holy fuck, he does have my list.

Shit. Shit. Shit.

What do I do? Do I go to the firehouse? The boys could stand to burn off some energy, and it's too cold for the park today. But if I go there, is he going to tease me about my list? What if he wants to help me with it? No, there's no way he'd want to do that. He'll probably just give it back to me and send me on my way.

Carl hands me our meat, all neatly wrapped, pulling me from my thoughts. I set Levi down, drop it in my reusable grocery bag, and walk out of the store, boys in tow, still unsure of my next move. When I get outside, Mike is nowhere to be seen, so I head toward our car.

Micah tugs on my hand. "I want to see the fire trucks."

"Fire trucks. Wee-noo-wee-noo!" Levi sings.

"Just get in the car," I say, buckling Levi into his car seat. Once I sit down, I grip the wheel tightly, willing away the intrusive thoughts overtaking my brain.

It's probably nothing.

He's probably just taking pity on an overwhelmed mom.

He probably offers up the fire trucks to every kid he meets.

He probably doesn't even have my list. I'm just imagining the way he emphasized that word.

That's it. It's all in my head.

"MAMA!" Micah shouts, startling me.

I turn in my seat to look at him. "What is it, baby?"

"I've been calling your name."

"Sorry, I have a lot on my mind. I didn't hear you."

"Can we go to the fire station? Mr. Mike said they have some cool Pokémon there. He has the game on his phone, and he said we could play sometime."

I don't even know how to respond to him. Micah does not like most men. A few visits with my dad ensured that. So for him to ask to spend more time with one, well, it's huge.

"Okay," I relent on an exhale. A chorus of cheers come from the back seat as we head towards the fire station.

I can't believe I'm doing this. Have I lost my mind?

We walk up to the front door of the station, and Levi yelps when Micah hits the doorbell before him. I'm trying to separate the impending fight when the door swings open and Mike's booming voice startles me.

"Just the kiddos I was hoping to see!"

Something about his admission warms my heart. He could have made a flirty comment and teased me more, but the fact that he seems genuinely happy to see my kids sets my mind at ease.

We follow him into the station, and Levi lifts his arms. "Uppies!" I'm about to lean down when Mike scoops him up like he weighs nothing. I should fight him on this, but I'm secretly relieved not to tote around an almost-fifty-pound four-year-old.

Mike continues the tour, showing us all the rooms in the station. I'm honestly in shock that they're not bored because we haven't even seen a fire truck yet. As I follow him down a hallway, Micah lets go of my hand and jogs to catch up with Mike. When he grabs Mike's hand, my heart skips a beat, and I blink rapidly, trying not to cry. This is dumb. Why is this making me so emotional? I mean, this is a huge step for him, but it shouldn't make me cry, for Pete's sake.

Quick, I need a distraction, something to take my mind off the sentimental nonsense running through my head. My eyes track over from their clutched hands to Mike's backside. Dammit, he has a really cute ass. I get why Levi grabbed it. It's thick and round, and I'm struck with the urge to touch it myself.

A throat clears, and I look up to see Mike peering at me over his shoulder.

"Enjoying the tour, Lucy?" He smirks, and I die a little inside. He totally caught me checking out his ass.

Fuck my life.

Before I have a chance to respond, he swings open a door to the garage part of the building. "This is the bay. It's where all the rigs are stored."

Saved by the fire trucks.

He sets Levi down, and he immediately takes off for the biggest truck, jumping up and down like he could reach the handle to open the door.

"Levi, no!" I screech.

Moving faster than I expected, Mike is right behind him, roping his thick, tattooed forearm around Levi's middle as he hoists him in the air. "At least lemme open the door for you, lad." He chuckles, and I blow out a sigh of relief. Micah lurks behind them, curious but cautious with his cast.

Mike sets Levi in the truck. Levi is in heaven, running his hands over everything in the cab, unable to sit still as his eyes go comically wide.

"Wanna jump in too?"

Micah nods, and Mike carefully lifts him into the truck. He sits in the driver's seat, watching his brother play whack-a-mole with all the buttons.

"He can't break anything in there, can he? Because I'm not sure I could afford to replace anything on my teacher's salary."

"He's grand," he says, still watching my boys.

I'm mesmerized by the way he observes my kids, like he can't look away. It would be easy to assume it's because he's worried about them breaking something, but he looks genuinely enthralled by them instead of scared off by their energy.

He must see a lot of kids come through here. This is just part of his charm. I mean, job. It's part of his job. He props his foot up on the bottom step up to the cab as he leans against the open door. The move makes his ass pop, and I can't help staring at it. Yeah, I definitely want to touch that.

"Whoa, you're having a party without me?" a voice calls from behind me. I startle, prying my eyes off Mike's ass as I turn, clutching a hand to my chest.

"Didn't mean to scare ya," he says, holding up his hands. "I'm Chief Sawyer." He extends his arm, and I shake his hand.

"Hi. I'm sorry. We're probably making too much noise, and you all probably have a lot to do. We'll get out of your hair."

"Nonsense, they're having fun," Sawyer says. "Stay as long as you like. Unless we get a call, we've got all the time in the world."

"Chief." Mike nods.

"Did you show them the button they're absolutely not supposed to touch under any circumstances whatsoever?" Sawyer asks. My blood pressure starts skyrocketing until I see the smirk on his face.

"No, I didn't. You want the honor?" Mike steps aside as the chief climbs into the cab and starts the engine.

My boys stare with rapt fascination as everything on the

dashboard lights up. Levi is sitting next to him, and I see the moment he loses his battle with his impulse control, but Sawyer throws his arm out, holding him back as he speaks in a low voice. "Whatever you do, don't touch that button," he says, pointing to the panel.

Levi's body vibrates with pent-up energy as his eyes flick back and forth from the button to the chief. Micah pulls his cast against his chest, using his other arm to hold it in place as he cautiously sizes up Sawyer, unsure what to make of him. I hold my breath, knowing exactly how this is going to play out since I've seen this scenario hundreds of times at home. I tell them not to do something, and Micah easily complies, but Levi's brain is set to destruct mode, calculating every angle of the situation. *Is it worth it? Do I care? How fast can I do it? Will Mama notice? Will Micah tattle? Fuck it, I'm doin' it!*

I see all that play out in Levi's head as he grips Sawyer's arm, shimmies over it, and slams his hand down on the button. I cover my ears as a siren blasts through the closed space and Mike doubles over in laughter. Micah looks terrified. Levi is whooping. And I'm oddly at peace for once that these two men are showing my kids some attention and they're eating it up. There aren't a lot of people I can depend on, and these two seem content to spend time with my kids, even if it is just for the moment.

Sawyer cuts the engine to the truck shortly after, which is probably for the best. He looks at Mike. "Why don't you give her a tour of the kitchen? I'll keep these two entertained." He then turns to my boys. "Have you ever seen the inside of an ambulance?"

"I have!" Micah says.

"I wanna see it!" Levi pipes up.

He turns back to me. "My kids are a little older than them, but I remember this age. I got this. Go take a break. Grab something to eat with Mike."

Before I can respond, he's chasing after my kids as they run over to the ambulance.

"Is he always like this?" I ask Mike, my gaze shifting back to Levi and Micah.

"A big kid? Yep. But he's a good guy. Even better father." We stand there in awkward silence for several moments before he speaks again. "You hungry?"

I am. But I've got groceries in the car I really should unload. They'll be fine in the cold for a bit, so it's not like I'm in a big hurry. But being in this man's presence is overwhelming, and I can't figure out why he has such an effect on me. My therapist would probably point out my lack of control. I don't like not having control over situations. I know it goes back to my shitty ex, Kyle. It's something I'm working on, but it's a damn hard habit to break.

Shit, he asked me a question.

I *am* hungry. Just not in the way he means, and definitely not for anything that can be served on a plate. My stomach tightens, heat pooling low as my brain insists on replaying the way he looked at me. The confidence. The ease. The fact that he knows exactly what he's doing and isn't the least bit sorry about it.

It's been years since I've felt the touch of a man. Years since I let myself think about one like this, about hands and mouths and the kind of attention that has nothing to do with responsibility or restraint. But I'm not about to tell him that.

Focus, Lucy. Food. Normal adult conversation. Being around kids all day at home and at school, I'm clearly starved for grown-up interactions. I just need to keep my mind out of the gutter.

Easier said than done when the gutter currently has his name written all over it.

"Yes? Maybe. I don't know. I just want to see how this plays out first." I nod toward the ambulance, but Micah seems to be taken by Sawyer just like he was with Mike. Maybe he's growing out of this phase of hating men. Maybe he just needs to be around more men instead of me and all my single mom friends all the time. Maybe he wouldn't be so skittish if my dad hadn't yelled at him for breaking a plate the last time I let him see them.

"They're really feckin' cute," Mike says as Levi runs around the truck, Sawyer chasing after him.

"Thanks."

"I know Micah already, but what's the wee one's name?"

Is he joking? "The number of times I've yelled it in front of you the past week should be a clue."

He chuckles. "Fair."

"It's Levi."

"Levi," he says slowly as if he's testing the feel of it on his tongue. "Not sure anyone could top our meet-cute." His head turns to mine, a smile lighting up his features.

"Really?" I look over at him, trying my best not to roll my eyes. "Our meet-cute was a train wreck."

"I was talking about me and Micah's meet-cute."

I shake my head, rubbing my forehead with two fingers as if I can iron out the wrinkles forming there as I hide my embarrassment. Of course he wasn't talking about ours. "Meet-cutes are usually between love interests."

"Anyone can have a meet-cute," he insists. "And Micah and I bonded over Pokémon. Best meet-cute ever, in my opinion. And then I officially met your wee one at Meat Cute. We had a Meat Cute meet-cute."

"Can you stop saying meet-cute?" I try to keep the frustration from seeping into my tone, but the slightly wounded look on his face tells me I failed. It's for the best. I don't want him getting attached to me or my boys, not when everything I touch ends in disaster. Best to keep things light. Casual.

"Sorry. Just saying I enjoyed spending time with your lad even if it wasn't under the most ideal of circumstances. But I hadn't been officially introduced to Levi, not counting the arse-grabbin'."

I feel bad for the way I shut him down with my comment, and I bite my lip, offering him a small smile. His eyes drop to my mouth, seemingly mesmerized by the movement. Is the firefighter hottie checking me out? Surely not. It's all in my head. I'm a walking disaster, as proven by our earlier run-ins.

There's no way someone as attractive as him would ever want to be with someone like me. I don't mean to put myself down, and I think I have very attractive qualities, but they're buried deep in the rubble that is my disaster of a life. I love my kids, and I was lucky to be able to conceive them, but my dating life often feels like a string of unlucky disasters.

"How'd you come up with the name Levi? I like it."

"It took me a week to pick a name for him. I was alone with a toddler, suddenly responsible for two kids on my own. And Micah kept getting annoyed with how attached Levi was to me, mainly because I was breastfeeding, so I looked up names and when I saw that Levi meant 'joined' or 'attached,' I just knew."

He furrows his brow. "Why were you alone? What about their dad?"

Knowing this isn't something I'm willing to share, I choose my words carefully. "Their dad isn't in the picture."

He nods once, and I exhale, relieved he's not going to press further. "Micah is a handsome lad. Has your eyes."

Our eyes meet, and I'm overwhelmed by the intensity I see there. *Is* he flirting with me? Or just examining my eyes to see if they match Micah's?

He lifts a hand and tucks a strand of hair behind my ear, and I shiver at the contact. No, definitely flirting.

"Where does Levi get the red hair from? Does it run in your family?" His fingers linger by my ear before he pulls back.

I drop my head, suddenly overwhelmed by his attention. "It must," I admit, and I squeeze my eyes shut, suddenly afraid he's going to pick that comment apart. Who doesn't know if something like that runs in their family?

But he doesn't press the matter, and I look up at him, silently wishing he would touch me again.

"It suits him."

"Thanks."

Mike nods and leans against the truck behind us, propping a leg up in a way that appears effortlessly cool, totally casual. Meanwhile, I'm a mess of chaotic thoughts and restless energy. What is his game here? Surely he'll get tired of me. He'll definitely get tired of my boys; they are a handful and a half. Is he looking for something serious or just a hookup? I've never brought men around my boys. I don't want them getting attached to someone who isn't going to stick around for long. And what if we did start something? Chestnut Mountain is full of gossips; it could get back to the boys. I've done a good job of isolating ourselves since they were born. I keep my circle small, don't go out much, keep to myself. Besides that, I don't like relying on other people, not even my friends. I learned at a young age that I could only count on myself, so I have a hard time letting people in.

I don't know a lot of people in our small town outside of my little friend group, so it's not surprising that Mike and I have never met before now. I've seen him around before, of course, but I can't seem to avoid bumping into him lately. With my luck, if we did start something and it ended, I'd never be able to turn another corner without seeing him.

Mike leans toward me and lowers his voice. "I want to help you." His clean, woodsy scent hits me, and fuck me, it smells good. Masculine. Sensual.

Shaking my head, I clear my thoughts, trying not to let the gravel of his voice or his hypnotizing scent influence the decision-making part of my brain. "We're good. Despite our recent run-ins, I promise I'm not a total shit mom."

He chuckles. "Never thought you were anything less than amazing."

I turn to look at him. "What?"

"With them. Your lads." He gestures to the ambulance and the excited squeals emanating from it.

"But that's not what I'm offering to help with." He winks.

Oh my *God*.

All the blood in my body rushes to my face as I try not to look at him again. My cheeks are on fire, my hands are sweaty, and my panties are damp. I try everything I can think of to calm down, every tool my therapist has given me, but nothing is working. I can't even control my reaction to him, and I hate it. Except I don't hate it. But I do hate that I like it so much.

Images flood my brain. Him shirtless, sweat dripping down his well-defined pecs, an axe on his shoulder. I swear I've already memorized every inch of his calendar photo and would recognize his body in a lineup while blindfolded, with only my hands to guide me.

Fuck, and now I can't stop thinking about that.

His hand brushes against mine, and I look down to see his pinky graze the back of my hand, tracing slow circles there. I feel it in every inch of my body, every nerve ending standing at attention. Even my clit pulses as he continues his movements.

It's impossible to look away from his hand. How is that one tiny movement the most erotic thing that's happened to me in years?

I need to get laid.

I need to fuck the hot firefighter.

I need to get a hold of myself.

As if sensing the switch in my mood, he hooks his pinky with mine, tethering me to him. In a move he must have practiced before, he slides his hand up and over the side of my palm, only letting go of my pinky at the last second as he presses his palm against mine.

He leans close to my ear. "Think about it. I'm more than happy to help." He squeezes my hand and then releases it as he slowly swaggers away from me. And I watch him go. Shamelessly. Because I clearly have no fucking self-control when it comes to this man.

It's only once he's gone that I look down and realize he's slipped a piece of paper into my hand.

Please don't be what I think it is.

I open it slowly, as if it's the most sacred parchment carrying life's greatest secrets to happiness.

Lucy and Mike's Get Lucky List
~~Lucy's Get Lucky List~~

1. Be less boring in bed – I can already tell you this doesn't need to be here. Care to replace it with something else?

2. Role-play – Yes ma'am

3. Have multiple orgasms – How many is too many?

4. Tie someone up – I have plenty of rope

5. Sit on someone's face – I volunteer as tribute

6. Spankings? – Giving or receiving? Okay, both it is

7. Hook up with a guy with an accent. Mr. March? I wish! – Your wish is my command

Underneath all his notes, he's included the words "Call me" and his number.

I glance around nervously, paranoid that someone is looking over my shoulder, but I'm alone. After I take a few calming breaths, I thank the fire chief and load up the boys in the car, determined to push this from my mind.

It's not until an hour after the boys have gone to bed that I pull out my phone and text Bella.

He has the list.

BELLA

And he's checking it twice?

This is serious.

Sorry, wrong holiday. Deep breaths. Putting on my serious pants.

They're a little tight, aren't they?

Yup. It's been a while since I wore them. LOL Tell me everything.

I ran into him again at Meat Cute and he invited us to the station. Of course I couldn't deny the boys a chance to see a real fire truck.

Ooh he's smart. Getting the kids involved.

Exactly

And right before we left, he slipped a note in my hand.

What did it say?

It was my list.

But he made some notes on it.

[sends pic of the updated sex list]

OH. MY. GOD. 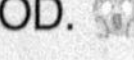

This is diabolical.

Never knew he had it in him.

Also, you're a little sexy minx and I love it.

You're not helping.

Are you going to do it?

No. Maybe? I don't know.

What do I do?

In the words of Aunt Delilah, you go hump the hot firefighter. 😏

CHAPTER 10

MIKE

It's nearly the end of February, almost a week has gone by, and I think Lucy has completely blown me off, when my phone lights up with a text from an unknown number.

I set down my ladle, put the lid on the pot, and wipe my hands on my apron as I lean back against the counter. When I'm satisfied no one is looking—I don't trust these fuckers not to tease me—I swipe up on my phone and pull up my texts.

UNKNOWN

Do you still want to help?

Depends who's asking.

If this is Lucy, then hell yes I do.

If this isn't Lucy, sorry, I'm waiting on this beautiful woman to call me.

The dots dance on the screen, and I second-guess my boldness as I add her contact to my phone. Did I read her wrong? Did I come on too strong?

MO CHROÍ

What do you get out of this?

This is going to be tougher than I thought. It would be fun to poke her a little, but something tells me I'm going to win more flies with honey with her.

Would it be lame to say the pleasure of your company?

Yes

Damn

Then I'm going to be honest.

I'm incredibly attracted to you.

And I found your list so I know you want me too.

I want to help you check everything off.

And if you're texting me, I take it that means you're on board with my amendments.

But why do you want to help me?

Woman, do I need to draw a map of your body and circle all the places I want to explore?

Because it would be a giant circle around your entire body.

Ummm

Okay

Damn. She's a hard one to crack. My dick is celebrating the news, but my head and heart are cautious. Clearly, she's not going to make this easy on me, but I'm up for the challenge.

> I want to be clear about what this is.

> And what is it?

> You're just helping me with the list.

> We're not together.

> And once the list is completed, we go our separate ways.

> What if I don't agree to all your terms?

> Are you open to negotiations?

I could easily complete her entire list in one epic fuckfest, if I hydrated and took breaks. At thirty-seven, I'm not a young lad and my refractory period isn't what it used to be, but that's what eating pussy is for. And I *love* eating pussy. I can bang a few things off her list, and if I get too close to finishing, I'll just feast on her cunt until I get myself under control.

Wait, what the fuck am I thinking? I want to draw this out, not end it all in one night. If I take my time, tease her, make her excited for more, maybe she'll keep adding to her list, or forget it completely.

> What are you suggesting?

> For every item we check off, I get one date.

> There are seven items on my list.

> So seven dates.

> Three dates.

> Five dates.

> And the boys can join us too.

No funny business. I just want to spend time with all of you.

That sounds an awful lot like dating.

It's not.

Unless you want it to be?

I don't date.

No? You just admire calendar men from afar?

Ugh you're annoying.

But you still think I'm hot.

Fine. Four dates, but they will all be at my house.

Embarrassed to be seen with me?

I don't need anyone spreading any gossip.

But also, the boys are easier to contain in their natural habitat.

What if I babyproofed my apartment? Would you come here?

It's cute that you think mere babyproofing could contain Levi.

That's fair. I accept your terms.

I can't believe I'm agreeing to this.

I promise you won't regret it.

Are you free tomorrow? The boys have a sleepover.

Shit, I'm on call all night.

Come to the firehouse.

What? No.

Do you trust me?

I don't even trust myself.

Afraid you'll fall?

Why did I say that? I was going for flirty, implying she would fall for me, but given that I have literally caught her falling thrice, I worry I've shoved my foot in my mouth. Shite.

Wow. Too soon, Mr. March.

You can just call me Mike.

Or Mr. O'Connor.

Or yours.

If I were to show up at the firehouse… is everyone going to know why I'm there? I don't want the whole town talking about this.

Come after 11 and text me when you get here. No one will know.

———

I do a quick sweep of the firehouse, relieved that it has quieted down for the night with most everyone in their bunks or the TV room. When I walk by Hardy's office, I notice the light on and pop my head in.

"Hey, Hardy, can I talk to you about something?"

"Why do I know that I'm not going to like the sound of this?"

"I would never normally ask this, but there's this girl I'm into, and she has childcare for only tonight. Do you think I could be off duty for a couple hours?" My phone buzzes in my pocket and I pull it out, noticing Lucy's "here" text.

He nods toward my phone. "That her?"

"Yup."

"She in the parking lot?"

"Emm…"

He spins his computer monitor around, showing me the image of a car idling in our parking lot.

"Feckin' hell. I can explain."

"Do I need to remind you that you're on call? That at any moment a call could come in that would require us to drop everything to go help someone?"

I nod, feeling like a royal arsehole.

Hardy stands, leaning over his desk as he lowers his voice. "Well then, I'm also going to remind you that the gym is the only room in the building with a locking door for some odd reason. And… oops, the camera just went out in that room. It does that sometimes. Someone really should fix it."

I blink at him in confusion, trying to decipher if he's being serious or fucking with me. Normally, I'm the one messing with him.

"If we get a call, you better haul ass to your rig. I don't care if you're balls-deep in your friend or not. Got it?" There's a harshness to his tone that lets me know that he means business. "And this is your one free pass. If I ever catch you pulling anything like this at this firehouse again, I'll go straight to the chief."

"Got it. One time. It won't happen again." I feel like I'm being punished, when he's actually given me the greatest gift. "Can I ask why you're doing this?"

"Bella told me about Lucy's date from hell. Said she could really use some good luck. Don't fuck this up. And for Christ's sake, clean up after yourselves."

I hurry out of his office, texting Lucy to meet me at the back door. When I see her walk up, I hustle her inside and down the hall toward the gym.

"Are we going to get in trouble?" she whispers.

Opening the door for her, I gesture for her to go first and I lock the door behind us. The fluorescent lights flick on, and she blinks as she adjusts to the brightness. "How many rules are you breaking right now?" she asks.

"Don't worry about it. Besides, you're worth getting in trouble for." I grip her by the hips and pull her against me.

Her hands land on my chest and she rests them there, pushing against me slightly. She looks around the room, taking in all the equipment. "That's a lot of mirrors." Her voice is quiet, a hint of nervousness in her tone.

"And I can't wait to see every inch of you in them," I say as I lean down to kiss her, but her words stop me.

"This was a mistake," she says, shoving my chest, attempting to break my hold, but I wrap my arms around her tighter.

What spooked her? "Talk to me," I plead, trying to get her to make eye contact with me.

There's a riot of emotions on her face, and I'm having trouble deciphering them as I'm still learning to read her.

"This just doesn't feel very…"

"Romantic?" I suggest.

She nods. "Sure, we'll go with that."

"It's not supposed to be romantic, we're not dating. Your rules, right?"

"Right." She looks around the room again. "Could we turn off a few of the lights?"

"It's all or nothing, and since this room has no windows, it'd be impossible to see anything with them off."

"That's good. Let's do that."

I lean back, trying to figure out why she's making such a

request. "What's really going on in that beautiful head of yours?"

"Look, I know this is just sex, but I don't want a quickie with you on a dirty gym floor in your fire station."

"Oh, Lucy. You underestimate my creativity," I say, clucking my tongue.

She cocks an eyebrow.

"I was going to let you tie me up to that bench press over there so you could ride me. The mirrors are just an added bonus."

Her eyes go wide before they flick over to the bench press. She shakes her head in an emphatic no when it hits me that she's self-conscious about her body in the mirrors and under the lights.

Knowing I'm not going to cure her body image hang-ups in the limited time we have, I opt for another approach.

"See that over there?" I nod to the old fire pole near the corner of the room.

Her head turns in that direction. "Yeah?"

"That used to be the fire pole for the station before we remodeled. Now all the bunks are downstairs, along with most of our living quarters. Instead of getting rid of the pole, they sealed it up and built the gym around it. Not sure if they thought we'd be in here pole dancing on it, but the chief said it felt like bad luck to tear it out."

"Why are you telling me this?" She's still looking over her shoulder at the pole.

I lean in, inhaling her fruity, floral scent as I get closer to her ear and lower my voice. "Because I want you to tie me to that pole and do whatever you want to me."

Asking her to please me feels like a selfish move for our first time together, but if I'm reading her correctly about the lights and the mirrors, she's a little self-conscious about revealing her body to me in these conditions. If I take the pressure off her and get her to focus on me, we can still complete item four on her list: tie someone up.

She looks at me skeptically, and I release her hips, putting my arms up in defense. I want her to know that she can trust me. Giving her all the power seems like the best option here.

I lock eyes with her, getting lost in her emerald-green depths. "You can tie me up and leave if that's what you really want. But your list mentioned wanting to tie someone up, and while I'd love to have you in a bed, we have childcare, school, and work schedules to juggle. I say we seize the opportunity we have, and you have a little fun with me. Whataya say, a chroí?"

"What does that mean? You keep calling me that."

"Nothing, just an old Irish nickname."

She crosses her arms over her chest.

"It's like 'my dear' in English." That's... not a complete lie. She already has my heart, but there's no way I can tell her that.

"I've never tied a knot before."

My heart races. Is she going to play along with this? "I can teach you."

She gives the smallest of nods.

I pull a rope out of the cargo pocket of my pants.

"So you planned this?"

"I like to be prepared."

"I can't believe I'm agreeing to this." She lets out a huff of a breath, and I hook my fingers under her chin, forcing her to look at me.

"You can stop this at any time. You hold the power here." If she only knew how much power she already has over me.

"Okay."

Uncoiling the rope, I show her how to make a simple column knot. After a few practice attempts, she makes a decent one and secures my left hand to the pole.

"Should I do your other hand?" She looks unsure. I know that if this is going to work, I need her to be in control.

"Depends on what you want to do to me."

Her eyes lower to my crotch, and I thrust my hips slightly.

"I'm not good at… that." Her voice is meek as her eyes drop to the ground.

I crook my fingers under her chin again, forcing her to look at me. "I don't believe that for a second, and whatever arsehole told you that wasn't worth your time anyway. Why don't you let me be the judge? I'm happy to assess your skills."

"Can I…" Her question lingers in the air as she runs her hands down my pecs and torso, and I shudder under her touch. When she hesitates at the hem of my shirt, I lift it up and over my head, letting it dangle on my bound arm.

"Get your fill, love." Her responding blush has my cock hardening in my pants.

Her delicate fingers roam greedily over my body, her nails dragging along the grooves and ridges of my muscles.

"It's not fair that you look like this."

"I spend a lot of time in this room, and my job is very physical. I've put in a lot of work to achieve this."

And all that time spent lifting means I had less time for others, something I'm desperate to change. I'd let myself get a little soft for the right woman, and something tells me that she'd be worth giving up hours in the gym. Worth eating shite food with her kids. Worth spending other ways to get in cardio.

When her hands reach my waistband, she pauses again. I undo my belt with one hand, letting the *thwack* echo in the space around us as I drop it to the floor.

Her eyes flick to mine and I nod, giving her the green light to proceed.

I can't look away as she undoes my pants and they fall to my ankles. She has me completely at her mercy, and I'm not sure she understands the full extent of that.

"Holy fuck," she rasps as I swell to match the size of my ego.

The tip of my cock pokes out of the top of my boxer briefs and she traces the head, then swipes a finger through the tip, smearing the precum collecting there.

A hiss escapes me as I silently plead with her to pull down my boxers so she can see the pot of gold at the end of my rainbow.

Fuck, that was bad, but I can't wait to see her reaction to my entire length and its hidden treasure.

My hips have a mind of their own as I thrust against her touch. After several seconds of exploration, she tugs down my waistband and my cock springs free.

Her eyes widen and her mouth drops open. "Are you pierced?"

"Aye."

She trails a finger down, playing with one of the gold barbells that make up my Jacob's ladder.

"How many are there?" she asks, still teasing the top one.

I grab her hand with my unbound one, taking her fingers in mine to help her explore. "One." I move her hand down an inch. "Two." Her eyes go wide. "Three." She licks her lips. "Four." Another inch. "Five." She gasps.

"Did it hurt?"

"Like hell."

"Will it hurt?"

Her question fills me with excitement. It means she's imagining it. Picturing us together. Maybe she'll give me a chance after all.

"I promise I will make you feel so good."

She drops to her knees, her face eye-level with my dick, and I hold my breath, waiting for her to take me in her mouth. Her skin is soft as she grips me by the base. When her tongue peeks out, licking her lips, a bead of precum leaks from my tip. Her eyes track the movement.

"I'm not good at this."

"Lucy, you've got me ready to blow my load just from the

way you're looking at it. There's nothing you could do to me at this point that I wouldn't enjoy."

"Okay." She exhales and the warmth of her breath against my dick has me shivering in anticipation.

Sensing her nerves and wanting to put her at ease, I grip her wrist as I speak. "I want your perfect feckin' mouth on me. Your plump pink lips. That wicked sharp tongue. You don't even know the mess you've already made of me without even touching me."

I release her wrist, and she guides the tip between her lips. The moment my skin hits the warmth of her tongue, I know I'm done for. I want to live in her mouth. Revel in her warmth.

"Feckin' *hell*."

When she hums in response, the vibrations make my balls draw up, that familiar feeling taking over.

Her hand tightens around my shaft, pumping in tandem with her mouth as her confidence grows.

"Yes, a chroí. Fuck, you're so good at that," I praise.

She slides down my length, attempting to take as much of me as she can. I grip her hair, holding her in place as I pulse into her mouth.

A line of saliva drips from her lips and I nearly come undone. "I'm going to come. Pull off if you don't want it." I release my grip and enjoy the view of her holding me in her mouth, challenging me with her eyes as if she's daring me to come.

My orgasm hits seconds later, and she takes all of it, swallowing me down. She pops off my dick, then uses a finger to wipe her lips.

How do I keep her? And who the hell told her she was bad at this? Feckin' eejit.

CHAPTER 11

LUCY

"Maaaamaaaa!" Levi's voice wails. I bolt up in my bed confused and disoriented. They weren't supposed to be back until ten. No, I was supposed to pick them up at ten. A quick glance at my lock screen tells me it's ten thirty. And there are a dozen missed calls.

Shit.

"I'm coming!" I yell as I scramble out of bed and pull on the nearest floor clothes I can find. When I run down the stairs, Summer's face greets me at the bottom with a knowing smile.

She places a comforting hand on my arm. "Hey! My kids are in the car, but yours have been washed and fed. Well, Levi's been washed. I wasn't sure if Micah could get his cast wet, so you may need to wipe him down."

"He's fine. Thank you."

"I was worried about you when you didn't show up at ten."

"I'm so sorry."

"And you weren't answering your phone."

"About that…"

She shakes her head. "You don't have to say anything."

I look over at the boys, relieved they're distracted by the TV, and glance back at Summer. Does she know?

"Don't be mad."

Fuck. She knows. "Who else knows?"

"Just me and Bella. When I couldn't get a hold of you, I started to panic. You never ignore your phone, especially with playdate stuff. But suddenly Bella was chill about everything. Too chill."

"Fucking small towns."

"It wasn't her fault. She was just trying to calm me down and then I knew that she knew something, and I made her tell me after Raven left."

"What did she tell you?"

"That you went up to the firehouse to… check an item off your list last night."

"Fudging popsicles."

"I want a Fudgsicle!" Levi cries.

"Of course that's the part of our conversation he hears."

"Can I have a Fudgsicle, Mama?" Micah asks.

I sigh. "You can each have one Fudgsicle, just eat them in the kitchen over the counter." I turn back to Summer. "That'll buy us a few minutes."

"So it's true? You and the firefighter hottie?"

I nod, unwilling to share more.

Summer keeps her squealing to a minimum. "Did you see anyone else while you were up there?"

"Nope, just Mike."

"Oh," she says, and I remind myself to ask her about that later. "Are you going to see him again?"

"I don't know. I'm not looking for anything serious. I don't want to bring someone into Micah and Levi's lives just to have them leave."

"What makes you think he would leave?"

"Everyone leaves. You and the girls are the only people I can count on."

"What about your sister?"

"Her too if she lived closer."

My sister and I didn't have the best childhood. Our father regularly cheated on our mom, and they bickered constantly. He'd always been a yeller. They finally divorced when I was in middle school, and when my mom wanted to move to start over in Chestnut Mountain, I went with her. But my older sister stayed with my dad. She was two years away from graduating and was planning to go to a school in state for college. Even though my mom has since remarried and left Colorado, I decided to stay. And it's in large part because of these women and the community we've found in one another.

Summer grips my shoulder and smiles, pulling me from my thoughts. "I'm excited for you, but I'd love to see you in a relationship if you decide that's what you want. You deserve someone who will treat you like a queen. Maybe Mr. March is up for the job?"

"I don't know. He seems nice enough, but he hasn't truly seen what my boys are capable of."

She chuckles. "They're a handful, but they're good kids. Try having three on your own. It's a never-ending cycle of chaos."

"No thanks. I'm good with my two."

"I'm gonna head out. I left the twins in the car, and they're liable to figure out how to hotwire it and turn it into their getaway vehicle."

"Thanks again," I say, pulling her into a hug.

"Seriously, though, Lucy—if you want something more with him you should go for it. You never ask us for anything, but any one of us would be happy to help with the boys more. That's what we're here for. I know I'd have a whole lot more grey in my hair if it weren't for Raven and Bella helping with mine."

"I'll think about it." It's not that I don't want the help, but I've just been doing everything on my own since they were born. And I've been doing everything for myself since I was a kid. I wouldn't even know *how* to ask for help.

I walk her to the door and say goodbye, shutting it behind her. When I turn back to check on the boys, Levi is missing.

"Have you seen your brother?"

Micah points to the bathroom. "In there."

My gut sinks. How long has he been in there? He could have half of his Hot Wheels collection in the toilet right now, using it as a car wash again. When I approach the door, I hear his soft little voice, and I crack it open to check on him.

"Pee-nis! Heehee. Poop. Poopoo in the potty. Peepee in the potty. Fart! Toot toots!" He makes a fart noise. I can't tell which end of his body it came from since I only have the door cracked.

It's hard to stifle my laughter, but I muster the strength.

I push open the door a bit more, and Levi startles. "What are you doing, buddy?" I use my sweetest voice, like I'm trying to tame a rabid raccoon. And since it's Levi, I pretty much am.

"I'm in the potty! You said I could use potty words in the potty. Those were the rules." He places his hands on his hips and pouts.

I get that he's trying to stand his ground, and he has some solid logic, but I stare at him dumbfounded, trying to suppress my laughter, impressed by how his mind works. I love this kid so much, and all I want to do is scoop him up and tell him how amazing I think his brain is—but I can't encourage this behavior, or his preschool will be constantly calling me. "Are you using the potty?"

He shakes his head.

"You came into the bathroom just so you can say potty words?"

He nods his head. "Am I in trouble?" His voice is soft, his eyes big, as he gives me "the face." You know the one. The face that all guilty kids make when they know they are in trouble and make themselves extra cute to avoid punishment. Except this time, he didn't do anything wrong. He probably thinks he's in trouble because I look angry when really I'm just trying not to laugh.

My sweet precious boy decided he wanted to use potty language, so he went into the bathroom to use it because I told him that potty talk is only allowed in the bathroom. It's so freaking cute. Inside, I'm dying of laughter. Outside, I'm composed, ready to handle my foul-mouthed preschooler.

"You're not in trouble."

"Can I have another Fudgsicle?"

"No, buddy, you'll spoil your lunch."

He runs out of the bathroom and launches himself onto the couch. Micah is still in the kitchen finishing his Fudgsicle.

"Micah, can you keep an eye on your brother for a minute while I grab my phone? Make sure he doesn't try to sneak another Fudgsicle."

"Yes, Mama."

"Thanks."

"Can you put the code in the iPad so I can play?"

Taking the device from him, I punch in the code, figuring it might keep them distracted long enough for me to actually check my phone and return some texts, not just grab it. I kiss Micah on the head and run upstairs with the fifteen minutes I just bought myself. There are dozens of missed texts from Bella.

BELLA

Hey! It's 10 and your kids are ready for pickup.

Lucy?

Are you on your way?

Where are you?

Okay I'm starting to get worried.

Hellllooooo

Seriously, are you okay?

Why aren't you answering?

Do you need an ambulance or are you just ignoring me?

Never mind

Just talked to Hardy.

He said you were up at the firehouse late last night. 😏

Lucy, you got some 'splaining to do!

[gif of Lucille Ball]

I'm just going to assume you had a late night and that you're dick drunk and sleeping it off.

Summer is going to drop the boys off.

Also, I may have told her about the firehouse.

She was worried since you weren't answering your phone.

I'M SORRY

Also, I'm going to need details!

Did you hump the hot firefighter?

I've been begging Hardy to bang me at the firehouse but he keeps shutting it down.

You're a lucky girl.

I'm alive. Sorry for the scare.

I pocket my phone and head downstairs before I'm gone too long and the boys get into trouble. Or make another mess like the poopocalypse of a few years ago. I shudder at the thought of a repeat of that disaster. My Bissell still looks at me with disdain. Is it normal that my longest, most dependable relationship is with a vacuum?

When I hit the middle step, I hear a deep male voice. A deep male *and slightly Irish* voice.

I look around the space, terrified I'm going to run into Mike while looking like a total bridge troll. My hair is in a bun —and not the cute messy kind—I have no makeup on, and I'm wearing clothes from two days ago that were on the floor of my bedroom. And no bra. Fuck my luck.

He wouldn't have shown up here the morning after our hookup, would he? I did agree to after-hookup dates, but surely, he'd give me some warning.

My boys wouldn't just open the door and let him in, would they?

Yes, they absolutely would.

I get to the bottom of the stairs and look around, praying I don't see his ridiculously handsome face, but the boys are sitting on the couch, eyes glued to the iPad.

"Do it again!" Levi laughs.

Micah's fingers swipe on the screen, and a loud fart noise comes from the tablet. Oh, thank God, they must be watching one of those stupid YouTube videos again. I walk over to the kitchen and start straightening up the island.

"How was that?" the familiar voice asks, and I pause my movements. "That one sounded real, right?"

"It did!" both boys squeal in unison, and another fart sound blares from the device.

Micah turns around from his spot on the couch and holds the tablet up, pointing the screen in my direction. "Mama, say hi to—"

All the blood drains from my face, and I don't hear the rest of his sentence because my eyes are glued to Mr. March staring back at me from FaceTime.

I drop to the floor, hiding behind the counter like that can save me from this nightmare scenario, except when my knee hits the floor, I don't see the LEGO until it imbeds itself in my flesh. "FUUUUDGE!"

"Oh no, Mama!" Micah cries.

"I want another Fudgsicle!" Levi whines.

Meanwhile, I'm writhing on my back on the floor, cradling my knee in my hands, biting my lips to keep the rest of the naughty words from spilling out. At least my tits don't fall out of my shirt.

When Micah appears in my field of vision, still holding the fucking iPad up so Mike can get an eyeful, I curse Lady Luck and the way she keeps shitting all over my life. I've got to figure out how to disconnect my iCloud account from Micah's iPad so this never happens again.

"Are you okay, Mama?" Micah asks right as Levi runs in, stepping over me on his way to get a Fudgsicle out of the freezer.

There's no way this man will want to have anything to do with me after this.

"Lucy, are you okay? Need me to bring my rig?"

"No. I'm fine," I groan, covering my face with my hands.

"Micah, can you set me on the counter so your mom can have a minute?"

"Okay."

I hear him set the iPad down and walk away. Levi tears open his Fudgsicle and runs into the living room, the wrapper of said frozen treat fluttering down like the last leaf falling off a tree in October and landing on my face.

"Lucy? Did I lose you? All I can see is your ceiling. I think there's something stuck to it."

I glance up, noticing the sticky ninja toy Micah threw up there months ago that I have yet to unstick. All I give Mike is a groan in response.

There're some shuffling sounds coming from the iPad and a muffled conversation, but I only hear every other word.

"Can...her kids...appreciate you...see...Monday." The muffled sound stops, and Mike's deep voice calls out again. "Lucy? You still there?"

"Barely."

"Bella is going to come get your boys for a few hours."

I bolt up, narrowly avoiding the drawer that's not closed all the way. "What?"

"Hang tight, a chroí." I hear the sound of the call ending, and I scramble to get up. When I see the dark screen, I breathe a sigh of relief when my phone vibrates on the counter.

BELLA

[gif of Mrs. Doubtfire saying "help is on the way, dear"]

I love you but you don't have to do that.

Getting in my car now

You and Summer had my kids all night last night.

Pulling out of the driveway

Are you texting and driving?

Talk to text

Seriously. You don't have to do this.

Five minute drive pit stop first pack kids

Sorry for typos period

I chuckle at her last two texts knowing her eye is twitching with the way talk-to-text butchered it. I grab an empty backpack and start stuffing it with a spare pair of clothes and some snacks, knowing she won't take no for an answer. Doing the mom math in my head, I calculate how much time it's going to take to get them to go potty, grab a car snack, and get their shoes and coats on.

Twenty minutes later, Bella is on my porch, a grocery bag in hand.

"What's in the bag?" I gesture for her to come in.

"Miss Carlisle!" Micah squeals as he runs over to hug Bella.

"You can just call me Miss Bella outside of school, silly." She looks around the room. "I'm missing one. Where's the little tornado?"

"He's pooping," Micah announces.

"Or he's in the bathroom so he can use potty words again."

"That's so cute," Bella says, taking the backpack from me as she hands me the grocery bag.

"It is until you get a call from his preschool three times in one week."

"Oof. We'll work on it. He's still got a couple years before he's in my class. You enjoy yourself for a few hours, I've got the boys. And check your phone before you open that bag."

"This feels like a setup. And I didn't enjoy the last one you were involved with," I say, thinking back to my terrible date with Temu Ben Affleck.

"Seriously, Lucy, the girls and I are all happy to help. I know you think you have to do everything on your own, but we're here."

Tears well in my eyes and I blink rapidly as she pulls me into a hug. I've known these women since middle and high school, but we only became close once we all started having kids. I've always wanted kids, but I never knew how isolating it could be, and these women saved me. Maybe I can lean on them a little more.

"Call me if they're too much—" I start.

"No such thing. I can handle a class of kindergarteners, this is nothing. And there's no such thing as too much between friends," Bella says against my ear.

She rounds up both kids and loads them up in her car.

Thankfully my car seats were still on the porch from when Summer dropped them off earlier.

Once I'm alone in my house, I pull out my phone to find a text from Mike.

> Hey gorgeous.

> I had Bella pick up some bubbles for you to drink and to soak in. I thoroughly enjoyed you last night and if you want to check something else off your list, or want some company in the tub, all you have to do is ask.

I open the bag, and there's a bottle of prosecco and a bottle of bubble bath. Do I want to spend time with Mike? Absolutely. Should I take advantage of this afternoon off from the kids and get caught up on chores around the house? I should. Am I going to? Hell no.

It takes me about thirty minutes to do a quick cleanup of the kitchen and living room. There are still food crumbs and school papers on the counters, but it's good enough for company.

As hard as it is for me, I'm going to do something for myself for once and put my needs before others. And I need to get laid. No, I need to get fucked.

> Meet me in the tub. I'll leave the door unlocked for you.

And then I text him my address, pop the top off the prosecco, and saunter upstairs full of false confidence that for once luck will be on my side.

CHAPTER 12

LUCY

"Knock knock." *I can do this. I will do this. I will do him.*

Arranging the bubbles so I'm covered, I take a big swig from the prosecco as I will my heart to calm down. "Come in."

"Jesus feckin' Christ." Mike's head peeks out from behind the bathroom door. "Can I join you?"

"Sure," I say with confidence I don't feel.

I've always been a bigger girl. My curves were my favorite part of my body, and I still love that part of myself. Most days. But the way motherhood has changed my shape has left me frustrated more often lately. Now my ass is bigger, and it makes finding jeans harder than ever, so I live in leggings. I'm used to my thick thighs, but the added stretch marks and cellulite have made me feel self-conscious about wearing shorts. The tummy pooch that won't go away has been an annoying addition. And the way my breasts hang after breast-feeding two children leaves me more insecure than ever. Also, why doesn't anyone prepare you for the boob sweat? It never used to be this bad or stink this much.

Don't get me wrong, I love my body, especially now that I've seen what it's capable of, but there are some days I wish I could go back to my pre-baby figure. It's not about being skinny; I've never really wanted that. I just wish I had enjoyed the body that I had before kids. I feel like I never truly appreciated it.

But seeing the way Mike's eyes light up when he looks at me, I feel like my old self again. I feel proud of my body and the way it excites him. I'd never felt more beautiful than I did when I was on my knees for him in the firehouse. The way he looked at me… well, let's just say that I want more of that.

He walks over to the tub, and I nearly swallow my tongue when I realize what he's wearing.

I take him in from head to toe. "Is that your Mr. March outfit from the calendar?" He's shirtless with a pair of pants that look like part of his fire uniform and black boots. Instead of a belt, red suspenders hold up his pants, and it takes everything in me not to snap them against his chest.

"Aye. Your list mentioned wanting to sleep with a guy with an accent. Mr. March, I believe?"

"Is that why your accent is thicker than normal?"

"'Tis. Dusted off me brogue just for you, lass." He takes a step closer to me, shrugging one strap off his shoulder. "This okay?"

I nod and watch in wonder as he strips all the way down and revel in the way he's already hard. "Is that because of me?" I ask, looking directly at his dick.

"Aye. It's always because of you lately," he says as he approaches the side of the tub. "Scoot forward so I can sit behind ya."

I follow his command, and once he joins me in the water, I lean back against his chest. His erection presses against my ass.

"Can I ask you a question?" I like the fact that I can't look at his face right now.

"You can ask me anything."

"Why were you making fart noises on my kids' iPad?"

He chuckles and wraps his arms around my waist. "They called me."

I drop my head back against his chest and groan in frustration. "Ugh, I'm sorry. They must've been mashing buttons on the screen. I really need to get Bella's son to fix that. He's a coding genius."

"S'ok. Was wrapping up my shift and I thought it was you. Levi started talking about poop and farts, so I just played along."

I smile, thinking about the little stinker. As much as their antics annoy me sometimes, I miss them when they're away. "Sounds like Levi."

"It made them laugh, which made me feel good." His arms tighten around my middle, and I try to relax against him. "Can I make you feel good?"

I nod, and he snakes a hand between my thighs, rubbing and teasing along my pussy and then parting me as he dips a finger inside. "Fuck, I can't remember the last time someone touched me like this."

"I'd like to be the only one you remember doing this to ya."

His confession lingers in the air. I should say something, shouldn't lead him on. He's just helping me with my list. This is only sex. But when his fingers find my clit, all rational thought leaves my brain.

Two fingers pinch my nipple, and I don't even realize he'd put his hand there until I'm moaning and arching back into him.

"You like that, don't ya, love?"

He makes slow circles around my clit, and I moan each time he hits a spot that makes my toes tingle. The more he repeats the motion, the louder I get.

"That's a good girl. So feckin' good for me. Your body's tellin' me exactly what ya need. Are ye gonna come for me?"

Oh shit, I am. How did he do that?

He moves his fingers back to the exact spot that made me

moan the loudest. As he lavishes attention to my clit, I squirm and buck my hips, gripping on to the side of the tub as my orgasm crashes into me. "Oh God! Mike. Fuck. Oh fuck."

"Feckin' hell, I really enjoy hearing my name come out of your mouth like that when ya come." He wraps both of his arms around my middle and grinds his cock against me. "I need to fuck ya."

I nod my head rapidly against his chest. "I want that."

He stands and reaches for a towel. I do my best to shield myself as I stand from the bubbles and wrap the towel around me, while he helps me out of the tub.

"You have another one of these?" He tugs on the end of the towel.

I've lived alone for so long that I'm used to just having one towel on the rack, and I hurry over to the linen closet to grab another one. Fuck my luck. Where are all the clean towels? I dig through, finally finding a kid's towel. It has a hood with Daniel Tiger's face and is comically small compared to his big body. "Here."

He chuckles and then dries off quickly, hanging the towel on the rack and tugging me into my bedroom. I clutch my towel against my chest, suddenly nervous that I don't have the bubbles for camouflage.

I walk over to my dresser and grab a T-shirt, slipping it on over the towel before letting it drop to the floor.

If he's disappointed in my attire, he doesn't show it as he comes up behind me and drags his hands along my outer thighs and up to my hips, dipping just slightly under my shirt.

He places kisses along my collarbone as goosebumps spread across my skin under his touch. "Do you have a condom?" I rasp.

"Aye. Get on the bed." He bends down to grab my towel and pops me on the ass with it before disappearing into the bathroom. When he emerges, he has a condom tucked between two fingers, and I marvel at the way he deftly rips it open with his teeth and rolls it on.

I shimmy up the bed, tugging at the bottom of my shirt to make sure it doesn't roll up too much.

The bed dips under his weight as he climbs over and settles between my thighs. I gasp when he bends down and places his head between my legs. The first caress of his tongue feels divine. The second has me panting. And when he pushes two fingers into my pussy, pulling my clit into his mouth at the same time, I can't stop the moan that escapes me.

"I knew I could make you scream for me," he says between flicks of his tongue. I grip his head to keep him in place as that familiar tingle starts to build.

Just as I'm about to crest over that waterfall and plunge into the depths of pleasure, he pulls back, his face glistening with my arousal. "The next time you come, it will be on my cock. Is that clear?"

"Then hurry up and fuck me."

Did I really just say that? What the hell has gotten into me?

Mike sits up as he grips the base of his cock in one hand. The firefighter in his tattoo dances as his forearm flexes with his movements. He teases my opening with his tip. Just when I think I can't stand it anymore, he pushes in and I gasp at the sensation, the fullness.

Holy shit, he's big.

"It'll fit," he says, reading my mind.

I grab his arms, desperate to touch his tattoo, needing to ground myself as I claw my nails into his skin while he slowly moves his hips in and out. It feels unlike anything I've ever experienced, not just his size, but the additional sensations his piercings add as they rub against my inner walls.

"So fucking tight, a chroí. You're squeezing me so feckin' tight. So good." He looks down at me with such longing, keeping his pace slow and tender like he's making love to me.

I panic, desperate to break the gravity of the moment and remind him what this arrangement is.

"Don't go easy on me. I'm not as breakable as you think I am."

"Never thought you were, love."

"If you want to fuck me again, you're going to have to give me more than that."

Something flashes in his eyes, a kind of desperation, and I know in that moment that I've fucked up. This man is going to ruin me for all other men.

"I'm not capable of holding anything back when it comes to ya. All you have to do is ask for something and it's yours."

He grabs my thighs and pulls me flush with him, holding me in place as my legs rest on his forearms. The new angle has my ass in the air, and I feel every barbell as he pistons in and out.

I reach back, bracing my hands on the headboard as he fucks me relentlessly. When his eyes move to the hem of my shirt, I look down and notice it's ridden up, exposing the roll under my belly button. Nervously, I watch as it jiggles with every movement he makes.

He notices my attention shift and pauses his hips, forcing me to look at him. "So feckin' perfect," he growls. "Every inch of ya." He resumes fucking me with more force. "Every"—*thrust*—"fucking"—*thrust*—"inch"—*thrust*—"of"—*thrust*—"ya."

My eyes roll back in my head as I get lost in every inch of him. Sex has never felt this good before. It's the piercings. That's all it is. Or his thick veiny cock. That's it. It could be the way he makes me feel too. Nope. Just focus on the dick. Not the feelings he's evoking. This is just sex.

Mike pulls out of me, flipping me over on the bed as he grabs my hips and pulls my ass in the air. The move takes me by surprise at how easily he's able to manhandle me. I should push up on my arms and work with him, but I lie there bone-less, ass up. He slides his hands into the crease where my hip roll meets the meat of my thigh, holding me in place as he fucks me like he hates me, but his words are anything but.

"This is my favorite part of ya. So round and perfect. You're a sight like this for me. Feckin' beautiful."

I can't begin to imagine how jiggly I must look from behind, but I push the thought from my head as his hands continue to roam over my entire backside, mapping it out like he wants to memorize every curve and dimple.

His piercings feel different in this position, rubbing against my G-spot, and it doesn't take long before I feel my orgasm building.

"I'm going to… Mike, fuck. Oh fuck, I'm—" I'm unable to finish the thought as waves of pleasure crash into my body, drowning me with an intensity I've never felt before.

"Tá mo chroí istigh ionat," he rasps as his hips still and his cock swells inside me.

As soon as he pulls out, my lower half collapses. I feel him climb off the bed, probably to dispose of the condom, but I can't move.

When he comes back in the room, he's fully dressed in his ridiculous calendar outfit. A tiny part of me is disappointed but I'm not sure why.

He leans over the bed and kisses the side of my forehead. "Get some rest before those mischievous little sprites return. You earned it."

"You're really playing into the whole Irish bit, huh?" I lean up on my arm as he talks.

"It's only a couple weeks till St. Paddy's. It's like Christmas to the Emerald Isle."

"Is it?"

He chuckles. "I don't know how to compare it, actually. It's a deeply religious affair to my folks. We head to Mass, have a big feast, and spend time together as a family. Similar to what some might do at Christmas. But there's no caroling or magical being bringing gifts."

"The leprechauns don't leave you a pot of gold if you've been a good boy?"

"They don't. The leprechaun originally was a derogatory symbol created to disparage the Irish. Americans have made it their mascot for the holiday, but a lot of Irish people take offense to it."

Shit. How do I keep putting my foot in my mouth with this man? "I'm sorry, I didn't realize that. I hope I didn't offend you."

"Nope. It doesn't bother me or my Ma, but my Da… it does his head in sometimes."

"Does his head in?"

"It fires him up. He's been known to get into a pisser about it."

"Ah, got it." I push up on the bed, sitting as he continues.

"And we don't dye large bodies of water green, or dye our beer, or even wear green for that matter. That's more of an American thing."

"You're gonna get your ass pinched if you don't wear green on that day around here."

"Trust me, I've learned that lesson. I was born in Ireland and moved to Boston in high school before we ended up in Chestnut Mountain. So I've seen many different ways to celebrate the holiday, and I honestly like the quietness of it here. I don't need a big parade, just time with my family and friends. And some Irish stew."

He strokes my cheek, and I lean into his hand as he kisses the top of my head. "Now get some rest with what little time you have left."

"Where are you going?" Did that sound as needy out loud as it did in my head?

If it did, Mike doesn't let on as he walks to the door.

"Headed to the store. Gotta pick up everything I need for tonight."

"What's tonight?"

He turns and grips the doorframe, leaning on it like one of those thirst trap book boyfriends on social media. "Our date."

CHAPTER 13

MIKE

"Oh my God, you're early," Lucy huffs, opening the door a crack like she's not going to let me in.

"Six, yeah?" I shift the bags of groceries in my arm and look at my watch.

"Shit. Is it six already?"

"'Tis."

"What's all that?" She nods to the bags. "I thought you were bringing dinner?"

"Dinner." I hold up the bags a little to make my point.

"That's not dinner, that's the ingredients for dinner."

"Exactly. And I'm going to cook these ingredients and make dinner." I arch an eyebrow in jest.

"You're going to cook?"

"I love to cook. I'm the resident chef at the station."

"Okay, but the boys are picky eaters, so I hope you have chicken nuggets in there, because that's about all they'll eat at this point. If it isn't shaped like an extinct animal, they don't want to eat it."

I chuckle, an idea already forming in my head. "Grand. Now can I come in? I'm freezing my balls off out here."

"Okay, but I need to warn you, I lost track of time,

and the two feral gremlins undid all the cleaning I did earlier, so do not judge me for the mess you're about to see."

"I spend most of my week in a firehouse surrounded by firefighters. Trust me, there is nothing that could shock me."

She blows out a deep breath. "I'm pretty sure my floor is composed of Pokémon energy cards and Band-Aid wrappers at this point. And if you see a juice box, don't step on it. Levi takes two sips and leaves them in random places. I've stepped on way too many Capri-Sun land mines, and my Bissell needs a break."

"Noted."

She opens the door and lets me in. It's honestly not as bad as I expected, but it's obvious kids live here, and I secretly love it.

"Lucky Charm!" Micah shouts as I walk into the kitchen.

Lucy's mouth drops open.

"Mikachu!" I shout back as he runs over and hugs my leg. I'm touched he still remembers the nicknames we gave each other the day we met.

"Choo-choo!" Levi parrots as he climbs onto the arm of the couch and flings himself onto the cushion, completely unbothered by my presence.

"You have nicknames?" Lucy asks, confused.

"Yeah, he's Mikachu, like Pikachu."

"And he sounds like the green guy on the cereal box in the ads," Micah says.

The horrified look on her face makes me chuckle. "Micah, that is not nice. You cannot call him that just because he's Irish."

"It's fine," I say, brushing it off, yet secretly loving that she remembered our earlier conversation. "I wouldn't recommend shouting it in Ireland, but I don't mind it."

"Can we have Lucky Charms for dinner?" Levi asks, now bouncing up and down on the cushions.

"No, and please don't jump on the couch, Levi," Lucy scolds.

She rubs her hands on her forehead like she's trying to relieve a stress headache, and I jump into action. "Come here, Levisaur," I say, walking to the couch and scooping him up. "I need your help."

"I'm Bulbasaur!" Levi growls, chomping his teeth in my direction.

"He certainly zaps all my energy," Lucy mutters. I give her a quizzical look as I set Levi down. "You know, cuz Bulbasaur draws energy into his back bulb, and that's what powers all of his moves."

"I was just playing off the dinosaur comment earlier. I guess I'm cleverer than I realized."

"Let's not get ahead of ourselves. You still have to get them to eat whatever it is you're making."

"Who wants to help me cook dinner?" I say with enthusiasm as I turn back to the boys. If I've learned anything about kids, it's that you can get them excited about boring tasks with some enthusiasm and a little competition, especially little boys.

"I do!" Micah raises his good arm.

"MEEEE!" Levi shouts.

I drop into a squat. "Okay, this is very important. Can I trust you two to do something for me?"

They both nod, looking at me intensely for further instruction.

"It's very important that we get all the germs off your hands so you can help. Can you do that?"

"I can!" Micah says as he walks to the bathroom.

Levi stomps his foot. "I don't wanna wash my hands. It's too hard."

"Then I guess Micah will be my assistant." I stand and cross my arms.

Levi runs off, and I chuckle when I hear the commotion and sibling fighting coming from the bathroom.

"Okay, that was a little impressive," Lucy says.

Moving closer to her, I take a minute to fully take her in. Her hair is in a messy bun, her face free of makeup. She looks beautiful.

The leggings that hug every delectable curve of her thick thighs make me want to take my time peeling them off her. But I mentally frown at the baggy shirt she's wearing that covers her perfect round arse. I didn't say anything when she put one on after our bath, but I want to rip it off and feast on every delicious inch of her. Instead, I reach out and tug at the hem, unable to help myself as I slip a hand under her shirt and squeeze her arse cheek.

She gasps and then looks at the bathroom before turning back to me. "Before they come back…" She pushes her lower lip out slightly. *Fuck, the things I want to do to that lip.* "Do I get a nickname?"

I lean into her ear, my cheek brushing hers as electricity courses through me at the contact. "I'm just going to call you Squirtle."

"Really?" She leans back, clearly unimpressed.

"Aye. Squirtle seems unassuming but has a hard shell that's tough to crack. And once I penetrate your shell, I'm going to make you squirt so hard, I'll ruin you for any other man." I slap her ass, making sure it's hard enough that the sting will linger while we cook. "And that spanking doesn't count for your list." I wiggle a finger at her.

"That's… umm…"

I don't have time to revel in her flustered look before the boys run back in ready to help.

Since picky eaters are involved, I decide to pivot and make dino nuggets for the boys and the chicken dish I planned for me and Lucy. If they get brave and want to try our dish, there'll be plenty to share. But I have something else in store that I think they'll really enjoy.

Levi helps wash the potatoes while I peel them over the

trash can. Micah is at the kitchen island, neatly placing florets of broccoli on a baking sheet.

Even though they both lose interest about halfway through the process, it's the most fun I've had in the kitchen in years.

While they're distracted watching an episode of *Numberblocks*, I pile mashed potatoes onto a baking sheet, forming it into a volcano shape while placing broccoli sporadically to look like trees. I pull the dinos out of the air fryer and arrange them into an epic battle scene in the mashed potatoes at the base of the volcano. Using two fingers, I create a channel in the potatoes for the gravy lava to flow, so it stays fairly contained in case they don't want it touching their food.

Lucy stares with rapt fascination as I work. It takes longer to assemble than I anticipated, but I finally finish my Jurassic creation. Mesozoic creation? What era was the one with the dinosaurs?

"Hungry!" Levi yells.

"Is dinner ready yet?" Micah asks.

"It is. Who wants to pour the lava?" I ask.

Two heads turn toward us and then they're up off the couch, running toward the kitchen. Levi climbs onto a stool, stretching out a hand to grab the gravy, but I hold it up, out of his reach.

"Is it really lava?" Micah asks, sounding unsure.

"No, it's just gravy." I show him the inside of the pot with the brown mixture.

"I don't like gravy," Micah says, looking at it like it's going to burn him.

"That's okay. There is plenty of lava-free volcano if you don't want any."

Micah folds his arms over his body, gripping his cast with one hand as if to shield himself from the gravy. Lucy gives me an apologetic look, and I smile in return.

I move closer to Levi and help him as he pours the gravy

into the volcano. It spills over the top, down the channel I created, and then pools at the bottom.

"Cool!" he shouts.

Micah peeks his head over to check it out, and Lucy sets out plates so we can dig in. She scoops a little potato and broccoli onto each of their plates and loads them up with nuggets while I pull our chicken out of the oven.

I set the hot pan onto a potholder on the counter and start to prepare plates for Lucy and myself when she screams.

"Levi, no!"

Levi has his eyes locked on the volcano, and he's doing a little shimmy like a cat about to pounce.

"Don't you do it!" Lucy shouts, jumping out of her stool to lunge for him.

It all happens so fast. Before she can reach him, he throws his hands in the air and shouts, "LAVA!" then face-plants into what's left of the volcano, flattening it as gravy goes everywhere.

Lucy stands there stunned, frozen in place. A million emotions cross her face, probably thinking about the mess she's going to have to clean up.

I feel bad for a split second and then break into a fit of laughter. It's a deep belly laugh, and I bend over clutching my knees trying to compose myself.

When Levi's head pops up, his arms still in the air, he breaks into a fit of giggles. Even Micah is laughing. Lucy has one arm crossed over her chest, propping the other up to cover her mouth.

"LAVA!" Levi bellows again.

The minute he smooshes his face into the baking sheet a second time, Lucy loses her battle with composure, letting out the most beautiful melodic laugh. Fuck, I want more of that laugh.

"I'm a lava monster!" Levi says, popping up again, and we all lose it, howling and cackling for a solid minute.

After I quickly scrub Levi with some wet paper towels, we settle in to eat our meal. When both boys finish all their food, Lucy nods her head toward me, giving me a silent golf clap in appreciation.

"Alright, boys, we definitely need a more thorough cleaning after that. Go get the bath started, and I'll be up there in a little bit," Lucy says before turning toward me. "You're so good with them."

"Thanks." I watch as Levi chases his brother upstairs. "It's probably because I never grew up myself."

She smirks as she sits on one of the stools at the island. I round the counter, dusting nugget crumbs from the stool onto my hand before sitting beside her.

"You ever think about having more?" I ask as I dump the crumbs onto a plate in front of me.

She shifts, taking a big sip from her wine glass.

Shite. I'm coming on too strong. Feckin' eejit.

"I don't think I could handle any more kids on my own. I love them, but I'm exhausted. What about you? Do you want kids one day?"

"At least four, maybe five."

She spits out her wine, spraying me with chardonnay. "Holy shit. I'm so sorry!"

I grab her wrist before she can scramble off her stool. "If you want to spit in my face or my mouth, you only need to add it to the list." I'm rewarded with the prettiest blush dusting her cheeks at my words.

"I… ummm… I should clean this up." She looks down at the counter, stacking plates as she reaches for the discarded napkins the boys left behind.

"Pretty sure you got most of it on me, a chroí."

"I should get something to clean your shirt with."

"It's white wine. Other than a few damp spots, I'm grand. I'd rather you sit with me while we have a moment to talk without wee ears around."

"Okay." She slowly leans back in her chair, and I tug her seat closer to me.

"That's better."

The smell of her fruity, floral scent hits my nose, instantly taking me back to the night we checked the first item off her list. I exhale, fighting the urge to pull her into my lap and kiss her senseless. "I've always wanted a big family. My parents struggled to conceive, and giving birth to me nearly killed Ma. She'd had several miscarriages and always considered me her good luck charm. Da always talked about how important it was to carry on the family name, and I want to be able to do that for him. And I love kids, and they seem to tolerate me."

Her body stiffens next to me, and I will her to look at me, wanting to search her eyes for the truth she's hiding from me. She doles out tidbits of herself like an iceberg, you think you're getting it all at first glance, but under the surface it goes so much deeper than she's willing to show. There's way more to her than what she shares, but I've caught glimpses of her here and there, and I really like what I see.

"I hope you get that one day," she says, staring into her empty wine glass, and I don't like her tone. It feels like she's pulling away from me, and I'm not sure why.

"Did I say something that upset you?" I place a hand on her arm, and she stares at it like it might burn her.

"No. I'm just thinking about everything I have to do once I get these two monsters down for bed." While there may be some truth to that statement, I can tell there's more going on in that pretty head of hers, but I let it go, squeezing her forearm once before releasing it.

"I can help," I offer.

"It's fine. You don't have to." She stands and carries the plates and silverware to the sink. "I'm going to go start the bedtime ritual. It'll probably take me about an hour with their bath now because of Micah's cast and the mess Levi made of his hair. You don't have to stay."

It's brief, but I see a flicker of something in her eye. Besides the sadness, there's a glimmer of hope, maybe? Or longing? Her gaze lingers on my lips for a second before she turns and heads for the stairs.

"Lucy."

She stops, refusing to turn around.

"I'll wait for ya."

Her head peeks over her shoulder and turns ever so slightly in my direction.

"If you need an hour to put them down. I'll wait. Go do what you need to do. But I'll be here when you're done."

"Why would you do that?"

"So I can give ya a proper kiss good night. This is a date, after all."

She nods once, giving nothing away, and then hurries up the stairs.

I survey the living room and kitchen, taking in the mess. I smile to myself as I remember all the times Ma would get on to me for not picking up after myself, and Da would say that the best memories are messy ones. I feel like we made some good memories tonight.

When I see the toy bin in the corner of the room, I decide to clean up the play area. She said she had a lot to do once she got the boys to bed, so maybe I can take some of the burden off her.

I'm not sure if there's a system for storing all this shite, but I do my best to cram it all in the bin. When it's clear there's too much to fit, I pull out some of the larger toy trucks and line them up neatly in front of the toy box. It takes a lot longer to clean the room than I expected, and despite my extensive workouts in the gym, my back aches from all the bending over.

How does she do this by herself every day? I'm in awe of this woman.

I head over to the kitchen next, gathering up any stray

snack cup or plate I see on my way. I hand-wash the dishes I used to cook our meal and all the other dishes that were lying about, and then I try my best to figure out where they go once they're dried. How can two tiny humans dirty so many dishes in a day?

There's a lot of laughter coming from upstairs, and I chuckle to myself each time I hear Levi shout the word "penis" at the top of his lungs.

I know she said that she doesn't want more than just sex, but my heart cracks a little thinking about the fact that they're up there and I'm down here by myself. We had a good time together tonight, and I want to show her that I'm serious about her and her boys.

Hanging out with Lucy and her kids gives me the same rush of feelings I get around my folks. Like a weight is lifted from my chest. Like the scary shite I have to do at my job is worth it when I get to spend my off days with them. Like I belong to something bigger than myself.

Once the dishes are put up, I wipe down the counters, taking extra time to clean some sticky syrup puddles off the kitchen table. I'm scrubbing furiously, moving my hand back and forth, putting as much elbow grease as I can into it. "Feckin' hell, this fecker is a tough one to rub out."

"Oh my God, what are you doing?"

Lucy's voice startles me, and I whip around, sponge in hand.

"Oh shit, you're scrubbing the table," she says, sounding relieved as she places a hand on her chest. I watch as her tits heave in her shirt.

"There was dried syrup. What did you think I was doing?"

"Well, you had your back to me, your arm was moving in a repetitive motion, and you were mumbling about rubbing one out." She makes a jacking gesture with her hand in front of her crotch.

"Jesus Christ." I drop the sponge and put my hands up in defense.

"I'm sorry, I'm sorry," she says as she breaks into a fit of laughter, the sound warming me from the inside out.

I close the distance between us, wrapping my arms around her as I pull her into my chest. She comes willingly for once but goes rigid when her gaze swings to the living room.

"Where are all the toys?"

"I put as many as I could in that bin, but the vehicles that wouldn't fit are lined up next to it."

She looks at the sink. "And the dishes?"

"Washed and put away. I think I found where they all go, but apologies if you can't find something tomorrow."

She places her hands on my chest and pushes me back, taking in the rest of the kitchen. "Did you clean and wipe down my counters too?"

I scratch the back of my neck, suddenly feeling like I fucked up. "Aye."

Two beautiful emerald eyes fix on mine, and I feel like I can finally exhale. The sadness is gone in her pupils, and she steps closer. I grip her hips, pulling her flush with me. She looks at me with so much longing, and I revel in it, relieved to see her peel back some of her armor.

When her eyes linger on my lips, I lean down, slowly going in for the kiss I've been dying to take since the day I met her.

"New rule," she says, her voice soft and breathy.

"What's that?" I ask, inching closer.

"No kissing."

I pause, hovering inches from her mouth. "Then you better stop looking at my lips like you want to devour them."

She untangles herself from my arms and takes a step back, leaning against the counter. "Why?" she asks, looking around the rest of the kitchen.

"You ask that question more than Levi does," I tease.

A small smile lights up her face as her mouth drops open in mock indignation. "You take that back."

"Is it so hard for you to believe that someone would want to spend time with ya?"

"In case it wasn't obvious, men aren't exactly lining up at my door to take me out. And the ones that might be interested, well, my kids scare them off real quick. I come with a harsh dose of reality in the form of two energetic, wonderful little boys, and they're a lot for people to tolerate. Not even my dad treats them like they deserve. And if they don't scare someone off, my baggage usually does."

"The right person won't merely tolerate them, you know that, right? Maybe you're looking in the wrong places for these guys."

"I'm not looking, period. I don't want my boys to get attached to someone that isn't going to stick around. I know I have a lot of baggage, and I haven't felt the same in my body since I became a mom. My clothes are too tight, I carry weight in new places, and the intrusive thoughts in my head are unlike anything I've ever experienced. When I'm not worrying about fucking my kids up for life, I'm thinking about what an awful mother I am, how I'm not good enough, how I have no clue what I'm doing when everyone else seems to have figured it out, and how I'm too afraid to ask for help out of fear that I'll be seen for the fraud that I am."

There's no truth I can offer her that she'd accept right now, so I tug her against me and give her a hug, squeezing tight. She fights me at first but gradually relaxes in my arms.

"What are you doing?"

"Hugging you."

"Because you feel sorry for me after I word-vomited all my scary thoughts?"

"No. I appreciate your honesty more than you know. I gather it takes a lot for you to feel comfortable sharing stuff like that. But I honestly like helping people. It's a big reason why I became a firefighter and a paramedic. And I can't help someone if I don't know what's wrong. And now that I know what you need, I'm hugging you."

"And what do you think I need?"

"I think you need to feel cared for because you spend so much of your time caring for others. I cleaned up so you didn't have to. And I think you need to lower your stress and blood pressure so I'm hugging you."

"So why aren't you letting me go?"

"Because ten seconds into a hug, oxytocin is released. And studies show that at twenty seconds, your stress and blood pressure decrease as more oxytocin and dopamine are released."

"I think it's been twenty seconds," she grumbles.

"This is really hard for ya, isn't it?"

"You have no idea."

"I'll start counting once you fully surrender. Right now, this isn't a hug, you're just trapped in my arms."

"Fine." She places her cheek against my chest, and as I count in my head, I slowly feel her relax against me. A few seconds in, I feel her arms wrap around my lower back, and I smile against the top of her head.

When I get to twenty, I wait for her to let go, and when she doesn't, I hold her for a while longer, basking in this moment.

"Okay. I think I'm good," she says, dropping her hands.

I search her eyes, enjoying the look of peace I find. "How do you feel?"

"I do actually feel better." She places her hands on my chest, holding my gaze.

I couldn't look away if I tried. I want her to look at me like this every day.

"Can I at least repay the favor?" she asks, starting to lower to her knees as her hands drag slowly down my abdomen, stopping on my belt.

"That's not why I did all this," I say, gripping her wrist and pulling her up.

"Are you actually turning down a blow job?"

"I can't believe I'm saying this, but I'd rather kiss your lips," I admit.

The hurt look on her face stabs at my chest.

"It's not that I wouldn't enjoy that," I rush to assure her. "I would. Immensely. But right now, I want the one thing you're not willing to give me. And while your lips wrapped around my cock is something I will fantasize about while I jack myself in the shower tonight, I'd rather kiss you until you're gasping for air, so consumed by my lips on yours that you'll want to throw away all your rules and restrictions."

"Oh." She blinks up at me. "We shouldn't."

I lean down and kiss her forehead. "Thank you for tonight. I had fun."

Not wanting to wear out my welcome, I turn and head for the door.

"Tomorrow!" she calls out, halting me as my hand grips the brass doorknob.

I turn around to look at her. "What's tomorrow?"

"The boys have a playdate in the evening for a few hours." She twists her hands in front of her. "If you want to grab dinner or whatever, I have some free time."

"I would love to take you out. Let me know when, and I'll be there."

CHAPTER 14

LUCY

There's not a Band-Aid wrapper in sight as I pace nervously in my living room waiting for Mike to show up. I cleaned up the house, shaved every inch of my body, and put on the sexiest panties I own.

What am I doing? Why would I agree to go out to dinner? We're just supposed to be hooking up.

Before I have a chance to second-guess myself, there's a knock at the door, and I'm instantly filled with relief. That's what this man does to me, calms down the swirling thoughts fogging my brain.

Except now, instead of my mind tugging me down rabbit holes of anxiety—worried about what could be, what this means, and where this is headed—it's running away with thoughts of all the things I want to do to him, have him do to me, and how good it feels when we're together.

When I open the door, he's standing on my porch, his brown hair perfectly styled and slicked to one side, and the light from my windows makes the slight reddish tint stand out. He flashes me a huge smile, his blue eyes lighting up at just the sight of me.

Closing the door behind me, I join him and pull on my

mittens as he takes my hands in his. We stand there staring at each other. It should feel awkward, but I feel surprisingly comfortable. His eyes take in every inch of my face as he tucks my hair behind my ear with his gloved hand.

Holy shit. I think I want him to kiss me. Whatever plans we had to leave my house fly out of my head. There's no way we can go out in public if this is how he's going to look at me. Everyone will know we're a thing. Are we a thing?

"Feckin' hell, a chroí, you look downright edible."

And now all I can think about is being exactly that for him. No one has ever made me come that fast while going down on me before.

"I think I'd rather stay in, if that's okay?" I ask as his penetrating gaze heats me from the inside out.

"We can do whatever your heart desires."

"Okay," I say on a big exhale, my breath making a cloud in front of me. I grab his arm and pull him inside, quickly closing the door before leaning against it. I tug my mittens off with my teeth as I watch him remove his scarf, gloves, and coat and set them on the back of the couch. Damn, his ass looks amazing in those jeans.

It takes him a second to realize that I'm not following him into the living room and he turns on his heel, slowly stalking toward me.

When he gets to the door, he presses his hands on either side of my face, caging me in. His nose runs along my jawline as he inhales deeply.

"Tell me again why we can't be more?" he asks, his lips ghosting over the shell of my ear.

I don't think I've ever wanted someone this badly before, but I shove it down, feigning indifference. I'm determined not to let him get too close, but it's getting more and more difficult each time I see him. "While I might be ready to put myself back out there, I'm not ready to get serious with anyone again. And I don't want the boys to get attached to someone who isn't going to be a permanent fixture in my life." The words feel like a lie, the line getting harder to recite when each time I see him I want more.

He pulls back, cupping my face in both hands, and I squirm under his intense gaze. He looks hurt, but I don't allow myself to examine it further, even though he continues searching my eyes as if he's going to uncover some hidden truth I'm unwilling to verbalize.

Just when I think I can't stand another second of his attention, he leans in. Slowly. So fucking slowly. I can feel his warm breath against my lips with each exhale, but his lips hover just out of reach.

Every nerve ending in my body is on fire. Do I want him to kiss me? Fuck, I want him to do more than kiss me. I reach up and grab his lapel and tug his lips to mine.

The move takes him by surprise, but he wastes no time crushing his mouth against mine. It's warm and perfect with just the right amount of lip nibbling and sucking, and I get lost in it as he melds his body against mine, pinning me against the door.

"You said no kissing," he says between kisses, though I make no attempt to stop as I dive back in for more.

His answering groan sends a bolt of lust straight through me, and I can feel my panties dampening as I wrap a leg around his hip, seeking out friction.

"Tell me to stop," I say.

"Like feckin' hell I will." He pushes his hips against me, peppering kisses along my neck and jaw, and I can feel how hard he is through his jeans. "Tell me you don't want my mouth on every inch of you." His lips brush along my jaw and chin as he works his way toward my cleavage.

"Oh my God, don't stop," I rasp as I thread my fingers through the hair at the base of his skull and move him lower while thrusting my cleavage out. He laps at my breasts greedily, making obscene noises as he lavishes my body with adoration.

And that's exactly what it is—pure and total adoration. I've never had anyone look at me the way he does, like I'm the most beautiful creature on the planet. Never had anyone have trouble keeping their hands off me the way Mike does, like it physically hurts him not to touch me. And I've never had anyone enjoy the way I taste like he does, like if he can't get a fix, he'll starve.

We're just friends with benefits. This is just sex. That's all it is. Even if it's never been this good before and I'm starting to want more.

I'm lost in my thoughts when I feel him slide a hand under my thigh, lifting me so I'm forced to wrap my legs around his waist. "Mike!" I squeal.

As a plus-size girl, I never thought it was possible to find a guy who could throw me around like I weigh nothing. But each time I think something is impossible or unlikely, here comes Mike proving me wrong in the best ways, resetting all my expectations and raising the bar for anyone coming behind him. Shit, will I even want someone else when this is over?

"Mike. Put me down. I'm too—"

"Shut that beautiful feckin' mouth of yours and let me make you feel good, love," he says, grinding his erection against me as I tighten my legs around his waist.

He doesn't give me the chance to reply as he seals his mouth to mine, kissing me fiercely, holding me tight. He continues devouring every inch of my exposed flesh that he can reach as my arousal builds. I'm probably making a mess of our clothes as I grind against him, and for once, I don't care. I don't remind myself about what I'm going to have to clean up after this is over.

"We shouldn't do this. What if HR finds out?" he growls into my ear.

I pull back, confused. What the hell is he talking about?

He cocks an eyebrow. "You know, because you're the CEO. And my boss. And I'm just a lowly intern desperate for whatever attention you'll give me. A weak pathetic man captivated by your strength. Your beauty. You have no idea the things I'd be willing to risk to fuck you right now. Even if it could get us both fired."

My list.

"Is that right?" I say coyly, trying to push down the inkling of disappointment as I fist the fabric of his shirt. "What do you want to do to me?"

He leans into my ear, and I steel my nerves. His dirty mouth was shocking at first—no one had ever spoken to me like that before—but now I've come to crave it, desperate for every little nugget he drops. "Nuh-uh. That's not how this little power dynamic works, Lucy. If you want to check this off your list, you need to claim your power over me. That's why you made the list, right? To take back your power? So fucking own me, a chroí, make me work for it."

Swallowing down my nerves, I lean into my role, even if it is way out of my comfort zone. "I want you to rub that giant cock of yours against me until you come in your pants like the needy man you are."

"With pleasure," he groans as he captures my earlobe between his teeth, giving it a not-so-gentle tug.

"And if you make me come before you do, I'll let you eat my pussy." I can feel all the blood in my body rush to my cheeks at my words. Who the fuck am I right now? I don't talk like this.

"Challenge accepted," he says, never halting his exploration of my neck and ear as he starts grinding his thick length against me, shifting me in his arms so the tip of his cock hits my clit with each snap of his hips.

He lowers his head to my cleavage. "Take this off," he says, biting the fabric of my bra and tugging at it with his teeth.

I let out a ragged breath. This isn't something I'm ready for.

No one has seen me topless since I became a mom, and breast-feeding two boys wasn't kind on my girls. They're not perky, not pretty thanks to the stretch marks, and all those hormones have made a few dark hairs sprout here and there. I have carefully cultivated a bra collection to make them look way more attractive than they feel, but I'm not ready to let anyone see the way they look naturally. Even letting him touch them in the tub was a huge step for me. It still feels way too daunting to let anyone see the real me.

Powering through the negative thoughts, I try to stay in character. "Needy boys don't get to make demands. They take what they're given. Now, are you going to be a naughty intern or my good boy?"

He blinks at me in surprise. "I'll be such a good feckin' boy for you, ma'am. Please let me prove how good I can be for ya. Feckin' hell, I want nothing more than to be with someone like you." His voice is soft, pleading, and it almost feels like he isn't pretending.

His confession washes over me, lighting me up from the inside out until I feel like I'm glowing, basking in the warmth of his praise. Is this what sex should feel like? We've had some great sex so far, but this feels different, more real than anything we've done.

But he's just playing along to check an item off my list. His words are just lines he's reciting, not true confessions. Right?

I can't get out of my head, can't stop thinking about what all this could mean.

"If you don't stop thinking about work, I'm going to bend you over your desk and smack that pretty arse until you come. I want you here with me in this moment. Want you to know how much I want to fill you and make you pulse around my cock. And I want your feckin' eyes on mine when I make ya come."

He snakes a hand down my leggings and into my panties,

gathering my wetness, spreading it around as he massages, teasing me.

"If you ever want to get ahead in this company, you're going to have to do better than that," I say breathily, needy for release.

A low growl emanates from his chest as he slips two fingers inside, grinding the heel of his palm against my clit. The dual sensations are overwhelming, like my body doesn't know what to focus on.

"Too much…" I rasp as my head lolls back and forth against the door.

"You can take it." He backs off my clit slightly, pumping his fingers faster as his cock grinds against my inner thigh.

"I—"

"It'll be worth it, ma'am. I promise."

The ache in my pussy builds, as that familiar tingle starts in my clit, but it feels… different. "Holy shit."

"That's it, come all over my fingers."

Why does it feel like I have to pee? I close my eyes, already in my head.

"Don't leave me, a chroí. Stay with me. Open those gorgeous feckin' eyes and look at me when you come."

My eyes fly open, and I see the intensity on his face. It's overwhelming how he's staring at me with such longing. How does he always know when I'm pulling away mentally? When a slight smirk appears, I exhale, knowing he's got me.

"That's my girl. Are you gonna squirt for me? It feels like you need to let go, doesn't it?"

I nod, confused how he could possibly know that.

"That's how it feels before you squirt. Jesus feckin' Christ, you're incredible. Give it to me. Cover my hand in your sweet cum."

He continues grinding against my inner thigh, his breathing increasing as his eyes bore into mine.

When my orgasm hits seconds later, it's unlike anything

I've ever experienced before. Waves of euphoria pulse through me as I shudder in his arms, trying to make eye contact until the intensity is too much and I have to close my eyes, gripping his shirt as I bite his shoulder to stifle my moans.

"Yes. Oh, fuck yes," he groans into my neck as his hips jerk erratically against me.

Oh my God, did he actually come in his pants? Why is that so incredibly hot?

Before I can process everything that just happened, he sets me on my feet and then drops to his knees, pulling my leggings and panties down as he goes.

"What are you doing?" I say, my voice breathier than I intend it to be.

"You said if you came before me, I'd get to feast on this delicious cunt. Since you squirted all over my hand, and I'm starving, I want to clean up the mess I made of ya." He throws one of my legs over his shoulder and takes my hand, placing it on his head. "Either use this to hold on or move me where you need me."

Then he forces my legs open wider with his broad shoulders and licks me like a man starved. With the way he's eating me, there's no way he's not making a bigger mess. And that mess feels so undeniably good.

I've never had back-to-back orgasms before. The closest I've come was yesterday when he made me come in the tub and then after on the bed, but there was a decent bit of time between. Multiple orgasms were on my list. This is just another item he's checking off, right? One step closer to this arrangement being over. Why does that suddenly fill me with dread?

He pulls back. "Thinking about your spreadsheets, ma'am?"

My cheeks heat, realizing he's caught me having wandering thoughts again. How does he do that? "Sorry."

"What is it going to take to prove to you that I want this? That I want to get ahead?"

Is he still in character? "You want a bigger role at this company?" I say, continuing the charade. Hiding behind this character feels safe.

His eyes connect with mine, and the look he gives me speaks volumes. "I want anything. Everything. All of it. All of you. All of this," he says, gesturing around the room with his head.

"At the company?" I say weakly.

"Anything more you're willing to give me." He punctuates the words in such a way, making it clear he's not playing this game anymore. And then he descends on my pussy, kissing, licking, and sucking it like it's the last time he'll ever do this.

He lifts me off the ground for a moment, one leg still over his shoulder, the other cradled in his arm as my orgasm hits, setting off the most magical prism against my closed eyes, like a rainbow of pleasure, each new color setting off a different sensation.

Despite my brain screaming warning signs at me, my heart slaps that bitch in the face telling her to be silent for once, as warmth fills my body and I convulse against his face.

I'm totally and completely gone for this man.

And I'm totally screwed.

CHAPTER 15

MIKE

Feckin' hell. I love this woman. Standing on her porch, staring into her eyes the other night, I knew. It was quick thinking on my part to role-play so I didn't admit too much and scare her off, but it took everything in me not to confess my feelings right then and there. Now I worry she's pulling away again.

It takes a few days to get Lucy to agree to another date. At least this time I came prepared with chicken nuggets.

She throws open the door, and I immediately know something is wrong.

"I'm so sorry to do this, but I completely forgot about the monthly PTO meeting tonight and I'm the teacher liaison, so I have to be there… in fifteen minutes. I need to help set up and all the girls are going too so they can't watch the boys. I'm probably going to have to bring them with me, and they're going to destroy half the school because Levi is a sneaky little ninja and never stays in the gym with the rest of the kids, and then Micah wanders off looking for him, and they always end up getting into something they're not supposed to. And they haven't eaten yet, which means we'll have to stop for food and that'll make me even later. And it's a school night, and this meeting is going to run long because we have to figure out all the details for the St. Patrick's Day program and the Easter egg hunt. And then they'll get to bed late, and Micah is a bear in the mornings when he doesn't get enough sleep—"

"Go," I say, cutting off her spiraling. "I've got them. We'll be grand here."

She's stunned speechless for several seconds, blinking at me before she speaks. "Are you sure?"

"Course. I've watched Micah before, that's how we met. And I brought nuggets." I hold up the grocery bag in reassurance.

"Are they dino-shaped?" she asks, putting on her coat.

"Does the shape matter?"

"*Does the shape matter?*" she scoffs.

I can tell she's still warring with the decision to stay so I decide to take matters into my own hands.

"Mikachu! Levisaur!" I call out toward the living room, getting their attention. "Want to have a boys-only night?"

"Yeah!" They both cheer in unison, and I tilt my head and shrug, giving Lucy a "Well, that's settled" look. "Guess you're going to have to go to your meeting after all. It's a girl-free zone tonight."

"No girls allowed!" Levi yells.

"You heard the lad," I say as I help her finish pulling her coat on before leaning into her ear. "We've got this."

She searches my eyes for permission one more time and then grabs her purse and keys, running over to kiss the boys. "You be good for Mr. Mike, okay?"

"Yes, Mama," Micah says.

"Make sure they're in bed by eight," she says as she answers her phone. "I know, I know. I'm on my way." She looks at me one more time, but I usher her out the door and close it behind her.

I take the bag of groceries to the kitchen and set them down on the counter right as Micah walks over.

"How's the arm doing?"

"It feels okay, but it's itchy."

"Casts can get quite itchy and stinky. Are ya getting it off soon?" I ask as I pull items out of the bag.

"I think so? What's all that?"

"It's dinner. Want to help?"

"Yeah!"

Micah is the perfect sous chef, grabbing everything I need as soon as I ask for it. He follows directions well. Levi runs in and out of the kitchen helping us with parts until he gets bored. I was worried they wouldn't like what I'd prepared, especially after Lucy's dino nugget comment, but my fears ease each time I catch Levi sneak in and steal an item off the tray.

"This is so cool," Micah says, placing the last bowl of dip down to complete our masterpiece. I snap a quick pic and then grab plates.

I've turned my back for less than ten seconds, and when I turn back around, I swear half of the nuggets are gone and there's dip everywhere. It's a huge mess I'll have to clean up later, but I don't say anything as I slide the plates to the side. If they're going to eat straight off the tray, so am I. I'm also a tiny bit terrified that they'll stop eating if I make any sudden movements, so we eat in near silence as *Paw Patrol* plays in the background.

Once we've nearly demolished the platter of food, I pull out my phone and text Lucy.

> Here's a pic of our dinner. You'll be happy to know they cleaned their plates. Actually we ate straight off the tray, so less dishes to clean.

> [pic of nuggets, fruits, veggies, and dips arranged in the shape of a rainbow.]

> omg

What's in the rainbow?

Strawberries, carrots, bananas, broccoli, blueberries, and blackberries.

And the clouds?

Dips. A sweet cream cheese one for the fruits, and ranch for the veggies.

And the nuggets are the gold at the end of the rainbow?

Aye

And they ate all of it, even the veggies?

There were a handful left behind, but they ate most of it.

Levi was covered in dip

[pic of Levi with a ranch mustache and beard]

That's my new lock screen photo. 😆

Sorry I have to get back to this mtg.

Thank you.

It's my pleasure.

I tuck my phone back in my pocket and finish wiping down the counter.

"Can we color? Mama said we aren't allowed to have any screens for an hour before bed," Micah says.

"Sure. You want to get all the supplies?"

He runs over to the cabinet in the living room and pulls out several coloring books and crayons. When he returns to the kitchen, he climbs up the stool and lays everything out.

My eyes flick over to where Levi is sitting upside down,

head hanging off the couch as he watches a dalmatian ride around in a fire truck. "Should we turn the TV off, then?"

"Yeah, but he's gonna scream."

I ponder what to do for a second and then realize I already know how to motivate Levi. Micah starts coloring a Spider-Man page, and I grab one of the coloring books he set in the pile.

"That looks so good, Micah. I wish there was someone that could help me color as well as you." I raise my voice so I can be heard over the TV and see Levi's little head pop up over the back of the couch out of my periphery. Seconds later, he turns off the TV and scrambles over the back of the couch and joins us at the kitchen island.

Levi climbs onto the counter and sits cross-legged while he colors. He slowly inches his way toward me as I stand across from Micah's stool.

"Look, he's pooping." Levi giggles as he holds up a drawing that he's scribbled on, not staying in the lines at all. But it's what's underneath the crouching Spider-Man that has him all excited as he points to a giant pile of poo. He's literally colored it so it would appear the superhero is taking a giant poop in the street. I burst out into laughter, and he follows suit.

When I look over at Micah, he's frowning. "Levi, Mama said you can't say that word unless you're in the potty."

Shite, I forgot about that rule.

"It's okay," I say to Micah. "I'll tell her I forgot. Let's just not say it anymore, okay?" I direct the last part at Levi.

We color in silence for several minutes when I feel Micah staring at me and I look up from my drawing.

"Your eyes look like Levi's eyes," Micah muses.

"Cuz we both have blue eyes?" I ask, holding Levi's face next to mine so Micah can compare. Levi squirms in my arms as I tickle him.

"Yep. Except yours are a little darker than his. Mommy's eyes are green like mine."

I release Levi as he refocuses on his Green Goblin. This one is getting what looks like a fart cloud behind him.

"My grandpa has green eyes too. But he yells a lot."

"Oh?" I continue working on my coloring, hoping he'll share more. Lucy had mentioned her dad before, and I wonder if this is where Micah's distrust in men comes from. When he doesn't elaborate, I ask, "What color are your dad's eyes?"

"I dunno."

His words are like a punch to the gut. Lucy hasn't told me much about her ex—practically nothing, now that I think about it. I wait for Micah to share more, but he keeps coloring. Who the fuck would create these amazing kids and choose not to be a part of their lives?

"That's okay if you can't remember. Is there anything you *do* remember about him?"

"I never met him," he says, so casually, like he didn't just drop the biggest feckin' bomb.

My blood is roiling thinking through all the possible scenarios Lucy must have gone through with their dad. Did he leave her before Levi was born and Micah just doesn't remember him? Did he tell her he didn't want to have anything to do with them? Did he sign away his rights? Do they even share the same father? Surely, they must. They look so much like each other and their mom.

I'm overcome with the need to ask her all my questions, but it's been like pulling teeth getting her to open up so far.

I don't know what else to say, so I sit in silence, coloring with the boys, hoping that one day their mom will share more of herself with me.

After coloring, Micah explains that they have to get ready for bed, so we put everything away and head upstairs.

I don't know what the protocol is for me helping with their bath, so I make them put on swimsuits. It takes them way too long to find them, and then I have to hustle them through washing. Levi keeps asking me to swipe a card, but I have no clue what he's talking about, and every time I open a drawer or cabinet to look for a card, they both start giggling.

It's difficult to keep water from spilling out of the tub, and I'm thankful I had the foresight to wrap Micah's cast in a garbage bag, because with the way Levi sloshes water around, the cast would've been soaked. Hell, I'm soaked.

Once I get the boys dressed and their teeth brushed, I'm exhausted. How does Lucy do this every night?

We walk into the boys' shared bedroom, and they go through a list of items they expect me to complete: three books, one bedtime story I have to come up with myself, five minutes of back scratches, and a rousing rendition of "We Will Rock You" by Queen—complete with stomps and claps.

I complete everything on the list and sit on the edge of the bed as they climb into the bottom bunk together. "That was way more than I got when I was your age. My Ma used to tuck me in with an Irish blessing and kiss me goodnight."

"What's a Ma?" Micah asks.

"It's what we Irish call our moms. Ma for mom and Da for dad."

"I wish Mama was here to tuck us in," Micah says through a yawn.

"I know, lad. But you'll see her in the morning. Would you like me to recite the blessing my Ma used to tuck me in every night?"

"Okay," Micah says.

Levi scoots over, making room for me between them, and I duck my head, careful not to hit it on the top bunk, and crawl up toward them. The bed isn't large, maybe a full-size, but I squeeze my big body between them, putting my arms around their shoulders so they don't fall out of the bed.

"May the dreams you hold dearest be those which come true, and the kindness you spread keep returning to you."

"That rhymes," Micah says.

"Aye, it does, like a poem."

"What's a poem?" Levi asks.

"It's a—"

"Do another one!" Levi says, not giving me a chance to answer his first question.

"May your thoughts be as glad as the shamrocks, may your heart be as light as a song, may each day bring you bright, happy hours that stay with you all the year long."

"We drew shamrocks in Miss Carlisle's class today," Micah says.

"You did?" I ask, pretending to be surprised.

"Yup. St. Patrick's Day is in two weeks, and we have an assembly at school." That must be the program Lucy mentioned earlier.

"You do? What's it like?"

"It's cool. We're gonna sing songs and wear costumes, and Miss Carlisle said we get to show off our drawings."

"That sounds fun."

"You should come." His voice is quiet, and my gut fills with hope at the possibility, but I don't want to insert myself any further into their lives without Lucy's approval.

I know what a big deal this is to her. She's mentioned not wanting the boys to get attached to temporary people, even though I'm determined to become a permanent fixture in all their lives. "I'd love to, as long as it's okay with your mom."

"She's gonna say yes."

"How do you know?" I wish I had this kid's confidence.

"Cuz I heard her talk about you with the moms when we were at Miss Raven's house."

Before I can process his words, Levi lets out a long, loud fart.

"I tooted!" he exclaims proudly.

Micah and I laugh at his antics.

"You sure did, pal."

"Did you know it was going to sound like that?" Levi asks.

"I didn't know it was going to happen, so no, I didn't." *Fuck, I love these kids.*

"You should guess what it sounds like before I do it." Levi leans against me in the bed, and I wrap an arm around him.

"Oh no, I have to toot now," Micah says.

Levi makes a fart sound with his mouth in response.

Micah's eyes flick to mine. "Hurry, Lucky Charm, it's coming!"

I decide to go in a different direction than Levi's rumble sound as I make a trumpet noise with my lips adding a brassy whine at the end.

Micah lifts his leg up and rips one, making a noise that sounds like neither of our guesses.

We all break into a fit of laughter until Levi wrinkles his nose and waves his hands in front of his face.

"It was a stinker," he cries, falling back onto the bed as he pinches his nose and holds his breath.

The stink hits me seconds later, and I grab my throat, pretending to gag as I cross my eyes and fall back onto the pillows.

Muffled giggles erupt from either side of me as the stench slowly dissipates.

"My fart was better!" Levi says, popping his head up.

"Yeah, but mine was stinkier," Micah adds.

I squeeze out from between them, scoot down the bed, and sit on the edge. "Alright, boys. I promised I'd get the pair of youse to bed and you have school tomorrow. So please help me out with your ma, yeah? I want her to see that I can do a grand job with you, and then maybe she'll let me do it again."

"Can you tuck us in tomorrow?" Levi asks through a yawn as he crawls under the covers and snuggles up to Micah.

"I wish, lad." I pat Levi's leg as he blinks slowly, eyelids drooping.

Micah stares at me, examining my face as I pull the covers up around them. "Do you like our mom?"

"Aye, I do," I say with no hesitation.

"Do you want to kiss her?" Micah asks.

I think about what to tell him, unsure how to answer his question honestly so it won't open the door for further questions.

"Can you do a blessing about farts?" Levi asks, interrupting the moment, and I mentally thank him for saving me.

Micah laughs. "Yeah, do a fart blessing!"

"Hmm, let me think." I tap my chin as I wrack my brain for the right wording. "May the road rise up to meet you, may the wind be always at your back, may your underpants stay clean as the air comes out of your crack."

A chorus of laughter erupts from them. "Do another one!" Levi demands.

"Greedy wee man," I mutter, grinning. "Alright. Alright. May the luck of the Irish be always at hand, and good friends always near you. May your farts always be silent, even when you've got to go poo."

"Another!" Levi shouts.

"I think two is plenty, lad." I ruffle his hair as I stand from the bed.

"Poo is number two," Levi says, and we all laugh.

It hits me, sudden and sharp, why my parents wanted this so badly. I spent most of my twenties looking for the perfect girl to start a family with so I could give my Ma and Da the big noisy clan they always dreamed of, the legacy they craved. By the time I hit my thirties, I was wrecked, tired of searching for *the one*, so I threw myself into a career and friendships instead.

For the first time I realize, I don't want a life dreamed up for me by my parents for their sake—I want it for myself. I want bedtime chaos and fart blessings and sleepy cuddles… feckin' all of it. And I want it with Lucy, with her two brilliant wee lads, and every tomorrow they'll let me have with them.

———————

Lucy's voice startles me an hour later. I shut off the TV, standing to greet her.

"Thank you for helping with the boys. I'm sorry I bailed tonight. I'm not sure what's come over me lately, I'm normally more on top of things. But we can reschedule. I won't count this as one of your four dates."

"Nonsense, it counts. And I was happy to help. We had a good time. Might be the best date I've ever had, actually."

She crosses her arms over her perfect tits and smirks. "Oh my God, you're actually serious, aren't you? I pity the women you've dated that two kids were more entertaining than them."

"Well, I've never had a fart contest on a date before. Not sure any woman will ever live up to that."

She laughs, and I relish the sound. "They did not."

"Aye, they did."

Her responding smile warms my heart. "They really are good kids."

"They are. I even recited two Irish blessings about farts. Not sure how you're going to top that one, Lucky."

The light in her eyes dims briefly, like she's pulling away right in front of me, and I reach out for her arm, desperate to keep the connection. Before I can make contact, she takes a step back. "I should go check on them, make sure they're really asleep. Levi's known to pretend and then sneak out."

I let out a deep exhale and shove my hands in my pockets. "Yeah."

"Friday," she says as she backs away.

"What's Friday?"

"When you get a redo at date number two."

I want to tell her that's not necessary, but I nod in response, not willing to turn down any opportunity to spend time with her.

CHAPTER 16

LUCY

I feel like crap. My period started unexpectedly, and the cramps have been unbearable. The procedure I had after Levi's birth was supposed to help manage my endometriosis, but this cycle is proving to be a rough one.

Micah and Levi are on the floor watching *Bluey* as I rot away on the couch with my heating pad and a finished bowl of ice cream on the table. They've been wild since we got home from school, and I'm thankful for the moment of calm the Australian dogs are providing me. There must be a full moon coming because even my students were more restless than normal today.

My bladder screams at me, so I sneak off the couch and creep over to the bathroom. As soon as they realize I'm gone, chaos will ensue, so I'm determined to make this quick.

Normally, I'd use the bathroom in my room during this time of the month since it has all my supplies, but I have to pee so bad that the downstairs bathroom is my only option. I hustle over to it, quietly kicking the door closed behind me so no kids come in.

It's my heavy day where I need a tampon and pad to contain the mess my uterus is trying to unleash. When I look down at my pad I silently curse. I've bled through another tampon, and I don't have any down here.

Fuck.

I wipe and pull up my pants right as Levi bursts through the door holding his iPad. "I play, Mama?"

Taking the tablet from him, I punch in the parent code.

"Why is that all red, mama?" He points to the toilet water that I had yet to flush due to his interruption.

Shit. What do I say? I'm not ready to have that talk with him yet, because I definitely don't need him repeating it to his entire preschool class. And he would.

"I... uhhh... That's what happens when you drink too much red Kool-Aid, buddy." Fuck, that was quick thinking. I hold my breath, waiting to see if he's going to buy my lie, but he shrugs and runs out of the room.

When I emerge from the bathroom, Micah hands me his iPad so I can unlock it, and both boys run upstairs to play. After I take care of my tampon, I collapse back onto the couch.

Yes, I'm using technology to babysit my children. I'm a terrible parent. Actually, scratch that, I'm a tired single parent with no one to relieve me, and I just need a fucking break sometimes. And they normally don't get more than an hour of iPad time a day. A few hours on a Friday night isn't going to kill them.

Besides, Bella's son Isaac is a coding genius and created a program that blocks them from talking to strangers that DM them in these games. It also has a feature that can tell if they're trying to play something beyond the age bracket I set. Instead of telling them they don't have access to it, it redirects them to an age-appropriate game, so they never know what they're missing. It's actually kind of genius. And he fixed my iCloud issue.

I lie there, watching an episode of *Bluey* that's still playing despite the fact that the boys left the room over thirty minutes ago. Oh fuck, it's the "Sleepytime" episode. This one always makes me sob. I watch as Bingo cries when Floppy leaves her to join her kind around the ring of Saturn. A few tears glide down my cheeks, and I swipe at them. Stupid perfect kids' show making me feel my feelings.

A knock sounds at my door, and my head pops up looking at it as though I'll be able to see through it. My phone buzzes on the table, and I see a message from Mike.

Open up, gorgeous.

Oh my God, I look and feel like shit. I stand, wrapping the blanket around me as I waddle to the door, cracking it open a sliver.

"Hey, I know I'm twenty minutes early, but I…what's wrong?" Mike takes a step closer, and I feel like a total asshole.

"Shit. I totally forgot we had a date tonight. I'm so sorry, it's been a long week at school," I say, defeated.

He grabs the door, forcing it open wider, looking me directly in the eyes. "What's wrong, a chroí?"

I chew my lip, hesitating as I figure out what to tell him. This is ridiculous, I am a thirty-three-year-old woman, I've had periods for most of my life, and yet I'm still scared to tell a man that I can't hang out with him because my uterus decided that she wanted to torture me three days early this month.

Before I can come up with a believable lie, he presses the back of his palm against my forehead. Even though I don't have a fever, the coolness of his hand feels refreshing against my warm skin, and I shiver against him.

"Sorry my hands are cold. Forgot my gloves."

"I don't have a fever."

"I know you don't. I just wanted an excuse to touch ya."

My responding smile is embarrassing, and I bite my lip trying to contain it.

"It's feckin' cold out here. Can I at least come in for a minute?"

I let out a sigh and nod, backing away so he can open the door. A cramp hits me suddenly, and I stumble for a second on my way to the couch.

"Feckin' Christ. What's wrong?" Mike asks, placing a hand on the small of my back as he guides me to the couch.

"It's nothing," I say as I close my eyes and flop down, curling on my side as I put the heating pad on my lower abdomen. I probably should be embarrassed by how pathetic I look, but I'm out of fucks to give at this point.

"Ah," Mike says as if he's figured out the answer to a riddle I didn't share with him.

The clatter of my spoon against the empty bowl startles me, and when I open my eyes, I see Mike walking with it into the kitchen as he puts it in the dishwasher.

"What are you doing?" I call out.

He walks toward me, his long legs eating up the distance between us in a few short strides. "I'm helping. I've noticed that the cleaner your house is, the calmer your brain is."

My mouth opens and shuts like it wants to speak, but I'm at a complete loss for what to say. How does he know that?

"What are we watching?" He nods at the TV and sits on the end of the couch near my feet. I secretly wish he would touch me, but he keeps his distance, and I grab the remote, unpausing the show. "Ah, *Bluey*. I love this episode."

I stare at him in disbelief. "You watch *Bluey*?"

"A few guys at the firehouse have kids, and they've put it on to entertain them during visits. And we may have left it on after their kids left. For hours. It's quite good. I'm mad about the grannies." He shrugs like it's not a big deal.

I don't know what to say so I lie back on the couch, and we watch several episodes together in silence.

When the show changes to *Caillou*, I reach for the remote. Fuck that whiny bald-headed kid. But Mike swipes it off the table first.

"What do you really want to watch?"

"I can't watch the mindless trash I really want to watch without worrying about little ears running in."

He flips through a few channels before landing on an episode of *Curious George*. It's one I've seen dozens of times.

"I'm convinced that Professor Wiseman has something going on with the Man in the Yellow Hat. Why else would they keep sneaking off together and leaving George alone to get in all that trouble? They know that monkey is always up to no good, yet they keep leaving him alone?"

He laughs. "And you think it's because they're feckin' horned up for each other?" It's not clear if he knows all the characters I'm talking about or if he's just humoring me, but for once I'm unbothered, just enjoying being in his company.

"Oh, they're definitely horned up. And don't get me started on Mayor Humdinger and Mayor Goodway on *Paw Patrol*. I think they create drama just so they can sneak off together."

"Do you always fantasize about cartoon characters doing it?"

"When you watch the same three seasons on constant repeat, you have to invent new storylines to hold your interest. And then when you start really paying attention, I swear you'll notice things, little clues the animators leave in."

"I think you're reading too many of your girly books."

"What do you know about my books?"

"I know you like to read them on your phone when you think no one's watching. And you think you have a good poker face, but whenever you get to a spicy scene, you'll look around quickly and then bite your lip as you continue reading. Maybe no one notices the way you squeeze your thighs together when you get turned on by the naughty bits. But I do. I see you."

Warmth fills me at his words. We've been hanging out for about a month, and I'm surprised he's already figured that out about me.

"Who's your favorite author?"

I sit up a little on the couch as he scoots closer, pulling my feet into his lap. "I've really gotten into this author named Ayana Cox. She writes the best characters. I've read everything in her backlist, and I've been dying to meet her, but she doesn't do signings or in-person events. She doesn't even show her picture online. Her characters feel like real people that I'd actually want to hang out with."

"And fuck?" he asks, squeezing my foot.

"If her male main characters were real people, I absolutely would. I might even add it to my list," I say with a smirk.

"Why does that make me want to beat their fictional arses?"

"I dunno. You really should work on your anger issues, friend," I tease, poking him in the chest with my toe.

He lunges toward me, pinning me to the couch, and I squeal, surprised by the intense look in his eyes.

"Does this feel like I'm just your friend?" He thrusts his hard cock against me, and I whimper.

His eyes search mine, and he leans down and runs his nose along my jawline. When he reaches my ear, he nips at the lobe. "If we were alone and there was no chance the boys could interrupt us, I would show you just how unfriendly I can be. Would you want that?"

I nod, exposing more of my neck to him.

"Good, cuz I'm going to light up this perfect, plump arse with my hand until your dripping all over my lap, begging me to fuck you."

"I'm on my—"

"Period? I don't give a fuck. A little blood isn't going to keep me away from this gorgeous cunt. But if you want to wait a few days, that's up to you." He tugs at my ear again with his teeth.

"Mama! The tablet died!" Levi wails from upstairs.

I shove Mike off me, and we separate on the couch just in time for Levi to walk into the room.

Levi sees Mike and drops the tablet, runs over to the couch, and launches himself into Mike's body.

I watch it play out in slow motion, and there's nothing I can do to stop it. "Levi, no!"

His knee connects with Mike's crotch, and Mike lets out a low groan that I can feel deep in my gut.

"I'm so sorry!" I say, pulling Levi off him.

"It's okay," Mike grunts. I feel so bad as I watch him slump over on the couch, hands between his legs.

"I sorry!" Levi says, patting Mike on the head.

"It was an accident, buddy," Mike offers, his words coming out in punctuated gasps.

"Kiss it, Mama! Kiss it better!" Levi begs, yanking on my sleeve.

Miraculously, I stifle my laugh as Mike lets out another keening groan. "No, buddy. Mr. Mike is hurt in a place where kisses won't help."

Levi examines Mike's slumped form. "On your pee-niss?" he whisper-shouts.

I bite my lip and nod. "Yup, you got him good. Let's give him a minute to recover."

How's the injury?

It's been two days, and I can still feel my nuts in my stomach.

I'm so sorry.

It happens. I felt bad about the way I left. Can I make it up to you?

You're fine. You walked out of here with barely a limp.

I cried in my car the whole drive home.

I'm not laughing, I promise.

You can laugh.

Good because I totally am. Getting hit in the nuts is never not funny.

He got me in the dick too. Impeccable aim, that one.

All things aside, not as good as the fart date, but still one of my favorite dates.

That was not a date.

It was a date. We have one left.

But that one doesn't count.

Just like the other one shouldn't count when you watched my kids.

It followed all the rules. At your house. With the boys.

I'm trying really hard to follow your rules here

What if you didn't?

Try hard?

Follow my rules.

Don't take pity on me because your kid nailed me in the balls. I want to earn your trust fair and square. I already broke your no kissing rule. And I know I fucked up at the hospital when I didn't stay with Micah like I said I would. I was going to, but then I saw you with him and I thought I'd give you time together. And I should have apologized for this sooner, but I'm sorry, Lucy. I've been trying to show you that you can count on me.

Instead of reading his text as a rejection like I normally would, I let his words sink in, letting them permeate my hard shell. This man has shown up for me and my kids since the moment we first met him, and I can't believe I've been so stupid to not see what he's been doing this entire time. Keeping him at arm's length, pretending this is just sex—just a list we're completing—is the biggest lie I've ever told myself.

Except for that one time at the hospital, he's done everything he said he would, and everything I've asked of him. He's told me how he feels, told me the truth even when I didn't ask for it, gone above and beyond to make me and my kids feel special.

We're not just friends with benefits. It's time I finally put on my big-girl panties and do more than just hump the hot firefighter.

CHAPTER 17

MIKE

"You want a Guinness? I think I might have a bottle of it in the back. Someone brought it for a poker night once, but I'm more of an IPA guy. It's yours if you want it," Hardy says as he walks over to the fridge.

"Didn't know we were ending our friendship today," I tease.

"I thought you liked Guinness?"

"Draught Guinness, not shite from a bottle."

"Yeah, don't have any on tap."

"I should just stick with water since I'm watching the boys."

He tosses me a water bottle and joins me on the couch.

"Daddy, Levi is jumping on my bed," Hardy's daughter Avery says as she runs down the stairs.

I start to bolt off the couch, but Hardy slaps a hand to my chest, pushing me back down. "Do you guys want to color in the kitchen?" he asks.

"Okay," she replies as she runs back upstairs.

"So much for being able to catch up," I say, sipping my water.

Hardy quirks an eyebrow, and I laugh. I've only been

around the boys for a little under a month, but it's impossible to have an adult conversation around them.

Minutes later, chaos descends the stairs in the form of two feckin' cute lads full of energy. Levi runs over and launches himself at me, hugging me as though he forgot I was here, and it fills me with warmth. I'm also thankful I've covered my crotch this time.

When he pulls back, he climbs up my chest like I'm not even here so he can perch on the back of the couch, feet dangling over my shoulders.

Avery flits around the room, gathering supplies and depositing them onto the kitchen table. When she grabs a bin full of glitter containers, Hardy stops her and shakes his head.

"Do we have any Sharpies?" Avery asks sweetly, and Hardy gives her a curious look. "I want to sign Micah's cast."

He walks to the kitchen, pulling out a pack of multicolored Sharpies, and Levi leans back, dangling over the back of the couch, doing quite the impressive back walk-over, before crashing onto the ground and running to the kitchen.

The boys are occupied for about fifteen minutes, coloring, though I wouldn't say quietly. Avery is doodling her name on Micah's cast next to the spot I signed, while Micah fills in a horse with a brown crayon in an animal coloring book.

Levi has added poop or fart clouds to almost every animal in a different book. He holds up a page for me to see. "Look, the chickens are pooping!"

Hardy chuckles next to me and then leans in, speaking so the kids can't hear. "Wait till they start drawing dicks on everything."

"I hope I'm around long enough to see it." I smile.

"You will be."

The front door opens, and Bella's son Isaac walks in, kicking off his shoes and tossing his coat over the banister. I expect him to take one look and bolt for his room, but he joins us at the counter. Bella and Hardy have been together since

Christmas, and I'm envious of the way they've blended their families together.

"How was your dad's?" Hardy asks.

"The same as it always is. What's going on here?" He nods to the boys coloring with Avery.

"Playdate," I say.

"Wanna see my poops?" Levi shouts at Isaac with a big grin.

"Levi, stop talking about poop, or I'm telling Mom," Micah scolds.

"That's gross," Avery says, wrinkling her nose.

"I'd love to see your poops. Are we talking little pellets or big logs?" Isaac asks as he joins Levi at the table.

"Eww!" Avery groans. "C'mon, Micah, let's go play with my ponies."

Micah shrugs and follows her upstairs.

"What's this?" Isaac asks, pointing to a page that is covered in brown.

Levi laughs. "That's a poo-splosion! The horse had to cha-cha really bad."

"Cha-cha?" Isaac asks.

"Yeah, like the song. Diarrhea cha-cha-cha," Levi says.

"Oh my God, I haven't thought about that song in years." Hardy laughs. "It's good to know that future generations are keeping it alive and well."

"Is this an American thing I don't know about? My folks didn't teach me any songs about feces growing up, and now I'm feeling like I missed out."

"Oh yeah, I think I know that one. You can keep making up rhyming verses," Isaac says.

We spend several minutes making up our own verses, and I secretly hope I don't pay for it later when I take the boys home.

When Lucy and Bella show up an hour later, my heart races at the sight of Lucy. Her long blonde hair cascades around her shoulders, and I imagine wrapping it around my hand as I fuck into her from behind.

And then Levi sings "Diarrhea cha-cha-cha!" and the spell is broken.

"Ugh, it took a week to get him to stop singing that song last time," Lucy groans.

I offer her an apologetic look as she walks into the kitchen.

"How'd it go? I see the house is still standing." Lucy looks around nervously as if she's going to find a giant hole in the wall.

"The boys were good. We had fun," I say.

"We colored. Look at my poops!" Levi adds, holding up a coloring book as Bella looks over her shoulder.

"Okay, but why is that actually good?" Bella asks. "That looks great, Levi. Very detailed."

"Do you like it, Mama?"

"I love it, buddy," Lucy says before turning back to us. "I really shouldn't be encouraging this, but he's gotten really good at drawing poop. Who knows, maybe he'll get into art when he's older?"

"As long as he's not drawing it with actual poop. They don't pay teachers enough to deal with all that," Bella says.

"How'd it go at the school? Did you get everything done for the St. Patrick's Day program?" Hardy asks.

Bella groans. "If I never see another shamrock again, it'll be too soon."

Hardy wraps an arm around her. "That bad, huh? Did Amber put you all to work?"

"She's going through a lot right now with the divorce. I think it was more about her wanting some friends to vent to than it was about prepping for the assembly. It's still a week away. We have time."

"Then she could have found another way to do it without giving us all carpal tunnel from cutting construction paper," Lucy mutters.

"Everyone deserves a second chance." Bella smiles, and I notice something pass between her and Lucy, like they're speaking about more than mean PTO moms.

I come up behind Lucy, wrapping my arms around her as I kiss the side of her head. The move is intimate, claiming, and she melts against me. Bella smiles at us knowingly, whispering something to Hardy, and I wait for Lucy to pull away from me, wait for her nerves to kick in and stop this semi-public declaration. We haven't officially come out as a couple to any of her friends, and I've managed to successfully dodge all talk about it at the firehouse. But to my surprise, she doesn't pull away. Instead she turns and wraps her arms around my waist, and I can't help the dopey grin that spreads across my face.

"Micah! Levi!" Bella calls, and the boys come running. "Isaac told me he needs help with a super top-secret project he's working on. Do you know anyone that can help with that?"

Micah raises his good arm. "I can help."

"MEEEE!" Levi says as he jumps up and down.

"Perfect. Why don't you guys head upstairs? And we have to hurry before it explodes. Oops, I've said too much." Bella mimes zipping her lips, and the boys hustle up the stairs.

Isaac saunters over. "What secret project are you talking about?"

"You know, the one where you watch them for an hour so the parents can hang out kid-free."

"Is that what you guys are calling it nowadays?"

"Thanks, Isaac." Bella pats him on the shoulder as he trudges over to the stairs.

"You owe me," he grumbles, but there's a hint of a smile on his face as he turns to climb toward the chaos I know is waiting for him.

"You kids have fun. We'll drop them off at eight since it's a school night. And don't worry, I'll make sure they're fed. Enjoy your adult time." Bella winks as Hardy wraps an arm around her.

"Don't do anything I wouldn't do," Hardy adds before kissing the top of Bella's head.

Minutes later we're sitting in the car as it idles in Hardy's driveway. She isn't saying anything and it's killing me. Is she mad about the poop song? Is she having second thoughts about how much we looked like a couple back there, and not just friends that are fucking? Is she having second thoughts about me?

We turn and look at each other at the same time, and relief hits me when I see the hunger in her eyes. Our lips crash together as she grips my face, pulling it to hers. She's kissing me harder than she ever has before, and it has more than my heart growing in size.

Her mouth explores mine, our tongues tangling together in a dance that feels choreographed despite our lack of rehearsal in that department.

"I'm so glad you got rid of the no-kissing rule," I say as she sucks my bottom lip into her mouth. "Fuck, I could do this for hours."

"We don't have that long. And I was thinking we could check off another item on my list," she says as she dives back into my mouth.

There are only a few items left on her list, and I immediately know which one I want to complete.

Reluctantly, I break the kiss as I back out of the driveway.

"Where are we going?" she asks as we drive through town and she realizes we aren't headed to her place.

"I've got a surprise for you."

CHAPTER 18

MIKE

"It's not much, but it's mine," I say, ushering her into the door of my one-bedroom apartment.

I watch as she takes in the space. It's pretty minimalist, just the essentials: a TV, a couch, and a small kitchen table with two chairs. She doesn't say anything, and I start to worry what's going on in her head.

"I know it's not much, but I don't need much. And it's clean. Besides, I'm at the fire station a lot so…"

She turns to me, a bright smile on her face. "It's quiet." She throws her head back, letting out a deep exhale through her nose. "It's perfect."

Her words calm my soul, and I tug her into the bedroom, guiding her to the queen bed. I reach down into the nightstand and pull out the bag I'm looking for.

"What's this?" she asks, cautiously opening the bag.

"I picked it up when I was in Denver the other day, so we can complete an item on your list."

She pulls out a paddle and hits it against her open palm, and the resounding thwack has my dick pressing against the seam of my pants. I wait for her to say something, but she's oddly quiet. When she sits on the bed, she looks down, spreading her hands over the comforter. "Is this navy?"

"Dunno, always thought it was dark blue."

She stiffens slightly. I reach for her, stroking her arms as I part her thighs with my hips so I can stand between them.

"You know what they say about guys with navy sheets." There's a hint of playfulness in her tone, but I can sense the tension in her body enough to know that she's in her head about something.

"I don't. Enlighten me."

"There's this trend on social media about guys with navy sheets belonging in the streets."

"I'm not following." I tilt her face up toward mine.

"The thought is that guys with navy sheets are just down for hookups. They're not guys looking for serious relationships. It's just my luck, that's all."

I can't stand the sadness in her eyes, and I grab her waist with one hand, picking her up as she wraps her legs around me in response, still clutching the paddle.

"Mike, what are you doing?" she asks, surprise in her tone.

I don't say anything. Instead, I lean over with her in my arms, and I pull the comforter and sheets off the bed. I struggle a little with the fitted sheet, but after a few tugs, I get it free from the opposite side of the bed and toss all the linens on the floor. Then I set her down and grip her cheeks in both of my hands.

"What do I need to do to prove to you that I want more than this with ya? You're more than just a hookup to me, a ghrá mo chroí."

I'm nervous about pushing her too hard, but if the color of my sheets upsets her because she thinks I'm not serious about her, I'll get rid of them.

She doesn't say anything, so I lean over the pile and pull out the top sheet, deciding to play it safe and refocus on her list. "If you want to check off another item, here." I hold the sheet out for her to take.

She eyes it suspiciously. "What do you want me to do with this?"

"I want you to tie me up and spank me. You said you wanted spankings, and I'm happy to give them or take them. It's up to you." I pull my clothes off quickly until I'm fully naked and bared to her. She pulls off her shirt and leggings, but keeps her bra and panties on.

A light flashes in her eyes as she takes the sheet from me. I hold my wrists together in offering, and she loops the fabric around it. The knot is big and bulky and isn't doing much to actually restrain me, but that's not the point of this. Once she secures the sheet, I turn and leave the room, feeling her eyes on my arse the whole time.

She follows me into the living room, and I walk over to the couch, leaning over the back of it. It's the only piece of furniture in my space that is the ideal height for this.

I can feel her body behind me, can sense her hesitation. "Spank me. Give it to me. I need to feel your hands on me. Or the paddle, I don't care. I want everything you have to give me."

The first slap is soft, timid, her hand lingering on my cheek as if she's exploring it.

"I know ya got more in ya than that, Lucky." I wait for her witty retort to the nickname, but it never comes. Instead, she smacks my arse with more force, and I groan, steadying myself against the cushions with the ridiculous ball of fabric binding my hands.

I don't know where the nickname even came from, probably all her talk about being unlucky. But she's far from it. And she makes me feel like the luckiest motherfucker on the whole goddamn planet.

She doles out several more swats, alternating cheeks as she increases the pressure.

The sounds that escape me are obscene, and I can feel the precum leaking from my tip as my cock rubs against the back of the couch. I should be embarrassed by the mess she's making of me, but I want to give this to her. Let her claim her power.

Her finger trails up and down my spine before I feel her palm shove my upper half down, my face now buried in the knotted sheet, forcing my arse higher in the air.

"Such a good boy for me, aren't you? So eager for anything I give you."

Fuck, if she only knew how much.

"Yes, ma'am."

Another crack of her hand echoes around the space, and I bite the sheet as the sting slowly eases into little pricks of pleasure against my skin. Then she uses the paddle, rubbing it around my flesh, before popping my left cheek with it, eliciting new sensations everywhere it lands. Who knew I would enjoy this so much?

She smacks the other cheek, and I buck against the couch. "Feckin' hell, Lucky."

As soon as the nickname leaves my lips, she smacks my right arse cheek again, this one harder than any of the previous ones. I let out a low growl of appreciation, and she pauses her movements, stopping to trace a finger over the bottom of my arse where it meets my right thigh. Every touch of hers feels goddamn amazing.

She continues teasing the spot below my cheek, and I push back against her, silently asking for more of whatever she has to give me.

"I think I like you like this." Her voice is quiet, yet full of power, as if she's been waiting for this moment for far longer than I realized.

"How's that?" I turn my head, trying to peek at her.

"Needy for me. At my mercy." Her hand snakes down between my thighs to grip my balls, giving them a firm tug.

"Fuck… I need…" I struggle to form a coherent thought when her hand reaches up and cups the base of my dick, her thumb playing with the barbell closest to my balls. "Oh fuuu-uck, that feels good."

She continues playing with me, toying with each barbell as she slowly makes her way up my shaft. I'm so distracted, so desperate for release that I don't notice her other hand bring down the paddle on my left side until it connects. "Jesus feckin' Christ. I'm…" Am I going to come? She's barely touched me.

"What do you need? I want to hear you beg for it again."

I have no shame when it comes to this woman. I will do anything. Give her anything she asks for. "I need your mouth on me. I want you to try to swallow as many of my piercings as you can while your hands stroke up and down the rest of my shaft. Please. I've been a good boy, taking my spankings. Please, Lucky. Please. I need to feel ya."

"Sit on the couch," she commands.

I push up on my hands, still bent over the couch and jump, swinging my legs up and over the back as I land somewhat sideways thanks to the knot of sheets.

The sound of her laughter makes me smile. When I look up, her head is thrown back as she clutches her chest. I live to hear this woman's joy.

"Oh my God, I'm sorry, this is probably the least sexy thing I could say right now, but that was a total Levi move," she says through giggles.

"Where do you think I got the idea?" I smile as I pull my hands out of the sheet knot.

"Sorry, I know I shouldn't bring up the kids when I'm about to suck your dick."

I sit up so she can stand between my legs. "S'okay. It's hard to turn off the mom part sometimes. But I meant it when I said I wanted all of ya. Every side of ya."

My comment sobers her, and she nods, slowly sinking to her knees.

All other thoughts leave my brain the moment my cock slides into her mouth. Her perfect, warm, delicious mouth. "Fuck, I love this mouth." The words slip out, and I squeeze my eyes shut and wait to see if she's going to react to what I said.

A low, deep moan escapes her throat, and I blow out a sigh of relief that she's not going to get hung up on my use of the L word.

When I open my eyes, I nearly come at the sight of her, on her knees, three barbells deep, saliva pooling from her mouth, as she does her best to swallow my cock. "Look at me, a chroí."

Her eyes lock on mine. She has the kind of eyes poets write about, a wild green, as fierce and beautiful as a storm rolling in off the Atlantic. Eyes that I want to spend an eternity memorizing every shade and nuance of as we build a life together with her boys. As we make love every night once they're tucked in.

But I don't voice my thoughts, instead focusing on her movements, wanting to make sure she gets as much pleasure out of checking this item off as I have. "Touch yourself. Put a hand in your panties and rub your clit."

Her hand moves down, slipping past the waistband and even lower. When she lets out another moan, I know she's followed my command.

"That's my good girl. I bet you're soaked for me, aren't ya? Making a mess of your panties just from sucking this cock."

The nod she gives in response is slight, but the thought of her dripping for me and the way she slides me to the back of her throat, working me deep with a swallow—that's all it takes.

"Fuck, I'm gonna come. Swallow it, Lucky. Every drop.

Ughhhnn, *fuck*." My cock pulses against her tongue, warm and hungry, as I spill into her mouth.

Seconds later, my cock is still between her lips when her orgasm hits and I feast on the sight of her as her free hand releases my dick and grips my thigh, anchoring her to me as she rides out her own waves of pleasure.

When she stills, I grip her arm, pulling her into my lap as I grab the hand that was in her panties and bring it to my mouth, sucking on her fingers as I clean her essence from them. "So feckin' delicious."

I pull her mouth to mine and thrust my tongue inside, wanting to lap up every inch of her mouth that I can. The taste of my release is still on her tongue, salty and tangy, as she matches my enthusiasm with gusto. I'm drunk on the taste of us—her on my tongue, and me on hers—mixing together as we get lost in each other, exploring and groping.

We sit there like that for a good bit, kissing and holding each other when something chirps on her phone, and she untangles from me. "Shit, we have to go. That's my alarm."

"You set a timer?"

"So we wouldn't be late. Bella's going to my house, and we need to be there when she drops the boys off."

I grab her hand, squeezing it to get her attention. When her eyes meet mine, warmth blooms in my chest at the admiration I see there.

"Plus, I know that if I didn't set an alarm, I'd be wrapped up in you all night," she adds with a smirk. And, fuck, do I love every little piece of herself Lucy shares with me. This admission is my favorite yet.

CHAPTER 19

LUCY

There's a knock on my door the next day right as I'm cleaning up after dinner and I stare at it from across the room like it's offended me. Why is it that as a kid I used to love when my doorbell rang, but now when it happens, I freeze in place, like if I don't move, they won't know I'm home?

"Lucy? I'm home!" Bella's voice rings out, doing her best impression of Desi from *I Love Lucy*.

"To what do I owe this pleasure?" I ask, swinging open the door. I'm stunned to find Mike standing behind her. I tuck my hair behind my ear, thankful that at least this time I was lucky enough to look halfway decent and not like a troll that just crawled out from under a bridge.

"Hey, Lucky. You look gorgeous." His blue eyes drag over me, igniting fires in places no one else has ever touched, and I shiver at the hungry look in them.

Bella clutches her heart. "Oh my God, he calls you Lucky! I love that. Wait till the girls hear."

Her excitement pulls me out of the trance Mike's attention has over me, and I take a step back, inviting them in.

"Not that I'm not thrilled you're here, but did I forget to

put something on my calendar?" I feel like I've been forgetting a lot lately, super distracted by the hot firefighter in my kitchen.

"I just left Delilah's, and I made you some *special* cookies." Bella says, flashing me a huge grin.

Mike lifts an eyebrow. "Are these like the magic brownie type of cookies?"

Bella laughs. "Nope, just normal ingredients. It's the design that makes them special." She places the container on the counter. "We've been baking all day to make treats for the St. Patrick's Day program at school, but these are just for you." She pops open the lid and pushes the container toward me.

"Thanks, but I'm not really hungry," I say.

"I'll take one," Mike says, reaching into the container and pulling out a cookie.

I quirk a brow at Bella. "You made those for the school? For the children?"

"Is this what I think it is?" Mike asks, moving his face closer so he can inspect the cookie.

"It is!" Bella laughs. "Since we couldn't make cockies for Christmas this year, Delilah and I decided to make some for St. Patrick's Day. These are just for the moms. I already dropped off Summer's and Raven's. I promise I made appropriate ones for the school."

I shoot her a dubious look.

"I did! It's Delilah you have to watch out for. Our principal may look all innocent, but she's a crafty one." She takes the cookie from Mike, waving it around as she speaks, using it to punctuate her point. "But isn't it pretty?"

She holds up the penis-shaped cookie, cupping it in her hand like she's showing off a prize on a game show. The testicles are decorated into two pots of gold, and she's turned the shaft into a rainbow that disappears into the cloud-shaped head of the penis.

"That's actually hella creative," I say, marveling at her creation.

"Thanks. The cloud was Delilah's idea."

"Do I want to know why you turned a penis into a rainbow?" Mike asks.

Bella smiles proudly. "Several years ago, my kid grabbed the wrong cookie cutters, and a new holiday tradition was born."

The clatter of footsteps approaches as Levi runs down the stairs and barrels into the kitchen. "I want a cookie!"

Before any of us can react, Mike snatches the cookie out of Bella's hand and takes a huge bite of the rainbow. "Sorry, lad," he says around a mouthful of peen cookie. "I couldn't help myself, I had to taste it. But you can have the pot of gold at the end of the rainbow." He holds the rest of the cookie out to Levi, who snatches it and finishes it in three bites before he runs out of the kitchen, a trail of cookie crumbs following him.

"Brush your teeth again!" I call after him as he climbs the stairs.

I can't contain my laughter once Levi has left the kitchen. "Did you just deep-throat a cock cookie to protect my child's innocence?"

"I didn't want him to see it and have to explain why the rainbow looked like a penis."

"Ooh, he's a keeper," Bella says, biting the tip off another cookie. She pulls out her phone and starts typing furiously.

"Who are you texting?" My phone vibrates on the counter, and I shake my head in defeat.

"What am I missing?" Mike asks, looking between us.

Bella smiles. "Oh nothing, the girls just owe me some money."

I want to be annoyed about their stupid bet, but we did the same thing to her, and for once I don't care as I lean against Mike's bicep. He wraps his arm around me, pulling me close as he kisses my forehead.

Bella puts the lid back on the container, and I stop her, deciding to try one after all.

As I bring the cookie to my mouth, I can feel Mike's eyes on me.

He holds his hands up in defense. "You can't put something that shape in your mouth and not expect me to watch."

I smirk and take a big bite off the pot of gold, and he winces in response, covering his balls with his hands.

"I'm loving this side of you," Bella says around a mouthful of cookie.

Both of our heads turn in her direction.

"You totally just forgot I was standing here, didn't you?"

Shit, I did.

"This playful side really suits you. And I don't think I've seen you this happy since…" She takes another bite of her cookie, intentionally drawing out her words. "Well… in a while. Ever, maybe."

"Is everything all set for the program?" I ask, shoving the rest of the cookie in my mouth.

Bella shrugs. "Fuck if I know. I have nothing to do with this one, I'm just doing what Amber tells me to do. I got my fill of being in charge after running Santa's Workshop, and we all know how that ended."

I groan. "I thought you'd have some inside scoop. Amber better not call another emergency PTO meeting like she did before the Valentine's party debacle. That three-hour one the other night was bad enough, and I still have a papercut from yesterday," I say, holding up my ring finger.

Mike grabs my hand and kisses the cut, his lips hovering over my finger as he holds it and looks at me. "Sorry. The boys keep saying that I should kiss your boo-boos, and this is one I can actually kiss."

A small squeal erupts from Bella, and I turn to her. She holds her hands up in silent apology.

"MO-OM!" Micah yells from upstairs.

"What?" I call back.

"Levi said Mike was here and I want him to tuck us in tonight."

When I look up at him, he's beaming, his smile stretching ear to ear. "Can I?"

"Go ahead." I nod as he kisses my forehead and takes off for the stairs. "But try to keep it to only one fart blessing this time, please."

"Yes, ma'am," he calls back.

"Ma'am?" Bella questions, looking at me with furrowed brows. "Oh my God, he checked another item off your list, didn't he? And based on the color of your cheeks, and the way he said 'ma'am,' I'm guessing it was role-play or spankings?"

I nod in confirmation as she jumps and claps her hands excitedly. "Oh my gosh, I love this for you. You're glowing! Spill."

"It was…" I trail off, suddenly nervous to share more. Normally I'd tell her everything, but something tugs at my heart, telling me to stop. What is happening right now? What does this mean? I've already told Bella about a few items we've checked off the list. So why does it feel like I'm breaking his trust if I talk about this now?

After what feels like minutes of silence while my thoughts spiral, I look up at Bella and she has a dopey grin on her face.

"Say no more. I know what that face is."

"What face?" How does she know what I'm feeling when I haven't even figured it out myself?

"Remember when you kept asking me what was going on with me and Hardy, and I kept deflecting?"

My mind races, struggling to put together the puzzle pieces she's dropping. "But we're just friends. This is just—" Just what? I don't even know what this is anymore, but it definitely feels like more than just hooking up.

"Are you sure about that?" She smiles, walking around the

counter, placing a hand on my arm. "You don't want to tell me about knocking boots with Mr. March, because his feelings matter to you now. You're worried about how he'd feel if he knew you talked about it. It's not just a hookup. And judging by the look on your face, you're just now realizing that. Shit, sorry. Why am I such an awkward turtle with this stuff?"

I pull her into a hug, catching her off guard. "Thank you."

She pats my back stiffly. "You're welcome? What are you thanking me for?"

"For being you. I'm not good at all this emotional stuff. But you are. And you blurt every thought in your head, and it's fantastic."

"Even the inappropriate ones?" She laughs against me.

"Especially those. That's who you are. And I love that about you." I release her and hold her shoulders as I look in her eyes. "And if you share what I'm about to say with the girls, I will deny it. But I think I needed you to be the one to push me—or that you'd be the only one who'd actually force me to admit what I've been thinking for weeks."

"That I'm your favorite? Don't worry, your secret's safe with me." She winks, and I laugh, thankful for her ability to bring levity to any situation.

"That, and that I might be falling for Mike."

"Good, because that man is so gone for you and your little boys."

I blink at her as my mouth drops slightly in shock. "What? When? How?"

"Who? Where? Why?" She laughs. "Sorry, were we not naming all the W questions?"

I teasingly smack her arm, but I can't stifle the giggle at her antics.

"As I was saying, that man is gone for you. He's always looked at you with such longing. And he brings you up all the time to Hardy."

"Oh God, does Hardy know about the list?" My gut twists at the possibility.

"No. I don't think so. I didn't tell him. I doubt Mike did. Besides, if Hardy knew about the list, that horny little firefighter would want to make one for us to do too. So that's how I know he doesn't know." She folds her arms over her chest, proud of herself.

"That's oddly good logic. Raven would be proud."

Bella smiles. "Hardy says Mike talks about you and the boys all the time. Like when he's cooking for the crew, he'll muse over whether you'd like his dish or not. They'll be out on a call, and he'll see a kid who looks like Micah and talk about how much he likes Pokémon. Or when someone says a curse word, Hardy will catch Mike looking around like he's worried Levi will hear it and repeat it. And Hardy pointed out that Mike curses less, and when asked about it, he just shrugged and said he was trying to cut it out because of the boys. You don't do all that for just a hookup."

I cover my mouth with my hand, blinking back the tears that want to fall. "He did all that? How come he didn't say anything?"

"He probably knew you weren't ready. You've been very clear about what you wanted. I think he was afraid to scare you off."

"I am scared," I admit. "Scared of how well he fits in with us. He looks and acts like he's part of our family already. He's up there tucking them in like a dad would." I gesture to the stairs.

Bella smiles. "I love this for all of you."

"Oh God, I'm going to have to tell him." I look at the stairs to make sure we're still alone.

"About—"

I nod. Bella is the only one who knows. "I think it's time. He needs to know now before this gets any more serious."

"I've seen the way he cares about you and the boys. I don't think he's going to care."

"He's mentioned wanting a family. Lots of kids, a whole clan of them to carry on his family name. It was important to his Ma."

A tear slips down my cheek, and Bella wipes it before I realize it's there.

"Then he deserves to know. I still don't think it'll change how he feels about you."

"This is why I wanted to keep it casual. Just sex."

"I don't think it was ever just sex for him."

I can't stop the train wreck of thoughts from spilling out, and before I know it, I'm confessing everything to Bella. "Of course I fall for the one man I can't have. The one man that wants something I can't give him. I don't think my heart can handle it if he walks away from this. How did I let it get this far? Why do I have the worst fucking luck in the world?"

"We make our own luck," Bella insists.

"You might. I'm over here wishing on rainbows and knocking on all the wood I can find." Bella starts to open her mouth. "Don't," I warn, a small smirk on my face.

Bella holds up her hands, letting my unintentional innuendo slide. "You of all people know the shit show my life was and how far I've come, and that didn't happen from luck. I'm not lucky because I have a hot man in my life who loves me and my kid. I mean, we *get lucky*." She laughs to herself. "But having a supportive partner isn't what makes me lucky. We've all had bad shit happen to us. But I've become an expert at squeezing those lemons."

"Is that a sex thing?"

She breaks out into laughter. "What? No! It's a metaphor. Not everything that comes out of my mouth is balls and dicks. Sometimes it's wisdom."

"Fair enough." I offer her a watery smile.

She tosses her hair over her shoulder. "I've learned how to

squeeze the lemons life has thrown at me. And it took a lot of practice, but I've finally made some damn good lemonade. Are you catching what I'm throwing down?"

"We make our own luck. And lemonade."

"Exactly. Now that you know what you want, go after it. Don't let little obstacles get in your way."

"It's not exactly a little obstacle," I say, gently reminding her.

"True. I didn't mean to imply that. But I honestly think it won't be as big a deal as you're making it in your head. Not that your feelings aren't valid, because they are. Jesus, Bella, just stop while you're ahead." She smacks her forehead, shaking her head.

"I know what you mean, and I know your heart. You never have to explain your ramblings to me, friend."

She smiles back at me, and my brain slowly starts to quiet, my nerves easing slightly.

I chew on my lip, trying to dispel the rest of the chaos of my anxious thoughts. "The last time I let someone in, he didn't want kids, and I did. And thanks to my shitty luck, now I don't want more kids, and Mike does, and my heart's involved. I've never felt this way before. And the fact that I'm scared of what he might say, how he will react, and terrified that he could walk away, it's too much. I don't know how to process it."

"I know I don't have all the answers, and I know you may not believe me, but I truly think you're it for him. There's something whispering in my ear, like a little leprechaun, telling me you should chase your rainbow to find your happy ending." Her face lights up like she's just had a revelation. "Two little leprechauns I don't think he'd ever walk away from. And I'm pretty sure he's fond of your pot of gold." She winks at me like she's proud of her terrible joke.

"That was bad. Like really bad." I try my best to say that

with a straight face, but when Bella sticks her tongue out at me, I snicker.

"I think those boys are your lucky charms. And you made them, so technically you did make your own luck."

"I am pretty lucky to be their mom, even if they do drive me batshit crazy sometimes."

"Amen to that. Now go tell your hot firefighter how you feel."

Once Bella leaves, I clean the kitchen, hoping to dispel my nervous energy. The sounds of farts and laughter filter down the stairs. Is this what it's like to have help? One of us corralling the kids while the other cleans up behind them? It's oddly domestic, and the idea of having more of this and maybe making it a permanent thing one day fills me with peace.

I let out a long exhale as the house quiets, and I hear Mike sneak down the stairs.

"Sorry to just show up tonight. Bella and I didn't plan that, I swear."

In all the chaos, I just realized he never said why he was here; only Bella had mentioned her reason for stopping by. "I'm glad you came. Do you want to stay and have a glass of wine? Maybe watch an episode of *Bluey*?"

"Please don't tell me you think the Heelers are doing it?"

I laugh. "They absolutely are, but I also think that Bandit and Chili run an international crime ring. Oh, and Chili totally reads spicy books."

"I saw the theory about the book."

"You did?" I sit on the couch, and he joins me.

"Aye, came across my social media feed when I was doom-scrolling one night. My phone must be listening to us talking about cartoons fucking."

"It was one conversation." I roll my eyes and playfully shove him. "But I do think they are smuggling artifacts. Think about it, he's an archeologist uncovering treasures, and she works in airport security. It's the perfect cover!"

"Or they're just dogs doing jobs that real-life dogs might do, you know, digging for bones or sniffing for bombs at an airport."

"I think my theory is more fun." I pout, sticking out my lower lip, and Mike leans over capturing it between his teeth, nipping on it, and then kissing me roughly.

When he pulls back seconds later, I'm breathless. "What was that for?"

"You can't stick that plump little lip out and not expect me to devour it, a chroí."

"Oh."

"I'm happy to watch *Bluey* with you, but can we watch the FaceTime one with Muffin? It kinda reminds me of our Face-Time run-in."

I can feel the blush cover my cheeks as I sink lower on the couch. "It's called 'Faceytalk.'"

He smiles at me, throwing his arm around me, and we watch the entire episode. Each time Mike chuckles at some-thing on the screen, I'm filled with warmth until I think about my conversation with Bella and what I need to talk to him about. When the episode ends, I let the next one play as I keep my eyes on the screen. "Can I ask you something?"

"Anything." He angles his body toward mine, and I twist my hands as I piece together how to word things.

"You said you wanted a big family."

"I did. Ma's been on me for years to settle down and start a family."

"I get that it's important to your parents, but is that something you want? Four or five kids? Or just something you say to please your folks?"

He searches my face before answering. "Aye. I do want that. Though some days I think that's too many kids."

"Trust me, it's too many. So what's stopping you?" I ask. There has to be a reason he's never settled down before now, and I cling to the delusion that maybe it's because he doesn't really want that many kids.

"I don't think I'd be a good dad. Got a lot of growing up to do."

I stare at him in disbelief. That was the last answer I was expecting. "Are you kidding me?"

"Nope. I know I'm a good time, but that's all I am. It takes more than fart jokes at bedtime to make someone a good dad. And I don't feel like I've had much more than that to offer."

His vulnerable admission stuns me. "Mike, you have to know you are so much more than that."

"Am I now?"

"Yes. You're incredible with my boys. They love hanging out with you. I think you'll make an amazing father one day."

"I make fart noises, and they laugh. I entertain 'em, that's all."

"Fart jokes are always funny. But you make my boys feel seen. You light up when you see them, and you give them your full attention when most people brush them off as nuisances to be seen and not heard."

"I could never ignore them. They're too feckin' cute."

"You make them feel valued and loved."

"They're easy to love." He stares at me intently, and while I normally would panic under such intense scrutiny, I can't look away.

"You would make an incredible father. Any kid would be lucky to have you as their dad. My kids would be lucky to have a dad like you."

"Careful there, Lucky. That's not casual talk."

I drop my head, looking down at my lap as I fidget with my hands, avoiding eye contact with him as I weigh out how much to admit.

Fuck it.

"What if I don't want casual anymore?"

"Thank fuck." He hooks a finger under my chin and tilts my head toward his as he closes the distance between us and seals his lips to mine, taking his time to devour me like I'm the last pint of Guinness at a crowded bar on St. Patrick's Day. "I didn't want to be the first to admit that," he says between kisses.

I pull back, placing my hands on his chest, preventing him from kissing me further. He's hinted at wanting more, but have I really been that daft not to see his sincerity? "How long have you felt this way?" My tone is gentle, laced with concern as my eyes search his for the truth.

"Longer than I care to admit."

My brow furrows. "Please. I need to know."

"Since the hospital."

"When I ran into a wall?"

"Aye."

"The whole time?"

"The whole time." His eyes are filled with warmth as he strokes my cheek.

Maybe I can tell him. It's clear that I mean a lot to him, that he might even love me. Surely, I could tell him the truth and it wouldn't blow up in my face. Maybe this is the time when Lady Luck is finally on my side.

"I wasn't lying each time I told you how I felt. It took everything in me to hold back how deep my longing runs for you. I didn't want to scare you off."

I swallow thickly, ready to give up a little piece of my shell. "People have always let me down. My dad. My mom. My sister, even though it wasn't really her fault. And all the men I've dated. Especially the last one. He didn't want kids, and it was all I wanted. It's made it very hard for me to want to let people into my circle. And my friends are amazing, but I have a hard time allowing myself to rely on them."

"I'm sorry to hear that, but I'd like to be someone you can count on. I'll probably make mistakes since I've never been a dad to anyone. But I will get better if you're willing to let me try. I want to try, for the three of you."

I nod like an idiot, and he grabs my hand, bringing the back of it to his mouth, placing a gentle kiss on it.

"That tickles."

"What does?"

"Your mustache."

He tugs me close, still holding my hand, then peppers kisses up my bare arm. When he gets to my neck, he hovers as if waiting for permission. I tilt my head, exposing more flesh to him, and he dives in greedily, sucking and nipping the sensitive skin there. "That feels—" I don't get the chance to finish that thought before his lips are on mine. His thick arms envelop me, pulling me onto his lap so I'm straddling him while he holds me in place, one arm cupping the back of my neck, the other wrapped around the back of my waist.

And for the first time in my life, I feel safe, totally at peace. There are no other thoughts in my head aside from the utter pleasure this man makes me feel. I'm not worried if my breath smells good enough, if my body isn't perfect, if I'm crushing him, if he'll leave after. And for once I'm not consumed with my pessimistic thoughts that I'll somehow fuck this up too.

All I can think about is the way this man holds me like he worships me. Like he wants me more than anything else on this planet. It's intoxicating knowing I have this kind of effect on someone. Me. A single mom to two little boys. A woman whose body isn't what it used to be. Whose mind is a scary, anxiety-ridden fever dream.

As if he can sense the subtle shift in my thoughts, he grips me tighter, sliding his hand from my neck into my hair, tugging gently as he breaks the kiss and licks and sucks down my neck and jaw.

The way his tongue moves against me feels divine, like an answer to a prayer when all I asked for was mind-numbing pleasure. An idea forms in my head.

"I want to sit on your face." The words come out of nowhere and I cringe at my boldness, but he growls against my neck and nips at my earlobe.

"Can you be quiet, a chroí?"

I balk at the eagerness in his tone. I expected some resistance, if not a downright refusal. "Just like that?"

"When are ya going to believe me when I say that I want to please ya? Explore every beautiful feckin' inch of ya? Lap at your perfect pink cunt as it drips all over me, knowing that it glistens only for me?"

His accent always gets more pronounced when he's aroused, and I love that I know that about him. That I've learned some of his mannerisms the way he's learned mine.

He taps my thigh, and I hop up, reaching over to turn off the TV as I set the remote on the arm of the couch. He leans down and hoists me over his shoulder like a sack of potatoes.

When I open my mouth to protest, he swats my ass with just enough force to suck the breath from my lungs. "If you're about to open that beautiful mouth and say something mean about this gorgeous feckin' body, shut it."

I can't help the lovesick smile on my face, and I'm thankful he can't see it. He carries me up the stairs, down the hall, and into my room, using his foot to close the door behind us.

"Lock it," I squeal as he tosses me onto the bed, and I land with a soft thud.

He turns back to the door, opens it, and pokes his head into the hallway. Once he's satisfied, he quietly closes and locks it. Then he walks to the bathroom, returning with a towel a few seconds later, shoving it against the bottom of the door.

I arch an eyebrow at him as he closes the distance between

us, stripping off all his clothes in the process. "I know how loud ya can be. Want to make sure we don't disturb the wee ones."

Why is that so hot?

His fingers glide up the tops of my thighs. Once he reaches the waistband of my pants, he yanks them off, along with my panties, and then straightens, making a show out of detangling my underwear from my discarded pants. "Already wet for me, eh?" he asks, bringing the fabric to his face as he inhales deeply.

He balls the cotton into his fist and crawls over me. The second his bare cock grazes my skin, all thought leaves my brain and I'm consumed by the heat of his touch as he leans down and gives me the most sensual kiss. This isn't friends-with-benefits kissing. This is a deep, soul-searching, feelings-confessing type of kiss. With one hand propped up beside me, fist still clenched around my panties, he uses his other hand to delicately caress my cheek.

All the air punches out of my lungs as he continues his meaningful exploration of my mouth and lips, leaving no trace untouched.

When he suddenly pulls back, I feel as though all oxygen has escaped me, as though his kiss was the only thing tethering me to life. I gasp for air, and I see the wickedly playful gleam in his eye as he takes my panties and stuffs them in my mouth.

"I need every scrap of fabric at my disposal to silence the sounds I'm going to pull out of this beautiful body, a chroí."

Oh sweet Jesus, do I want that.

I nod like a love-drunk idiot and watch as he pushes off me and climbs up the bed, tossing pillows aside as he positions himself next to the headboard.

"Get over here and sit on my face, love. I've been dying to check this off your list."

I pull the panties out of my mouth. "Are you su—"

"Absolutely feckin' sure. Now come make my face your throne and show me the power you wield over me."

My nerves get the better of me. I'm not a small woman, and I've never done anything like this before. "But I'm—"

"There are dozens of words you could use to finish that thought. Were you gonna say beautiful, powerful, amazing? How about fierce, stunning, breathtaking? Anything less than that is unacceptable. You are incredible, every inch of ya. Your big heart, your capable mind, the way you care for others and protect the ones you love."

I'm at a loss for words, stunned at his confession. Is this how he sees me? "Can you—"

"I can do anything you want right now, but the thing I want most is your pleasure. I want to see you come apart on my tongue. I want to feel your thighs squeeze my face when you're on the edge. I want to taste your cum on my tongue knowing I earned every drop of it. Can you do that for me?"

Nodding hesitantly, I slowly crawl over to him, panties clutched in my hand. Even though his words fill me with a warmth and comfort I've never known, I can't help but feel nervous about putting all my weight on him. He must see the concern in my features.

"What is it, Lucky?"

I blink at him, stunned. He's called me that a few times now, and it stops me in my tracks every time. "What did you call me?"

"Lucky?"

Do I tell him? Not even the girls know this part of my past. "I've been avoiding that name my entire life."

"Why?"

"I am the unluckiest woman on the planet."

"Don't think that's true. You've got two beautiful boys, a job you love, and a supportive group of lassies."

"Is that all I've got?" I search his eyes for more, hoping his confession isn't complete. I want to tell him how I feel, but I'm too afraid to say it first.

"I think you know the answer to that. But I'll humor you since I'm so feckin' gone for ya."

An embarrassing smile lights up my face, and I bite my lip trying to play it cool.

"I called ya Lucky because that's how ya make me feel. Lucky we met. Lucky you finally let me help ya with your list. With your boys. And so damn lucky every time ya look at me like that. And while I'm dyin' to get lucky with ya right now, I'd be even luckier if we ditched the friend title and I could enjoy all the benefits of calling ya mine."

All words escape me as I nod emphatically.

"Can we tell the boys?" The eager look on his face nearly does me in.

"I'd like that," I say.

He pulls me against him as he presses his lips to mine.

"So damn lucky." He pulls back, searching my eyes. "Does it bother you when I call you that? Lucky?"

"It shouldn't."

"Why's that?"

"Because it's my name." I sit up and twist my hands in my lap.

His brow furrows and he blinks several times in confusion. "Like your nickname, yeah?"

"No. Like the name on my birth certificate."

A wide grin lights up his face as he chuckles. I swat at his chest.

"If you haven't noticed, bad luck follows me wherever I go, so the thought of being called Lucky felt too ironic when I'm the definition of unlucky. Also, Lucky Lovejoy? The teasing was relentless. So I dropped the K and started going by Lucy once I moved here with my mom in middle school."

"I love it. And I'd love it even more if you came over here and sat on my face."

"It's just…" I trail off, unsure how to finish that sentence.

"What? How can I set your mind at ease, love?"

"I'm not a small person."

"Feck no, you're not, and it's damn sexy," he says gliding his hands up my thighs as he digs his fingertips into the flesh on my hips. "This body is feckin' incredible. I have enjoyed every inch of you already, and if you think I'm going to deny you the pleasure of coming on your man's face, you're wrong. Now get your fine arse up here and ride me."

Empowered by his declaration, I nod and inch my way up his body when he places a hand on my stomach and frowns. "I know ya like to leave the shirt on, but I've been dying to see this part of ya," he says as he palms the area around my belly button. "And I'm going to need you fully naked so I can watch those perfect tits bounce while you ride my face."

I let out a breath and slowly peel off my shirt and bra trying not to let my nerves get the better of me.

"Christ, Lucky. You're feckin' exquisite."

His words fill me with warmth. I haven't revealed this part of myself to anyone since becoming a mom. But with Mike, it's not as scary as I thought it'd be. Nothing with Mike has been.

He reaches up and cups my breasts, rolling a nipple between his thumb and forefinger as my head drops back in a small moan. He halts his movement and grabs the balled-up panties still sitting on the bed, shoving them in my mouth before he grabs my thighs and helps position me over his face.

Oh my God, what if I crush him?

"I'm not gonna do a lot of talking, but I will make noise. Do not stop, no matter what. If you need me to move to a specific spot, just grab my hair and move me. Other than that, hold on to the headboard and ride my face so I can feast on this delicious cunt."

Ever so slowly, I lower myself until I can feel his warm breath tickling my pussy.

"None of this hovering shite, Lucky. I told you to sit." He

wraps his arms around my thighs and pulls me onto his face and then proceeds to eat me like a man starved.

Every lick and suck of my flesh makes my legs shake as my core tightens. One of his hands releases my thigh and then I feel fingers push inside my pussy. I moan into my gag; thankful he had the foresight to use it.

He latches onto my clit, pulling it into his mouth while his fingers stroke my inner walls. I buck against him and dig my fingers into the wooden headboard to steady myself.

I can feel him moaning against me, the vibrations creating an indescribable feeling against my skin. He continues his efforts for several minutes, and while it feels amazing, I can't help but worry that I'm crushing him, that he won't be able to breathe.

Suddenly, his fingers and mouth are gone as two hands grip my thighs, pushing me up in the air like he's doing bench presses, and I tighten my grip on the headboard to keep my balance as I peer down at him in confusion.

"I can feel your hesitation, and I can assure ya I'm fine. As you can see, I have no problem lifting you to put you where I want ya. But Jesus feckin' Christ, if you don't get out of that pretty little head of yours and ride me like you mean it, I'm gonna spank your arse and cunt until you want to come so bad you're begging me to fill ya."

All I can do is nod my enthusiasm as he lowers me back down and begins eating me with a fervor I've never experienced. His fingers are back, filling and stretching me as he taps out a rhythm on my G-spot, and my body responds as if it knows the rest of the melody to the song he's creating with my muffled moans, his deep growls, and the dirty sounds his mouth makes against my soaking center. My orgasm hits quickly as I buck and grind against him, threading my fingers into his hair as my nails graze his scalp.

I struggle to catch my breath as I come down from the high. When I slowly push up on my knees, he slides out from under me, swatting my ass as I yelp into the fabric still balled into my mouth.

My hands are gripping the headboard as I attempt to catch my breath. There's some jostling around behind me, but I'm too spent to look.

Warm hands grip my waist, and then Mike is pressing his big hard body against mine. His hands glide up my stomach as he rests them right under my breasts and grinds his hard cock against my ass.

He lowers his head next to mine and I can feel his breath tickle my ear. "Can I truly make ya mine, love?"

I nod my head in agreement as I push my ass against him, creating more friction.

"Do you know what I'm asking ya?"

He pulls my panties out of my mouth, and I inhale deeply as I turn my head to look at him. "I want you to fuck me bare."

CHAPTER 21

MIKE

There is nothing more beautiful than the sight of this woman stripped completely naked before me. Her body is spectacular. I know she gets in her head about it, but she's been withholding more than just her body with me since I met her, and I'm thrilled that she's bared all for me tonight.

"I've been tested, and I'm clear," I say as I rest my hands on her hips.

"My last test was clear, and I haven't been with anyone since the boys were born."

"Birth control?" I ask, more for her sake than mine. I'd put a baby in her right now if she'd let me. But I know she may not be ready for that.

"I have that covered," she says softly, refusing to make eye contact with me as she turns back toward the headboard.

The last thing I want is for her to get lost in her thoughts again and pull away. I'm desperate to keep her with me, in this moment. "I want you to ride me so I can watch you stretch around my cock as your perfect cunt swallows my piercings."

She hesitates for a second, turning to look at me over her shoulder again. "I–I've never done that before."

Jesus feckin' Christ. I'm filled with rage and excitement at her words. What kind of feckin' eejits has she been with that have denied her this right? But fuck, am I thrilled to be the first person that she gets to experience the pleasure of riding a man and having full control over him.

"I'll let you ride any part of me you want. My face, my cock, you name it." I wrap my arms tighter around her as I delight in the warmth of her body against mine. She feels perfect against me, every plush curve.

"Do you feel that, a chroí?" I thrust my cock against her plump arse, and she gasps in response. "Do you feel how much I want you? There is nothing you could ever do to change that, but I want you to be comfortable."

She leans her head back against my shoulder, the move pushing her tits out. They're round and lush, and I want to bury myself in them. I glide my hands up her sides and cup her breasts, then tease one of her nipples. Her body melts into mine and my pulse steadies.

"Fuck. No one has touched me there in years."

I let her words sink in, the gravity of them tethering me to her. She hasn't felt comfortable sharing this part of herself with anyone since the boys were born, except me, and I feel honored by that admission. I'm grateful for every piece of herself that she's shared with me.

"Tá tú foirfe." I kiss a path up her neck, hovering close to her ear. "So fucking perfect."

She shifts on the bed, turning so we're both on our knees facing each other. When she nods, I don't need her to even say the words. I seal my lips over hers as we devour each other, hands groping, teeth nipping, as if neither of us can get enough. I will *never* get enough of this woman.

Something has shifted between us, like some unbearable weight she'd been carrying on her shoulders has lifted and she can finally breathe, finally take what she wants. And I'm thankful as fuck that what she wants is me.

I break the kiss, unable to contain how I feel any longer. "Tá mé i ngrá leat. Tá an t-ádh dearg orm go bhfuil tú agam."

"I love you too."

My heart leaps out of my chest as my head tilts and I examine her face. "How—?"

"The first couple of times you spoke to me in Irish, I got curious. But I could never remember what you'd said by the time I went to look it up. So I looked up how to say 'I love you.' I figured I could at least recognize it if you ever said it. I don't know what that last part was, though."

I cup her face in my hands. "I am so lucky to have you." I kiss her between each word. "I love you, Lucky. Every feckin' inch of ya."

"I know." She smirks, and it fills me with joy.

"Say it again," I tease, tickling her side.

The sound of her laugh as she tries to speak is music to my ears. "Mike. Stop. Okay, okay."

She places her hands on my chest, digging her fingertips into the smattering of chest hair there. "I love you. You're the best thing that has ever happened to me and my boys. I'm sorry it took me this long to see it, and I know it feels fast, but I also feel like I've known you forever. Like we've known you forever. You're such a good man. To me, to my boys. So patient and understanding. And thoughtful. You make me feel like the luckiest person on the planet because you chose me."

"And I would do it a thousand times over, in every life after this." I lean in and capture her mouth against mine as I kiss her like I've been waiting a lifetime for this, and in many ways I have.

Her answering moan has all the remaining blood in my body coursing to my dick. I gently guide her toward the top of the bed as I sit, leaning against the headboard. "Unless you want a mouthful of your panties again, you better sit on this cock and claim it as yours while I take this perfect feckin' mouth."

She doesn't hesitate and I delight in the way she moves, lifting herself over me as she sinks slowly down on my cock. I let out a groan and she stops, pausing halfway on my length. "Am I going to have to shove my panties in your mouth?"

"Feckin' hell, woman, don't make me blow my load before you've even ridden my cock." I grip her hips and pull her the rest of the way down, watching as every inch of me disappears into her until she's fully seated. Then I pull her lips to mine, swallowing the small moan that escapes.

"Oh my God." Her voice is frantic, needy. "This feels…"

"Incredible."

Her eyes pinch shut, but I can't take mine off her as she slowly starts to move, bucking her hips against me. "Your ladder… Fuck. It feels so good like this."

Hands still on her hips, I guide her, moving her back and forth, showing her how she can grind her clit against me. "You can control the pace in this position if you want. You can go back and forth and rub that messy cunt all over me…." I move her hips, showing her. "Or you can go up and down and rub against my ladder." I grip her, holding her up so I can fuck up into her, showing her how good it can feel.

"Oh fuck. Mike." Her voice is soft and desperate, as though she's concentrating on coming, eyes still closed as she starts bouncing up and down on her own. "Oh God, I like that."

I let her continue to explore, finding different ways to make herself feel good. When she bites her lip and starts bouncing faster, I know she's found what she needs to take herself over the edge. But she stops a few seconds later as her brows pinch and she opens her eyes, nearly in tears.

"What is it, a chroí?" I hold her face in my hands, our noses millimeters apart.

"I… I think I need your help," she says softly, as though the admission pains her, and I know instantly what she needs. This woman does so much for everyone in her life, yet she has a hard time asking others for help. Since we've started seeing each other, I've watched her be on the brink of an orgasm, only to lose it to her spiraling thoughts.

"I've got you, love." I kiss her hard, thrusting my tongue in, stealing her breath and her thoughts. "I'll always have ya." I wrap my arms around her waist, holding her in place as I begin fucking up into her in brutal strokes. The sound of our skin slapping together sounds dirty, erotic, and I get lost in it. Lost in her. Her eyes are locked on mine and I'm drowning in their emerald depths.

Slowly her lips part and I capture them in mine before the moan can escape. She tastes sweet, fruity, with just a hint of salt from her sweat-soaked skin.

She wraps her arms around my neck and in seconds she's shuddering against me as her pussy clenches around me, pulsing and squeezing, her orgasm pulling her under.

Watching her let go is the sexiest thing. I can barely hold back as I continue thrusting up into her. "Are you going to take every drop of this cum you milked from me, Lucky?"

"Wait."

I halt my movements, searching her face for some kind of clue as to what's wrong.

"Is it too much?" My balls are screaming at me to keep going, dying for release, but I'm suddenly filled with concern that I've hurt her.

She eases off my dick and lies down on the bed beside me. Her delicate hands glide up the curve of her body, and I can't look away as they dip and roam up her stomach, finally landing on her tits as she pushes them together. "I want you to fuck me here."

"Jesus feckin' Christ, woman." I shouldn't be looking a gift horse in the mouth, but I want to be sure. She just told me that she hasn't shown them to anyone, and letting me fuck them seems like the biggest gift she could give me.

"You said you wanted to claim me. Mark me and cover me with your cum. Make a mess of me."

She doesn't have to tell me twice. I straddle her in two moves, hovering over her as I grip the base of my shaft and spit onto my dick. When she repeats the move, spitting onto her chest, I nearly come at the sight.

I push into the channel between her breasts. It's warm, enveloping me in a way that feels uniquely different from her cunt and mouth. Each time I thrust in, she pushes her tits together tighter, and the squeezing sensation has my balls drawing up as my orgasm approaches. "Take it, a chroí."

"With pleasure, a stór." The look she gives me is molten, lighting me up from the inside out as I let go, spilling hot ropes of cum all over her chest and neck as my release overtakes me.

I collapse back onto the bed, utterly spent. "I'll clean you up, just give me a second to catch my breath. You stole it along with my heart when you spoke in perfect Irish."

A feline grin spreads across her face. "I may have picked up a phrase or two to surprise you with."

I lean up, pressing a kiss to her stomach. "I'll be right back. Don't move." It takes more effort to get off the bed than I'm proud of. This woman has sucked the strength out of me, and I don't want to leave her side. I find a cloth in the linen closet and warm it up under the water.

When I turn back toward the bedroom, I'm stunned by the sight of her as I lean in the doorframe of the en suite. She is splayed out on her bed, golden hair fanning around her gorgeous face, looking like a debauched version of a pin-up model from my wet dreams. "I could wake up to this view every morning, a chroí."

She pushes up on her elbows, making eye contact with me. "There's something I want to talk to you about."

"This sounds important."

"It is."

My gut sinks at the seriousness in her tone, and I search her face. It doesn't look like she's pulling away. She just told me she loves me… surely, she's not ending this?

I'm halfway across the room when I hear a buzzing on the floor. Leaning down, I pull my phone from the pocket of my discarded pants and see dozens of missed calls from Hardy and Sawyer. "Shite." I hand her the washcloth as I scroll through my phone.

"What is it?"

"There's a bad accident up near Highland Ridge. Three vehicles involved, one went off the side of the cliff and is on fire. They need all hands to help contain it so it doesn't start a wildfire." I pull on my clothes as I type back one-handed that I'm on my way.

It kills me that I can't be here, cleaning her and holding her after we made love, but duty calls, reminding me of another reason why most of my relationships haven't worked out.

"I had a tubal ligation. I can't have any more kids." She stares at me, like she can't believe what she's just blurted out.

My phone rings again, and I curse my luck when I see it's the chief.

"I have to go, I'm so sorry."

CHAPTER 22

LUCKY

When I call Bella, she answers after one ring. "He's on his way."

"Lucy? Are you okay? Who's on his way? What's wrong?"

"Mike."

"Oh?"

I pull the phone back from my face as if we were on a FaceTime call and I could see her. Did he lie to me just to get out of here? Surely, he didn't.

"Lucy?"

"I'm here."

"You said Mike's coming here?"

"He said something about a crash and a fire?" I say weakly. "He got called in. Hardy was looking for him."

"Oh! I'm sorry, I was confused. Hardy's at the station. He texted me to see if I thought Mike was with you, but he didn't say why he was looking for him."

"So there was a crash?"

"Probably. What's going on? Are you spiraling?"

I clutch the phone, feeling like my chest is getting tighter as spots dot my vision.

"Lucy?"

"Yeah?" My voice is shaky, on the verge of breaking.

"Shit. I'll be there in five."

I manage to pull on some leggings and the undershirt Mike accidentally left behind. It's not as baggy on me as I'd like, but it smells like him, and I sit on the couch holding the neckline over my nose as I take deep breaths to calm myself.

I hardly notice when Bella slips in quietly and sits on the couch next to me, placing a hand on my shoulder.

I practically leap into her arms, pulling her into a hug. She stiffens briefly, probably not expecting my reaction, before she wraps her arms around me making "shhh" sounds as she rubs circles up and down my back.

"Is this the first time he's been called in since you've been dating?"

I nod against her shoulder.

"It's going to be okay."

"But what if it's not?"

"Then we make lemonade until it is."

I pull back and search her face.

"Want me to make you a dick cookie that looks like a glass of lemonade with two lemons for the nuts? Because I think I could do it. The glass may not hide the shape of the tip very well, unless I used an ice cube or added a straw…" She rambles on as if she's having a creative breakthrough, and my nerves slowly ease as her ridiculousness calms me down. "I know it may seem like I'm not taking this seriously, but you calmed down a little, didn't you?"

A shaky breath escapes me as I nod.

"Good. Now what's really bothering you. Tell me everything, all your scary thoughts. Get them out now so we can deal with them and move on."

"I told him I love him, and he said it too and then we made love, and I was so close to telling him the truth. I mean, I was scared, but it felt like the right time. And then he got a call about a wreck and a fire, and right as he was headed out the door I blurted out that I can't have any more kids."

"Then what happened?"

"Then his phone rang, and he said he was sorry, and he left. The last words I heard him say on his way out were 'Feckin' hell,' and I'm not sure if that was because of what I said or if he was on the phone. And now I'm overthinking everything."

"Either way, he's allowed to have feelings about what you said. It doesn't mean he won't be okay with it."

"But what if he walks away? What if he wants kids and a big family more than he wants me? What if we're not enough for him? What if I'm not enough for him?"

"You're enough." She pulls on my shoulder, forcing me to make eye contact with her. "You are enough. And he loves you and your boys. I don't see him walking away from any of you."

"How do you do it?"

"Do what?"

I scrub a hand down my face. "Put yourself out there. Trust someone with your heart?"

"You build trust. It's in the little things they do, the consistencies, the way they show up and walk the walk. If he treats you anything like he has the firehouse crew, then I think I already know the answer to that one. I've never met a more consistent person. Every time I go up to visit Hardy, Mike is there, offering me a bite of his latest creation."

"He does that for us too."

"That's good. So what makes you think something changed? Is it because you finally admitted your big feelings out loud and you're feeling vulnerable?"

"Yeah. I think so," I say, feeling some of the tension leave my body. Bella's always been able to read my thoughts without me having to voice them.

"What is this really about?"

"I feel like I finally found someone, and now I'm terrified that I'm going to lose him, either physically to an accident at his job, or emotionally because I can't give him the kids he wants. Carrying on his family name is important to him. What if I can't give him that?"

"That's a lot to unpack. Let's start with the job part."

"Okay." I swallow, trying to calm my nerves.

"Mike is by the book. In all my experiences with him, he's never made a rash decision, never let his emotions get the better of him. He'll look at a situation from all angles before deciding how to approach it. It's what keeps him safe, it's what keeps all the guys safe."

"You're right. I know you're right."

"Still doesn't make it easier thinking about our guys out there, running toward the danger that most people run from, while we sit here safe in our homes." She places a hand on my thigh and squeezes.

"No, it doesn't. And I think deep down, the rational part of me knows that he's okay."

"That's why I have hobbies. Why do you think I've started baking so much? I need something for myself, a routine I could create that would help me focus on something else when things get scary. Something I could control when my world starts to feel out of control. And I have you and the girls to keep me company too. You can always call any one of us, and we'll be there to talk to you about your intrusive thoughts."

I pull her into a hug, whispering against her shoulder, "But what if he wants more than I can give him? I don't think penis-shaped cookies will distract me from that one."

She laughs as she pulls back to look at me. "Look at you making dick jokes. Maybe I am rubbing off on you."

"Don't say it."

"That's what she said." We speak at the same time, and the laughter that erupts from us eases the ache in my chest.

"So, we addressed the job part, now let's talk about why I

think you're really spiraling. I know you said Mike wants a big family and that carrying on his family name is important to him, but there are ways he could do that."

"I don't have the ability to produce more offspring."

"He could adopt the boys."

"I hadn't thought about that." I blink at her as I think over her suggestion. "But it wouldn't solve the problem of him wanting more kids."

"You guys could always adopt more if you were open to it."

"But technically none of them would be his. It wouldn't be carrying on the bloodline, just the family name. What if that's not enough for him?"

Bella purses her lips as she searches my face. "You won't know until you talk to him. Maybe it's good that he had to leave when he did. It'll give him time to think through how he feels about your news and process it before he sees you again."

"Maybe."

She squeezes my thigh, redirecting my attention. "He loves you. And I've seen him demonstrate that in just the few times I've been around you two together. I've never seen a more considerate person than Mike. Hell, the man shoved a cock cookie in his mouth to protect your kid's innocence."

"He did."

"Just give him some time to process this."

I nod, feeling slightly reassured, but still worried about what this means for our future together.

CHAPTER 23

MIKE

"Feckin' hell," I mutter as I jog down the stairs and rush out the door as my phone vibrates in my hand. It physically hurts my heart to walk out of her house. I feel like I'm leaving my heart behind the minute the cold air hits me. I want to stay there in the warmth of her house, in the warmth of her embrace.

But I'm reminded that duty calls and I have to answer.

Normally, I'd head to the station and ride in one of our vehicles, but this is all hands on deck, and I'd lose time if I went back toward town, so I head toward the scene. If there's a chance that this could start a wildfire, every second counts.

With each mile that I get further away from Lucy, my stomach sinks. She finally opened up to me, admitted her feelings, and then dropped that bomb. All I want to do is hold her right now. Assure her that this will be okay, that we'll be okay.

Will it be okay? Choosing her means giving up my dream of continuing the family line. It's what I've been working toward my whole life. My dream.

What the fuck am I saying? I love this woman and her kids. They are my dream. It doesn't matter to me that they don't share my blood. I could adopt them, and they could carry on my family name. And if Lucy's not okay with that, then I'll happily be the last of the O'Connor clan, because there's no way in hell I'm losing this woman. Or Micah or Levi.

There's a parking lot several hundred feet down the road meant for tourists to park and enjoy the mountain views. Once I find a spot, I run up the steep road till I get to the incident commander. "Where do you need me?"

"There's extra turnout gear in the truck, go suit up."

I go through the motions, but that rush of excitement, that race of adrenaline is missing. It's not that I'm happy to show up on a scene—some are absolutely devastating, or even terri-fying—but I'm the happy-go-lucky guy. The constant that others depend on for my optimistic outlook. When a rookie encounters their first catastrophe, I'm the one they count on to help guide them through it, keep them focused on the task, provide levity, and prevent them from spiraling out.

It's exactly what I've been doing for Lucy. When she gets overwhelmed and lost in her thoughts, I step in, distract her. Every skill I've honed on the job, I've been able to use with her and her boys. It's as though I've spent my entire career, my entire life, preparing to be theirs. I've fallen for her and her boys, and even though the boys aren't mine, even if she can't give me my own, I want to be in their life, be a father to them, love them as much as I love their mom.

For the first time in my life, there is something more impor-tant to me than fighting fires. Someone. Three someones.

"O'Connor! Get your ass over here," Chief yells, and I hustle over, trying to clear my thoughts and focus on the task at hand.

"What are we looking at?"

Stress lines crease Chief Sawyer's face as he fills me in. "Two cars collided going around the bend, the northbound vehicle overcorrected and struck the guardrail so hard, it teetered on the edge of the cliff. The driver was able to bail before the vehicle went over and the impact caused an explosion. Another car rear-ended the southbound car while taking the turn too fast. Rescue is transporting victims, no casualties. At this point, we're trying to contain the fire from the impact since it landed in the brush. We've got a crew at the bottom of the hill and one up here hitting it from all sides. Wildland Fire Patrol is down there dousing the surrounding area to block it off and keep it from spreading, and they've got choppers on the way. They're trying to contain it to this area, but the trees are dense in spots so it could be dicey getting it to stay isolated. We're going to be here all night."

"Feckin' hell."

"We could use some of your uplifting spirit right now. I've got a rookie already freaking out."

"Who? RJ?"

"Nah, the other one. Shit, what's his actual name? I'm so used to calling him Sparky."

"Aye, Reggie," I say.

"Yeah, that's it. Can you go check on him at the bottom and fill in if he needs a breather? That truck should be full. The crew from Longmont just relieved engine 2 so they can go back and refill. I got a couple more on the way to swap out once the tanks are dry since we don't have access to water up here."

"Aye, Chief."

I hitch a ride from one of the cruisers on the scene and make my way down to the bottom of the cliffside. Once I get Sparky settled, I step in to help.

It's hours before we're even making progress and morale is low, and I'm feckin' useless to change that for once in my life. It feels like I've lost everything I ever wanted in one night, and pushing through the emotional pain and physical exhaustion is the hardest thing I've ever done.

By the time the sun comes up, we've had several other towns send replacement engines, and it's finally starting to feel like we might get this under control. Another round of choppers shows up a couple hours after daybreak, and the fire lines the Wildland crew dug out seem to be holding.

All I want to do is climb into Lucy's bed, hold her, and get some rest.

I'm so wrapped up in my thoughts that I lose sight of Sparky.

"Hey, Blaze! Have you seen Sparky?"

Jesus Christ, all these nicknames make us sound like cartoon characters. Normally, I'd crack a joke about that, but now all I can think about is watching *Bluey* with Lucy or *Paw Patrol* with the boys.

"He was going to refuel. Something about a snack? I dunno."

The hairs on the back of my neck prickle. When rookies start, I like to learn about them, especially when I'm making their meals in case they have any allergies. Didn't he tell me he was diabetic? If my head was on straight, I'd have remembered this and looked after him better.

I do a quick scan of the area, calling out his name, and don't see him. "When did you see him last?"

"Kinda busy here, man. I'm not keeping tabs on probies," Blaze calls back.

Something's not right, and I race over to the truck so I can radio up to the incident commander. When I climb in the cab, the sight of boots in the back seat sets my mind at ease.

"Hey, Sparky, you okay?" I reach over the seat and tap his shoulder, but he doesn't respond. "Sparky?" I tap harder. Nothing. I spring into action, climbing over the seat and checking his airway, relieved to find it clear and find him breathing on his own as I take his pulse.

I radio in for rescue, and it doesn't take long for Hardy to pull up with the ambulance.

We work in silence as we get Sparky loaded into the back of the vehicle. I chew on my lip as I decide what to say to Hardy. Do I ask about Lucy? Send her a message through him?

"What's up with you? Everything okay up here? It's been quiet down at the station."

"I think we've finally got it nearly contained."

"You good? You seem off."

"No, but you need to get him to the hospital. Just… let Lucy know that I love her and nothing could change that."

He looks at me quizzically and nods as I hop out of the rig.

I sigh, surveying the rest of the landscape around me as Hardy drives off. We probably still have several more hours before we'll be able to leave, but I get to work checking on the whole squad, making sure everyone has food and is hydrated so we can power through.

I'm too exhausted to drive home so I hitch a ride with Blaze. When I stumble into my apartment much later, I take the quickest shower known to man and collapse on the bed naked, pulling my new clean white sheets over me, too tired to even throw on underwear as I pass out from exhaustion.

CHAPTER 24

LUCKY

BELLA

Just heard from Hardy.

Mike is okay.

Hardy saw him on the scene when Mike
saved a rookie who passed out and Mike
asked Hardy to tell you that he loves you and
nothing could ever change that.

Were those his exact words?

That's what Hardy told me.

Okay

This is good news.

Then why haven't I heard from him?

I don't know, but Hardy said the fire was
almost out when he saw him.

Said he looked miserable and exhausted, but
he was fine.

He probably went home and crashed.

What if I scared him off?

What if he doesn't come to the program tomorrow?

Micah invited him. He'll be there.

I hope so.

OMG I just realized that they are Micah and Mike! How cute is that?

Yeah

Lucy!

[gif of Lucille Ball sticking out her tongue]

Sorry

Hang tight. We're on the way.

We? We who?

Bella?

It's a school night.

Aren't the boys in bed?

Yeah

[gif of the Sex and the City women walking in slow mo]

Thirty minutes later Bella, Summer, and Raven are on my couch.

"Sorry, I know I'm normally the life of the party..." I trail off, unsure how I even want to finish that thought.

Summer places a hand on my arm, rubbing small comforting circles. "What's going on?"

I sigh, trying to decide where to start. "So I've been seeing someone."

"We know," the girls practically answer in unison.

I look between Summer and Raven. "I figured Summer knew because I missed pickup at that playdate, but how do you know?" I ask Raven.

"Ned said he saw you two driving through town together one night last week. Said you stopped at the light in front of the store, and he saw Mike lean over and kiss you."

That must have been the night we went to his place. I look at her apologetically. "I'm sorry I didn't tell you. I feel like an asshole."

"Eh, I figured you'd tell me when there was something to tell. Despite working at a newspaper, I don't think every bit of gossip in this town is newsworthy. You know me, I'm not really one to get FOMO about stuff."

"So what happened with Mike? Are we here for the big talk-you-off-the-cliff speech?" Summer asks.

"Yes. No? I don't know." I sigh. "I know I tend to be tight-lipped about my past, but I had some really shitty exes, and the last one really fucked with my head and my self-confidence. He called me boring in bed and would make little comments here and there about my weight, and how my clothes fit, and whether I should really be eating that," I say, doing an impression of Kyle. "And my body changed so much after having the boys that I just started to feel like, I dunno… not myself."

"I totally get where you're coming from," Summer says with a warm smile. "Motherhood is hard. But you don't have to do it alone. You have us."

I return her smile as I continue sharing my truth. "My ex never wanted to have kids, and Levi was so difficult. I knew I couldn't handle any more kids on my own, so I had a tubal ligation. It was also supposed to help with my endometriosis.

But then I met Mike. And he's amazing, but he wants a big family, and I can't give him that."

"Oh, Lucy," Summer says, pulling me into a hug.

"Please don't tell me this one was calling you a good girl in an ambulance too, or on a firetruck." Raven lifts an eyebrow.

We all burst into laughter at Raven's unexpected joke.

"Look at you cracking jokes. That's my job!" Bella playfully says.

"He did not call me that in an ambulance," I say.

"Good, because I just don't think that's very professional."

"I agree with Raven. I think it's hot in a book, but I don't think I'd like it in real life," Summer says.

"Oh, trust me you would," Bella and I say in unison.

"Please tell me someone has at least called you a good girl before," Bella says to Raven.

"Nope, and I'm not sure I'd like it if one did," Raven replies.

"Okay, you need to read *Hitched and Tied* by Ayana Cox," I tell her.

"Oh my God, I don't think I've ever realized how much her name sounds like 'I wanna cock,'" Bella squeals.

"That was probably intentional," Summer adds.

"I wouldn't put it past a romance author to come up with a cheesy name," Raven scoffs.

"Well, this book will definitely change your mind about romance books and men who like to praise their women. It's the first book in her cowboy romance series, and the mouth on this man is delicious. It's a fake marriage to save the ranch story. You will definitely like *good girl* after reading that one," I say.

"And *darlin'*," Summer adds.

"And *mine*. And the way that man growls *my wife*? Ugh." Bella shimmies her shoulders, and we all get quiet, probably thinking over our favorite scenes from the book.

Raven scowls, crossing her arms over her chest. "I'm just not really into romance."

Summer leans forward on the couch. "But these ones are different. The characters feel so real, and the stories feel cinematic, like you're watching a movie in your head while reading."

"Ayana's books are always a one-handed read for me, if you catch my drift."

"Bella, you could have your kindergarten student with the worst penmanship write it out for us, and we'd still know exactly what you were talking about." Raven playfully rolls her eyes.

"All I'm saying is if you want to let loose, you should check out Ayana's books. She might really open your mind to some things." Bella winks.

Raven visibly stiffens, and I chuckle. Every so often, Bella says something crass that makes Raven uncomfortable, and it's comical to watch them tiptoe around each other.

"So, what happened with Mike? Does he not want to be with you? Is that why we're here, to beat his ass?" Summer asks.

Bella claps her hands like she's calling her classroom to order. "Mike got called into the fire up on the ridge last night, but he told Hardy to tell me to tell Lucy that he loves her and that will never change."

"So, what's the issue?" Raven asks, flicking her hand. Her practical approach to every situation is calming. While she might come across as cold or uncaring to those that don't know her, that couldn't be farther from the truth. She grounds our group, is the order to Bella's perverted chaos, the balance to Summer's romanticized naivety, and the calm to my anxiety-ridden storm.

"I think I'm just panicking because I told him I can't have kids and then he left for the fire, and we haven't talked since."

"He's probably just resting after the fire. RJ said they were up there all night," Raven says.

"RJ was there? He's okay, right?"

Bella and I exchange curious glances at Summer's question. Sounds like someone is still hung up on her first kiss.

Raven nods. "Still an idiot, but otherwise okay."

"Oh! I've been dying to tell you ladies. Guess what Mike calls Lucy?"

"Please tell me it's darlin'," Summer says with a wistful look in her eye.

Bella shakes her head. "It's Lucky!"

Summer lets out an audible sigh.

Raven rolls her eyes. "What's with your men adding letters to your names for nicknames? Bells, Lucky. Am I the only one who understands how nicknames are supposed to work?"

Summer swoons. "I think it's cute."

"It's technically not a nickname when it's what's on your birth certificate."

"Wait, what?" Bella gasps.

"I dropped the K and shortened it to Lucy in middle school. I just never believed that I lived up to the name, and it made me feel like shit every time someone called me that. I've always been unlucky. In love. In life. But when Mike calls me Lucky, it feels right for the first time in my life."

Summer sighs. "I love that."

"He's your person," Bella adds.

"Do we need to start calling you Lucky instead of Lucy then?" Raven asks.

"No, Lucy is fine."

Raven nods. "So, what are you going to do about Mike?"

Summer claps her hands as if she's had the biggest revelation. "You know what you should do?"

We all stare at her in anticipation.

"You should propose!"

"I can't believe I'm saying this, but I agree," Raven adds, and we all gawk at her. "Mike is the Irish one, right?"

"How did you—"

"Ned."

"Sounds about right," Bella says.

Raven continues, "Tomorrow is St. Patrick's Day, and according to an old Irish legend, St. Brigid was annoyed that women had to wait on men to propose. So, she complained to St. Patrick, and he agreed to let women propose too, but they could only do it on Leap Day. Small victories, I guess, but we're still getting fucked by the patriarchy."

"There's no Leap Day this year," Summer says, sounding defeated.

"Who says she has to wait till Leap Day? If St. Patrick allowed it, she could do it on his day," Bella declares.

"I need to plan this out," I mutter, mind racing. Am I really considering this? "And there's something else I'm waiting on that I'm supposed to get tomorrow."

"A delivery?"

"Sort of. It could be nothing, but it's something I wanted to look into."

"It better not be a house listing with another realtor. If you propose and Mike moves in, you better use me to sell your house or his."

"Of course." I nod at Summer.

"I'll watch your class tomorrow. Go do what you need to do, just make sure you're back in time for the assembly," Bella says.

Fuck you, Lady Luck. I'm off to make my own luck and get the man of my dreams.

CHAPTER 25

MIKE

I wake up to the sun beating down on me. Stretching like a cat, I bask in the warmth of it and wiggle against the sheets.

Am I naked? I peek under the covers. Definitely naked. Why am I naked?

What time is it?

Why is it so bright in here? It's never this bright in the morning. Only in the afternoon.

Any rest I felt vanishes when I bolt up in bed and reach for my phone. Shite. I never plugged it in. I tear out of the bed and run into the living room, dick flopping with the motion as I check the time on the oven. Fuck, it's nearly one. The St. Paddy's Day program is at two.

And my car is still parked on the mountain.

Feckin' hell.

I plug in my cell and throw on some clothes. Once I'm dressed, I fidget as I sit on the bed, anxiously glaring at the phone as if doing so would charge it faster. I'm aware of every sound in the apartment building as I sit there helpless with no way to contact the outside world. No home phone. No computer. Just this stupid useless feckin' brick charging at a snail's pace.

Getting frustrated, I race out to the kitchen again to check the time. It's quarter after one. If someone gave me a ride to my truck, it'd take twenty minutes to get up there, another thirty to get to the school, and that's assuming they could get here within minutes of my call, so I'd have to add even more time to that.

Fuck.

I have to try. I can't let Lucky down. And Micah is expecting me to be at his assembly, so I have to find a way. I can't break my word to either of them again.

The sound of buzzing pulls me from my thoughts, and I hurry back to the bedroom and pick up my phone, swiping through all the notifications popping up now that it's powered back on. I'll check them later, but right now I need to find a ride. I frantically tap Hardy's contact info and call him.

He answers after one ring. "Hope you're wearing green—"

I cut him off as I try to get everything out. "I need a ride to the school. I got in late from the fire and I never charged my phone, and I overslept, and I have to be at the school because I promised Micah."

"Slow down, Mike. Does your accent come out only on St. Paddy's Day, because it's thicker than normal and I'm having a hard time understanding you."

Before I can repeat my mess of thoughts, he bursts into laughter. "I'm just fucking with you. Look in the parking lot."

I race over to the window, and when I peek through the blinds, I see Hardy in his truck waving at me through the windshield.

Relief washes over me and I take a deep breath as I gather up my phone and keys. I dig around my nightstand drawer for my wallet, and my attention snags on something underneath it. I pocket both items and rush out the door.

When I climb into the cab of his truck seconds later, I almost don't recognize him from the dopey grin on his face.

"I'm here to give you a ride to the assembly at the school."

"How did you know?"

"Bella told me you needed to be there, and she tends to be right about a lot of things. I also figured you'd left your car when I heard Blaze mention that he gave you a ride."

"Thanks, man."

"No problem."

The parking lot is full when we pull into the school. It looks like the whole town is here. Hardy and I end up finding seats in the back row of the auditorium right as a line of students marches in, heading for the stage.

I spot Micah searching the crowd, and I wave, hoping he's looking for me. He could be trying to find his mom, but when he sees me, the biggest smile lights up his face. Damn, I love when this kid smiles at me. My chest warms at the sight. He doesn't share as many smiles as his brother, but when he does it's damn hard to look away from the joy radiating from him.

My eyes scan the room looking for a familiar blonde ponytail when I spot it in the front row. It's obvious she's working, corralling kids and miming the movements for them to copy as she mouths the words to the songs they're singing.

It's amazing how quickly my body calms at the sight of her. She is my peace. All I want to do is go over there and kiss her, pull her into my arms, and reassure her that she is more than enough for me. Hell, she and the boys are all I want.

Instead, I sit through the program, my eyes bouncing between Micah and Lucky when something tugs at my pants leg. Looking down, I see Levi on all fours peering up at me like he's a dog. He climbs up my leg and I lift him, depositing him on my lap as he fidgets to get comfortable. I lean down to press a kiss atop his crown, feeling my pulse finally even out.

I lean over to Hardy, lowering my voice to a whisper. "Hey, can you—"

"Already on it." He holds up his phone to show me the text he's sent Bella to let her know we have Levi.

When I look down at him, he's conked out. I rope an arm around his waist, holding him in place as his head droops onto my bicep.

The program feels longer than it should be, probably because it's the only thing left standing between me and Lucky, and I'm dying to talk to her.

Once it ends, I stay in my seat, not wanting to move and wake Levi up. Hardy stays seated beside me.

"I meant to ask, is Sparky okay?"

Hardy nods. "He's good. It's lucky you found him when you did. Coulda been really bad if you hadn't checked on him."

The auditorium clears out, and I lock eyes with Lucky as she emerges from backstage.

"Here, I got him." Hardy pulls Levi from my arms and stands. "Go get your girl."

I nod, my eyes never leaving Lucky's as he shuffles by me. As I make my way to the stage, I take her in. She's wearing a bright green shirt with the words "One lucky teacher" printed over her perfect tits and a dark green skirt covered in shamrocks.

Da would hate it, but I think she looks feckin' beautiful.

"I'm sorry I had to leave ya the other night," I say, my voice rough since I haven't used it much today.

She tilts her head, examining my face as if she's waiting for me to say more.

"I didn't want to leave ya. I never want to leave ya. Nothing will change that. You and those boys matter more to me than any bloodline or name. And I don't care if you can't have more. You are enough for me, all of ya."

Her fingers twitch and I watch as she reaches into the pocket of her dress and pulls out a folded piece of paper, handing it to me with a shaky hand. Is she nervous? Why is she nervous? And why hasn't she said anything?

Something tightens in my gut at the way she's acting. It's not like her. Her eyes flick to the paper, gesturing for me to open it.

I blink in confusion. When I unfold it, I realize it's her list. Everything we've completed is checked off. The only unfinished item—"be less boring in bed," along with my suggestion for her to pick a new item—is scratched out, and next to it she's written the words "marry Micah and Levi's dad."

Is this her way of telling me she's getting back with her ex? That she's done with me now that I've completed her list?

"Lucky…" My voice goes rough. "What is this?"

She doesn't answer as she sinks to one knee in front of me like she's done waiting on luck to dictate her choices.

"Mike O'Connor, you are my person, the love of my life. You bring me and my boys so much joy and laughter. Our lives are better with you in it. And I want you to be part of our family forever. Someone told me there's this old story about St. Brigid making St. Patrick give women Leap Day to propose, but I can't wait until the next one, so I'm asking on St. Patrick's Day. Will you marry me?"

I haul her up, forehead to forehead, hands shaking on her waist. "A ghrá mo chroí, go deo."

"What does that mean?"

"It means love of my heart forever."

I lean down and kiss her, soft and sweet, filled with overwhelming joy at this turn of events. I thought she was about to end things. And then the words she scribbled on her list hit me and I break the kiss, pulling back. "But—Lucky. This says…" I tap the words with my thumb. "It says you want to marry their dad."

"You are their dad." She's beaming, her smile radiant as though that fully answers my question.

I stare at her. Properly stare. "So… you want to marry me so I'll become their dad?"

"I mean…yes, marrying you makes you their dad in every way that matters." She reaches up and cups my jaw as her voice softens. "But, Mike… you are their actual dad. Biologically."

"But we only just met recently. I would have remembered hooking up with ya years ago, especially twice."

She shakes her head, seemingly unbothered by my confusion. Thank Jesus she has the patience of a saint, because I'm at my wit's end trying to figure out this puzzle she's dropped in my lap.

"Do you ever remember going to Bright Beginnings Bank?" She smiles as I try to process what she's saying.

"The sperm bank?"

She nods.

I went there once, early in my twenties out of desperation to give my Da some kids one day. My heart beats rapidly in my chest as a riot of emotions overwhelms me. "Holy feckin' shite! They're… you… they're actually mine? My biological kids? I'm their dad? I have two sons?"

"You do. I used the same sample—your sample apparently —twice."

I pull her into my arms, lifting and spinning her around as she laughs against me, the sound music to my ears.

When I set her back down, I cup the back of her head and pull her lips to mine. How is it possible that this woman is going to be my wife and is also already the mother of my kids?

"How? How did this happen? How long have ya known? How did ya find out?" I feel like Levi, bombarding her with questions, and it fills me with warmth to think about how many other traits we must share.

"I was watching you and Levi the other day while you were coloring, and you scrunched your brow the same way he did. And then Micah said something about you having the same color eyes."

"He said that to me too, the night of the PTO meeting, but tons of people have blue eyes, so I didn't think anything of it."

"I didn't either at first. The facial expression and the eyes didn't immediately set off alarm bells. This is going to sound crazy, but stay with me. It was the night we checked item six off my list."

"The spankings?" Visions of that night flash through my mind, and I search my brain, trying to remember what part of that encounter she could be referring to.

"To be more specific, the part where I bent you over the couch and spanked you."

"Aye, that was fun, but what does that have to do with this?"

"You have a little birthmark at the top of your thigh, right under your ass."

"The one that looks like a clover?" Holy fuck. She wasn't tickling me; she was tracing my birthmark.

"That's the one. With all the ways we've done it, that was the first time I'd ever noticed it. It's kinda hidden when you're standing, but when you were bent over, I could see it clearly. I thought it was familiar at first, but it wasn't until I was giving the boys a bath a couple days later and Levi asked me to swipe the card that I realized why."

"I meant to ask you about that."

She chuckles. "It's a nicer way to say wipe my ass. I swipe through their cheeks with a washcloth, like a credit card swipes through a machine, only now we insert a chip, so I realize I'm showing my age. Anyway, when I was wiping him, I noticed a spot between his cheeks. At first, I thought it was poop, so I kept wiping but then I remembered he had a little birthmark there."

"In the shape of a clover?"

"Yup." Her smile is infectious, and I revel in it.

"I did not swipe the card, and I made them wear swimsuits. I just want that on record."

She laughs. "I know, the boys told me the next morning. But it was after the bath I gave them that I had a hunch. The eyes, the mannerisms, the distinct birthmark, it was too much, so I did one of those home DNA tests that takes a few days for results. Micah said you used a toothbrush when you tucked them in the other night."

"I was showing them how to brush their teeth better because Levi was rushin' through."

"Well, I used that toothbrush. I'm sorry, I know it's a huge invasion of your privacy and probably not ethical, but I had to know."

"I don't care about that," I say, hanging on every word of her story.

"Well, I'm glad I did it, because I got the results this morning, and it confirmed what I suspected."

"That I'm their father?"

"You're their father. Not many people know that they were conceived by artificial insemination. This town loves to gossip, and I didn't want to add any fuel to that fire. I'd rather people think I slept around than know the truth."

"And what's that?"

"That I couldn't find anyone to love me and give me the life I always wanted, so I made it happen for myself. It was embarrassing how desperate I was to be a mom and not be able to find someone who shared that dream. And then you came into my life and you wanted all the same things as me, and I got scared because I've gotten my hopes up before only to be crushed in the process. I've always had such terrible luck."

"Feckin' hell, that's all I've ever wanted, and I had no clue you were right under my nose this whole time."

"And little did I know, I was looking for four-leaf clovers in the wrong place."

"Levi did try to tell ya with all the poop drawings."

"Oh my God, how did I not put it together sooner?"

I bark out a laugh and grip her tight. I'm never going to let this woman go. "There's something I've been meaning to tell ya." I release my grip on her and reach into my pocket, dropping to one knee as I hold out the ring box to her. "You're not the only one who was planning a proposal."

Opening the box, I hold out the ring. It's a brilliant green emerald, surrounded by diamonds that encircle the entire band. "This was my granny's ring, and I want you to wear it."

She holds out her hand, and I slide the ring onto her finger, relieved that it's a perfect fit. "It's beautiful."

"You're beautiful in every possible way. I know you feel life hasn't been kind to ya, that luck hasn't been on your side, but I think it made you into who you are today. And I love you. You're exquisite. Messy. Perfect. Unpolished and a little rough around the edges, but you still shine more brilliantly than any diamond. That's why I chose this ring, with the stone that matches your eyes."

"I think Micah was right. You are our lucky charm."

We're in a school, her place of work, but I can't stop myself from pulling her into me and sealing my lips over hers in an embrace less chaste than our earlier kiss.

A throat clearing from across the gym breaks our trance. We pull back, breathing heavily as we stare into each other's eyes, neither of us able to look away.

"Did he say yes?" Bella calls out.

We laugh, realizing neither of us actually said the words.

"Yes," we say in unison.

"I know this is fast, and this town is going to think we're crazy rushing into this, but I don't want to live one more day without you as part of our family," she whispers against my lips as I rest my forehead against hers.

"Your place or mine?"
She laughs. "I think you know the answer to that one."
I nod.
"But bring the couch."

CHAPTER 26

MIKE

"A re we there yet?" Levi whines from the back seat.

"Almost, Levisaur." I smile as I grip Lucky's thigh from the passenger seat. "Ma and Da are going to be excited to meet ya."

"They won't be mad that you missed St. Patrick's Day with them?"

I shake my head, squeezing her thigh tighter. "They understood, and they're thrilled for us."

"Fudgsicles," Lucky mutters as red and blue lights illuminate the car.

"I want a Fudgsicle!" the boys beg in unison.

Lucky pulls the car to the shoulder as I reach into her glove box to retrieve her paperwork and hand it to her as she lowers her window.

"License and registration," a voice booms.

"Doug!" I say, smiling at the officer.

He looks between us, frowning at Lucky before his eyes and flashlight land on me and a smile crosses his features. "Mike!"

I lean across Lucky and extend my hand as Doug slaps it in our practiced shake.

Lucky's head swivels between us. "Umm, you two know each other?"

"This is Doug. We met on a call a few years back. Doug, this is my fiancée—"

"Lucy," he finishes.

"You two know each other?" I chuckle, looking between them.

"We went on a date once, a couple months back," he says with pursed lips.

Lucky locks eyes with me. "We had lunch the day Micah broke his arm."

Doug crosses his arms. "I didn't know you were already seeing someone."

Ah, the first date from hell she told me about. I bite my lip to hold back my grin. "Sorry, mate. We ran into each other at the hospital after that. I knew there was no way I could let this one go." I squeeze her thigh and lock eyes with her. "When you know, you know."

"It's just as well." Doug taps the side of the car, breaking our trance. "Think I'll let you off with a warning this time. Have a nice night."

Once he's back in his car, Lucky breaks into a fit of laughter, and I grip her cheeks in my hands, planting a kiss on her lips.

"Eww, kissing is gross."

"Sorry, Mikachu," I say, breaking the kiss as Lucky pulls back onto the road.

My folks greet us on the porch and the grin on Ma's face when she sees the boys eases my racing heart. We're ushered inside, and Da pulls me into a hug. "Good to see you, Mac."

"Michael Nolan O'Connor. You didn't tell me you were bringing such handsome lads," Ma says as she bends down to greet them. "And who might you two be?"

"I'm Levisaur!" Levi growls as Micah hesitates behind him.

I lean down and extend my arms, silently asking him for

approval. When Micah nods, I lift him up, holding him tightly against me. "This is Micah and Levi. And I want you to meet their mom, and my beautiful fiancée, Lucky."

"It's lovely to meet ya, dear," Ma says as she pulls Lucky into a hug.

"I'm so sorry that Mike missed spending St. Patrick's Day with you," Lucky says, giving me an apologetic look.

I can't stop the smile from lighting up my face at the fact that this woman remembered my St. Patrick's Day tradition with my parents. Micah shifts in my arms and I'm pulled back to reality.

"Micah, I want you to meet my Da."

His head lifts from my shoulder, and he offers Da a small wave.

"It's nice to meet you, lad."

Dinner is chaotic in the best possible way. The boys won't sit still, and it's pure joy watching my Ma and Da dote on them, showering them with praise and attention, even if the lads are being picky eaters.

Lucky is buckling the boys in as I finish my goodbyes with my folks. "There's something I need to tell ya."

Ma looks at me expectantly.

"This sounds serious," Da says.

I glance over to the car, and Lucky's smile gives me the encouragement I need to continue. "I know how much youse wanted a big family, how important it was to carry on the bloodline and name."

"Do ya know how many O'Connors there are in Ireland, Mac? It's not dying out with ya."

"Where is this coming from, Michael?" Ma rests a comforting hand on my forearm.

"I heard the two of ya talkin' about it all the time. And, Ma, you ask me when I'm giving ya grandkids practically every time we talk on the phone. It was a lot of pressure on me, and back in my twenties when I didn't think I could give ya what you wanted, I donated my sample to a sperm bank. I figured that I'd give ya that big clan one way or another."

"Ya feckin' eejit. It wasn't that big a deal to us. You probably overheard the two or three conversations we ever had about it. Feckin' Christ."

"We just want you to be happy." Ma nods at the car. "The blood doesn't matter as much as the family does. And those wee lads are your family. It was obvious the moment you walked in."

I can hear my heartbeat in my ears. Have I really banjaxed this? All these years spent worrying over something that was a passing conversation. "Aye, they are my family, but they're my blood too."

"What are ya saying?" Ma stares at me with tears in her eyes, while Da's mouth hangs open.

"I don't understand," he splutters.

"I wanted to give ya a full clan, and I had no clue that Lucky'd been trying to build her own by herself. She used my sample twice. I had no idea that they were mine when we started dating. We just found out, but we haven't told them yet."

"Jesus, Mary, and Joseph." Ma pulls me into a hug, and I release a shaky breath, wiping the tears from my eyes. "This changes nothing. They would've been my grandkids regardless."

"I expect to see ye and those boys around more," Da says.

"Aye."

It takes a few days for the excitement of our double proposal to wear off with the boys. When we told them that we were going to get married, they were excited but not surprised. Micah already thought we were together, but he gave me the longest hug. Levi had a bunch of questions including what room I was going to stay in, could it be their bedroom, where would all my clothes go because Mama's closet was full, and if I fart in my sleep. Lucky and I both agreed that the proposal news was a big enough change that we didn't want to overwhelm them with too much at once and tell them that I was also their father.

That changed quickly when Micah had a nightmare and came running into Lucky's bedroom looking for me in the middle of the night. It was the one night I spent at my apartment since I needed to do laundry and grab clothes ahead of my shift the next day. Lucky told me he was crying so hard from the dream that he started to say "dad" at one point but caught himself. It nearly broke me that I wasn't there for him, and we both agreed that we didn't want to wait any longer to tell the boys. And I physically couldn't bear spending one more night away from my family.

My family. My sons. My soon-to-be wife.

So, I packed up as much of my shite as I could, recruited the rookies to help with the rest, and I've been here ever since.

"Levi, Micah, can you come down here?" Lucky yells.

Seconds later the patter of little feet races down the stairs. Levi beelines for the couch, hopping over the back of it as he flops onto his side. Micah walks over calmly and sits next to him.

"There's something we want to talk to you about," Lucky starts.

"Levi did it!" Micah says, assuming they're in trouble. I can't help but chuckle.

"No, I didn't," Levi whines.

"It's not about that." I look down at them as their big eyes stare up at me expectantly. "Your mom and I—"

"Is this about kissing?" Micah interrupts.

Lucky lets out an exasperated sigh next to me. "It's not about kissing."

"Well, I *will* be kissing my wife," I say, winking at her.

"Eww, kissing," Levi says.

"That's gross," Micah says.

"Not the point, lads."

"What Mike and I are trying to say is—"

"When are you getting married?" Micah interrupts again.

"Why are you getting married?" Levi asks.

"Because we love each other," Lucky and I say in unison. We smile at each other as a chorus of "ewws" erupt from the boys.

"Are you going to be our dad now?" Levi asks.

This is it. Tears well in my eyes, and I blink rapidly to clear them.

"It turns out that I already am your dad."

Micah gets really still, his mouth slightly parted as he blinks up at me. I hold my breath waiting for his reaction. He jumps up off the couch and runs over to me, plastering himself to my leg in the tightest hug his cast will allow. I can feel the small hiccupping breaths causing tremors in his body, and I bend down to pick him up, pulling him against my chest as he rests his head against my shoulder. My palm covers his back as I rub soothingly up and down.

"I love you, Mikachu," I say against his cheek as I plant a gentle kiss there.

"I wanted you to be my dad," Micah says through small sobs.

"Levi, what do you think about this?" Lucky asks. I search his face for some sort of clue that he's okay with everything. He's still sitting on the couch, completely unbothered, leaning into the cushion and kicking his legs off the edge as he shrugs.

"Can I have a hug?"

"Okay," Levi says as he does a tuck and roll off the couch, landing on all fours before he army-crawls under the coffee table. He pops up next to my leg, and I instinctively cover my crotch in response.

"Uppies!" he says, doing grabby hands. I lean down and

scoop him up, pulling his body against mine. He weighs nearly as much as Micah, and I grip them both tightly, as if they were balloons that could float away.

I look down at Levi. "Are you okay with this, lad? Is there anything you want to know? Any questions you're dying to ask?"

He thinks for a second, and then a Cheshire grin lights up his face. "Can I have a Fudgsicle?"

CHAPTER 27

LUCKY

A month into our new living situation, we're finally starting to find our rhythm. I'm making breakfast for the boys while Mike packs their lunches.

Every chance he gets, he's touching me, kissing me. Most times it's simple touches—grazing my waist as he reaches around me to grab a utensil, slapping my ass when I bend over the freezer, a peck on the shoulder when I'm cooking. He touches me with such reverence, like he can't believe I'm real.

I remove the pan from the stove and start plating scrambled eggs when Mike bumps my hip and leans close to my ear.

"Still thinking about the way I woke you up this morning. I really hooked you with my ladder."

It's an effort not to roll my eyes. "Leaning into the dad jokes, I see."

"Or was it the flavor saver that won ya over?"

"You're ridiculous." I shake my head, but I can't hide the dopey grin he's put on my face.

"What's a flavor saver?" Levi asks, and I inwardly groan. This kid has the worst timing.

Mike's eyes flash to mine in panic, but I only offer him a smirk in return. "Yeah, what is it?"

He hasn't yet gotten used to Levi repeating the things he says at the most inopportune times.

"It's… It's a…" he splutters, looking for the right lie to give him. "It's a piece of bread, like on a sandwich. It soaks up all the… juices."

His eyes dart to mine, pleading for help, but I just gesture for him to continue.

"What kind of sandwich has juice on it? Like orange juice?" Levi asks.

"Yeah, Mike, what kind of wet sandwiches are you eating?"

"Not orange juice. It's more like when you have peanut butter and jelly, and the jelly is extra runny."

"That sounds gross."

"Trust me, you'll love it when you're older." He squeezes my hip on the last part, and I can feel my cheeks heat in response.

"Micah, hurry up!" I call up the stairs right as he comes running down. "Oh, there you are. Breakfast is ready."

"Yes, Mama," says my perfectly sweet oldest child.

The boys sit at the island stools eating their breakfast as they watch *Bluey*.

Mike puts lunchboxes in the boys' bags as I rinse off the last of the dishes. When he finishes, he wraps a forearm around my shoulder, pulling me against him. "We make a great team, a ghrá mo chroí."

"We do—"

"Can we get a dog?" Micah asks, interrupting our peaceful moment.

"Dog! I want a dog!" Levi adds.

Everyone turns and looks at me as if I'm the ultimate canine decider. I stare back at them unsure what to say. My Bissell finally got a break; I really don't want to sully our relationship with dog shit.

As if he can sense the impending no, Mike leans into me. "Every lad needs a dog." He turns back to the boys. "I used to have a dog when I was your age. It was a corgi named Benedick Longbottom the third. But I called him Benny for short."

Oh shit.

I scrub a hand down my face, covering my mouth with my hand as I try to keep the boys from hearing me. "Shhh, don't say that word. I'll never get him to stop repeating it."

"What word? Bottom?"

"DICK!" Levi shouts as Micah covers his mouth with his hand, looking horrified.

I drop my head, shaking it in defeat.

"Ohh, that one. Sorry."

"He's definitely getting kicked out of preschool for that one."

"I guess we need to get them a dog." He winks at me.

I poke a finger in his chest. "You're cleaning up the poops." I turn to the boys. "And you're going to have to help walk it and feed it. And you'll have to pick up your toys every night, so the dog doesn't eat them."

Micah looks horrified at the thought. "Is it going to make messes like Levi?"

"I don't make messes. You make messes."

"Do not."

"Do too!"

"Lads, settle down. We'll just get a dog that doesn't make messes."

I burst into laughter. I love this man, but he has no clue the chaos he's unleashing with this plan. "This is going to be fun."

"So, we're getting a dog?" Micah asks, voice full of hope, green eyes round and pleading.

"I guess we're getting a dog."

Cheers erupt from all three of them, and I laugh at the thought of a dog running around every morning, eating floor eggs and scraps of bacon the boys sneak it under the table. I sigh. There's no way I'm saying no to this.

I look at the clock on the microwave. "Bella's going to be here any minute. Go brush your teeth and then get your shoes on, boys."

There's a knock on the door and Levi darts over to it, pulling it open before we can stop him.

"Hey, stinker!" Bella calls out as she walks in. Hardy started dropping her off on the way to work so we can carpool and then the guys ride in together.

Mike kisses my forehead on the way out the door. "See you tonight, Lucky."

I'm totally aware of the lovesick look on my face as I linger in the doorway watching them pull out of the driveway, when Bella's words slap me back into reality.

"Uhh, Lucy, we've got a situation in here. Code brown."

Cocking my head at her, I walk over to the bathroom and immediately see what she's referring to.

"Who pooped in here?" I shout into the void as the boys conveniently scatter, both shouting about brushing their teeth. Bella and I look at each other. "Sure, this is the one time they actually take dental hygiene seriously."

"Look at that turd in your toilet." Bella says, standing in the doorway behind me. "No fair, it doesn't even stink in here."

"That's a weird thing to be jealous of," I say.

"Wait till they're teenagers. Teenage poops are terrifying."

"Moreso than adult poops?" I ask, walking over to the sink to wash my hands.

"Yes, and don't ask me why. It's probably all the puberty hormones or something. Want me to flush it?" she asks, walking over to the toilet to examine its contents.

"Well, I'm not saving it!"

"Isaac used to save them to show me the ones he was proud of. Now they're massive. And scary. And I wish he'd stop showing them to me. Back then they were all little, tiny poops in funny shapes. Is it weird that I kind of miss those days?"

"Yes. Yes, it is."

"Why are boys so gross?" she laughs, flushing the toilet.

"I dunno. Do they ever learn to flush their turds?"

"No, they do not."

———

Later that night, Bella takes the boys home with her, giving me and Mike a much-needed night alone.

"Are you sure you want to stay in? The boys will be gone for the whole night. We could go out? Have a meal with no interruptions? Come home and bend me over the couch?" I wiggle my eyebrows at him and love the way his cheeks blush in response.

"Oh, I will be bending you over several pieces of furniture tonight. But I'm keen to stay here."

I give him a knowing look. "You miss the boys, don't you? They can be exhausting, but as soon as they're gone or asleep and the house is quiet, you miss the chaos they bring."

"Yeah, what's up with that?" He rubs his shoulder against mine as we sit on the couch.

"One minute you're fishing a scorpion out of a toddler's mouth, questioning your decision to have kids because you're terrified of bugs and these tiny humans keep forcing you to touch them. The next minute, you're lonely because they've been asleep for thirty minutes so you decide to sneak into their room while they're sleeping because they're just so cute, but then you wake one up and they stay up for three more hours."

"Those are oddly specific examples."

"They are." I sigh wistfully leaning into him.

"Can you show me more pictures of them as babies? Or videos? I feel like a broken record asking again, but I could stare at them all night."

He continues rambling on, getting more and more animated as he talks, slowly inching forward in the same way Levi does when he's excited about something.

I lean away to look at him. "Is this really how you want to spend our last official date together?"

"This doesn't count."

I scoff, dropping my jaw in faux indignation. "Doesn't count? Mr. 'I'm counting the time I babysit the kids as a date?'"

"The rules clearly stated that I would get a date when we checked an item off your list. There is still technically one item remaining."

"Close enough." I say, holding up my hand to admire the beautiful emerald ring again.

"Once I get to call you my wife, I'm going to take you out on a real date. Outside of this house. Kid-free. We will eat fancy food neither of us has to cook, and we will sleep in a bed we don't have to make. Don't get me wrong, I love our family dates with the boys, but I want to take you somewhere nice and make you come so many times you lose count."

"I think that's just called a honeymoon."

He leans in, his lips ghosting the shell of my ear. "Sounds like I'm not the only one getting spanked tonight, Lucky." Then he sits back against the couch like he didn't just whisper filthy promises in my ear. "What's one of your favorite memories of the boys?"

"There are too many to count."

"We have time." He flashes me a panty-dropping smile and it's hard to concentrate for a second.

But I calm myself and think through some of my favorite memories of the boys. "When I brought Levi home from the hospital. I was breastfeeding, but I hadn't had a lot of success getting him to latch, so I was pumping a lot. The first day at home with two boys was chaotic, but Micah was very helpful. I was stuck on the couch a lot, either tied to his brother or the pump. He was very observant, and I'd catch him staring at me. By the second day, I could tell something was bothering him and I was worried. You never know how kids are going to react to their new siblings, and I was concerned he would feel slighted or jealous."

"Was he?"

She laughs. "Nope. He was concerned about something else. He'd watched me pump for two days and seemed fascinated by it. I was in the middle of pumping when he approached me, his eyes full of concern. He pointed to the pump parts on my chest and said, 'Are you…are you a robot, Mama?' He sounded so hopeful, so excited at the prospect, and I about lost it because I had to tell him that I was not, in fact, a robot. Poor thing got stuck sharing my attention with a new baby, and he didn't even get a robot out of the deal."

Mike throws his head back in laughter, wiping away tears as he tries several times to speak and fails. "I can picture the look of disappointment on his face. Poor lad."

I tap my chin, trying to think of another one. "And Levi has been enamored with farts since he was born." I pull out my phone and search through my camera roll until I find the video I'm looking for. I point the screen at Mike and press play. A four-month-old Levi squirms on the couch, Micah hovering over him. Levi looks up at his big brother with such love and adoration. And then Micah makes a long, loud fart sound with his mouth as Levi bursts into laughter.

"That's…" Mike sniffles and wipes a tear from his eye. "Can you send me that?"

"Absolutely."

"I hate that I missed out on all that time with them. Missed their first words, first steps, all these milestones."

"I know. But we're together now. And I have pictures and videos of a lot of that."

He nods and pulls me against him, kissing my head.

"What about Christmases and birthdays? Halloween costumes?"

"I have all of that captured."

"I want to see it all. Fuck doom-scrolling on social media, I want to go down that rabbit hole. Hear their little voices as they age. See how they grow and lose their baby fat."

"You haven't missed every milestone. Neither of them has lost a tooth yet."

He sits up, excited. "I get to play Tooth Fairy?"

I chuckle at his enthusiasm. "You can, but we have a system for that."

"We?"

"The girls and me. We have a whole set of rules for Santa, the Tooth Fairy, the Easter Bunny. Basically, any mythical creature that you want kids to believe in. Admittedly, the Santa Rules are the most elaborate, but we have some fun tricks for the other ones."

A thought hits me, and I push up, sitting taller on the cushion. "Do you think it's possible that you could have other kids out there? When I chose artificial insemination, I knew that was a possibility, that the boys could have siblings out there they might never meet."

"Does that bother you?"

"That they could have siblings? No. I mean, it makes me sad to know they could have brothers or sisters they'll never know, but I knew that going into this. Does it bother you?"

"Nah. I only donated because I was shite at dating in my twenties and figured that if I never met the right girl and couldn't give my Ma and Da the family they always wanted, well, at least someone could create a family with my donation. It was kind of a rash decision one night after I had too many pints. I never regretted it. If it carried on the bloodline then it wasn't in vain. But I did have second thoughts about the fact that me and my folks might never know for sure if there were more of the O'Connor clan running around. And sad that I might never meet them if there were."

I think through his words, in awe of the way this man has always put the needs of others first, with his parents, the crew at the station, and with us.

He looks at me, taking my hand in his. "Does that bother you? That there could be more mini-Mikes running around out there?"

"No. There could be even if we'd never met. Knowing you now doesn't change that for me. I kinda hope that someone else was able to create a family with your donation like I did, just as long as I don't have to have any more kids, because these two are more than enough for me. But it makes me happy for you that your bloodline could be carried on by others. It's funny that you *donated* because you couldn't find the right person, and I was *looking* for a donation because I couldn't find the right person either. You gave me the best gifts ever."

"Aye, I got more where that came from if you want me to give ya another gift later." He nips at my ear, teasing me, and I'm filled with gratitude that I gave this man a chance.

We spend the rest of the night scrolling through memories on my phone and laughing. One video after another and I'm pausing and stopping, interrupting as old memories resurface. And I share it all with him. Every thought. Every laugh. Every fart and poop story. It's the perfect evening; all that's missing is our little chaos monsters.

EPILOGUE

MIKE

"Fuck, I love you in green." My hand glides over the smooth skin of Lucky's ass, tracing the lacy fabric of her lingerie. I check my knots one more time to make sure they're secure. "What's your safe word, love?"

"Cabbage."

I can't help the chuckle that escapes. "Cabbage, eh?"

"Yeah. Never liked the stuff, so if I say it, you know I'm done."

I nod, impressed by her logic. "Makes sense."

Her eyes pinch shut, and I take a minute to admire my wife's curves. That's right. My wife. I am the lucky man who gets to spend the rest of his life with this perfect creature.

"On your side."

She rolls obediently wrists bound in a prayer tie overhead, body offered up like she knows exactly what she does to me. The ropes frame her perfectly, pressing her curves into something sinful, and perfect, and all fucking mine. I trace a finger up her hip, moving across the dip of her waist until I reach the basic chest harness I gave her. Fuck me, her tits look incredible like this, round and full. I lean down and caress her breast, pulling a nipple into my mouth.

She gasps and moans as she rolls onto her back, pushing her chest out in presentation to me. Knowing how far she's come since I first met her, I waste no time, licking her breasts and teasing both of her nipples.

"Mike," she breathes, already wrecked on nothing but anticipation. "Fuck."

"What do you need, wife?"

She moans as I pinch a nipple between my lips and tug.

"I need to come."

Releasing her nipple, I hover over her, silently demanding her to use her words. She knows by now that if she doesn't, I will edge her until she does.

"I want to fuck your thigh while you play with me until I come."

A slow smile pulls at my mouth as her legs part in invitation, and I seize the opportunity to push my leg between hers. "And for your second orgasm?"

"Do you need a list?" Her head pops up, a smirk on her face, half teasing, half exasperated.

"I'd love a list. A Lucky List." My tongue lightly brushes her nipple with nowhere near the amount of pressure I know she needs.

She lets out a frustrated little sound. I love this game, this back and forth we have where I push her to take control, and she teeters between total surrender and total domination.

"One thigh. Two Squirtle. Three hard and from behind. Four on my throne. And if you think you're capable of anything beyond that, surprise me."

Her shorthand makes me chuckle as I lower my head and nip at the flesh of her breast as she starts grinding on my thigh. I tug on her rope harness, moving her to where I want her on the bed and she gasps when I bite a nipple.

"Harder. Yes, fuck. I'm close."

My teeth close around her tight bud as I increase the pressure, careful not to break the skin. My wife likes it right on the edge of pain and pleasure, and the moment I give her what she's asked for, she breaks exactly the way she always does. Shuddering, shaking, breath stuttering like she's trying to hold herself together while falling beautifully.

"Let's see what kind of mess you made, wife."

"Lap it up like a good boy. I know how desperate you get for my cunt."

Fuck, I love this woman. Love the way she has come into her own, taking exactly what she wants without apology.

"Yes, ma'am." Those are the last words I utter for several minutes as I lap at her pussy like I haven't eaten it in weeks. There's no way I could go more than a day without feasting on her and she knows it.

I can tell she wants to move her hands, but she's unsure if she's allowed to or not, so they writhe above her head as her hips buck against me.

"Oh shit. Mike. Oh God."

She only says "shit" when she's about to squirt. I know this because it takes her by surprise each time despite how often I've made her do it. I rest my forearm across her hips, holding her in place as my other hand strokes her G-spot in a come-hither motion.

And I'm rewarded seconds later when she gushes for me, covering me in her cum. This is my favorite part of eating her pussy, when she comes so hard her body shakes in tiny after-shocks for several minutes while I clean her with my tongue.

Before she has a chance to recover, I drag her to the edge of the bed and flip her over, forcing her thighs open as I line myself up with her entrance. We both groan when I push inside. I move slowly at first, rubbing each golden barbell against her walls. The feel of them sinking into my wife's cunt as it greedily swallows each one has me pausing my movements to keep myself from coming.

"You're so desperate for me you're going to come soon, aren't you, husband?"

"Feckin' hell." This vixen knows what she's doing. I pinch my eyes shut, reciting football stats in my head as I continue at a glacial pace.

She wiggles her ass against me, and I slap it. "Behave," I growl.

It takes a whole minute for me to get myself under control. That's what happens when you have the most beautiful woman on the planet underneath you.

The dips in her hips are my favorite part of her, and I sink my fingers into them as I start thrusting into her with more force.

"Is"—*thrust*—"that"—*thrust*—"all"—*thrust*—"you"—*thrust*—"got?" she says each word between thrusts.

The death of me. That's what this woman is going to be.

I know my fingers are going to leave bruises on her hips, but she asked for it, and I give her what she wants. Always will.

When I feel the familiar flutter of her cunt around me, I snake an arm down to her clit and play with it until she's coming again.

"Three," I murmur near her ear. "You going to make it to four?"

She looks over her shoulder at me. "Are you?"

I pull out of her and climb onto the bed, grabbing her bound wrists to guide her onto my lap. "You can try, wife. If you come first, I get to fill this cunt full of my cum. Fill you until you leak all over me. Till you're swollen with my child."

Her eyes flash with heat. I was pleasantly surprised to discover that my wife has a breeding kink, and I have thoroughly enjoyed feeding into it. I think there's something about the role-playing, knowing that she can't actually get pregnant, that excites her.

"And if you come before me?" she asks.

"Try it and see what happens."

She sinks down onto my cock slowly, like she's savoring

the power of it, and I can't look away from the place we join. But I need to if I'm going to make her come first, so I pinch my eyes shut and resume unsexy thoughts.

"Eyes on me, husband."

I slowly drag my gaze up her body before I lock onto her eyes.

"I want your cum. Need it. Fucking fill me up. Breed me, a stór."

Not the Irish. Feckin' Christ, her perfect pronunciation is going to make me blow my load. Fuck, she's incredible.

Taking a nipple in one hand, her clit in the other, I play her like an instrument until she's clamping down on me. I don't even wait for her orgasm to finish; I flip her onto her back and hover over her, pushing in slowly.

"A ghrá mo chroí, go deo," I rasp, pistoning into her.

Needing her connection, I grip her chin and force her to lock eyes with me. "Fuck, Lucky. I can't hold it back anymore."

"Give it to me."

I let go, snapping my hips with ferocity as I succumb to my orgasm. She holds me as I groan and shudder against her. "Fuuuuck."

When I finally still, every ounce of energy drained from me, I look at her. "I'm sorry."

Her head tilts in confusion. "What? Why?"

"I didn't make it to five," I say, panting, still trying to catch my breath.

"Your fingers don't need to recharge, do they? Besides, I need you to push every last bit of your cum back inside." Challenge flashes in her eyes, and I pull out of her slowly, trying not to spill a drop. Minutes later she's screaming, coming on my fingers, and I finally collapse back onto the bed, entirely spent and thoroughly satisfied.

Her head lolls to the side, resting on my bicep as she smiles at me. "Best date ever."

I smirk. "Best honeymoon ever."

STAY IN TOUCH

Want more Lucy and Mike? Download the bonus scene here:
https://dl.bookfunnel.com/4hfhn5xuai

I hope you enjoyed this book and would consider writing a short review and posting it on Amazon, Goodreads, Bookbub, or anywhere else you share book love.

Even a single sentence review helps other readers decide to take the chance on a new-to-them author. It can make all the difference for indie authors like me.

Want to know when I have a new release or get exclusive access to my works in progress? Let's keep in touch!

Follow me on Goodreads:
https://www.goodreads.com/author/show/55362142.Mya_More

Follow me on Amazon:
amazon.com/author/myamore

Join my reader group:
https://www.facebook.com/share/g/1ZnWm8uSUT/

ACKNOWLEDGMENTS

Thank you to my boys and the endless laughter you bring me. Dingdong, yes this is your fault and I'm so grateful for that. You have no idea the joy and laughter you've brought others because of your silly peen doodles. Sweetcheeks, you have inspired characters in several of my books and you don't even know. I love you and your chaos, but please stop eating all of the popsicles. Mess, my silly little storyteller. I can't wait to read every idea that pops out of your brain and I'll happily help you edit your stories if you promise to keep inspiring mine.

Levi is a combination of my boys, but the inspiration for the name comes from a dear friend who lost her son in a tragic drowning. I may not have a huge platform, but I would be remiss if I didn't talk about this while I have your attention. According to the CDC, drowning is the number one cause of death for children 1-4 years old in the United States. It isn't talked about enough. Please educate yourself. I didn't know and now that I do, I won't shut up about it. https://www.face book.com/WaterGuardiansLevisLegacy/

Thank you Sarah. Without you all my characters would be winking idiots. People would read my books and think…"Do their eyes work normally? Who winks that much?" Seriously, I have grown so much as a writer in the past two years and you are a huge part of that. Thank you for pushing me, poking at my characters, and encouraging me to do more with this world.

And my other Sarah, because apparently I only hire Sarahs to edit my books, thank you! It is a joy working with you. Thank you for always squeezing me in. For capitalizing all the words I forget, for adding commas when I don't, and squealing in the comments. I, promise, I, will, use, commas, correctly, one, day. Did I do it?

To my alpha reader, Amanda. Thank you for always lifting me up. Besides my husband, you are the first person to read my stories. The first person to fall for my MMCs and root loudly for my FMCs. And the first person asking when you can get more chapters. The amount of joy and encouragement you bring me cannot be stated enough. I hope this book brings you joy, comfort, thigh squeezing, and a big warm hug. I also hope you don't wake up with a dick to the face.

To the real life Webster. You are so greatly missed by your humans, including those you never met. It doesn't feel like enough, but I hope your memory lives on well beyond this story. And I hope you are getting all the belly scratches, treats, and nose boops over the rainbow bridge.

Erin you are a wee bonnie lass and I love ya. Thank you for your Irish sensitivity read. Your suggestions and feedback are so appreciated. Thank you for taking the time to help me shape this story. Now start writing, you left me on a cliffy and I need to know what happens to your characters!

To my Romance Era book besties. I love you all. We need another trip. We need 100 more trips. Even though we are spread out across the country, I feel like you're right next door with every voice memo, text, and reel you send. We need some tipsy pantry calls real soon!

Thank you to all of my lovely beta readers! Amanda, Angelica, Becka, Hannah G, Jen, Rachel, and Stacey. Thank you for loving these characters. Every comment brought me life. I appreciate each and every one of you. Thank you for helping shape this story!

Rachel, thank you for letting me pick your brain about the EMS elements. I thoroughly enjoy your voice memos and filthy Friday posts! Now excuse me while I go wash my hands.

Repeating this, because I don't think I could ever sum it up any better: Being an indie author can feel isolating at times, but I am so thankful for this community of women who have helped me along the way. Berlin, LJ, Erin, Mauve, Sky, Taccara, Loren, Ruby, Jen, and Kay. From Sleep Token clips, way too many voice memos, TMI stories (there's no such thing!), multiple timezones, not entirely enough thirst traps, supportive husbands, sprints, blurb dodging, creamy peens, raccoons and possums, and all the laughs. You ladies have lifted me up, supported one another, and offered comfort and advice and I appreciate all of you. Let's conquer this romance world, one good pegging at a time!

Thank you to all my Amores! I have the most supportive street team! Thank you for loving my books and sharing them with others. Thank you for supporting each other. I couldn't do it without you all!

Hey Coach, I love you. I know you're tired. I know you're grumpy. But you do it anyway. You show up for us every day. And I love you. Aren't you glad we aren't swiping cards anymore? You are my ultimate HEA and I love you, grumpy bear.

have no clue how to pull off the effortless kind of holiday magic my late wife did. I need help.

When I walk into the local PTO meeting, I don't plan to volunteer to help my daughter's teacher. We make a deal: She'll be my Christmas coach and teach me the Santa Rules, and I'll help her build the most magical Santa Workshop.

Bella

I'm determined not to be the *hot mess* everyone thinks I am, so I volunteer to create the biggest and best Christmas event the PTO has ever seen…along with my student's hot dad.

He swears he can't fall in love again—and isn't sure his daughter is ready for him to try—but somewhere between decorating trees, making questionable Christmas cookies, and *defiling Santa's throne*, we start breaking more than just **The Santa Rules**.

The Lucky List

A rom com with a tired single mom, 2 active little boys, an Irish firefighter, and a whole lot of luck.

Sometimes, luck isn't found—it finds you.

Lucy

I'm a single mom to two boys, fiercely independent, and painfully familiar with things going wrong. Luck has never been on my side, so I've learned to rely on myself—and expect nothing from anyone else.

Then a series of embarrassingly unlucky run-ins throws me right into the path of Chestnut Mountain's ridiculously hot Irish firefighter. When my resolve finally cracks, I agree to one reckless deal: friends with benefits—and a chance to put myself first for once.

Mike

I don't believe in coincidences. Especially not when the woman I can't stop thinking about keeps crashing into my life. She swears she's unlucky, but I see a woman who's strong, stubborn, and already has everything that matters… including two boys who steal my heart.

What starts as casual quickly turns into something deeper. I fall for all of them, hard. But the closer we get, the more she pushes me away, determined to keep it casual. She doesn't trust luck—or love.

Too bad I'm Irish, relentless, and very good at tempting fate. This St. Patrick's Day, I'm not leaving things to chance—I'm finishing **The Lucky List**.

The Summer Plans

Sometimes love deserves a second chance.

Summer

All I wanted was a quiet summer. When my best friend offers me a free stay at her beach house in exchange for helping her sell it, it feels like the reset my three kids and I desperately need.

What I don't need? Her brother showing up.

RJ was my first kiss. My almost-forever. The one man I never quite recovered from. Now he's back, looking just as devastating as he did the day he broke my heart. I came here for peace—not for unfinished business.

RJ

As the oldest rookie at the Chestnut Mountain Fire Department and a single dad, I'm focused on proving myself and building something steady for my daughter.

Then I walk into that beach house and find Summer. Fate might have separated us once, but it just handed me another chance. And this time, I'm not letting her slip away.

She may think this is just a temporary escape—but I have every intention of rewriting **The Summer Plans**.

The Haunting Plot

Coming fall 2026

ALSO BY MYA MORE

The Broken Series

All Her Broken Pieces

Bridget and Ethan's story. An age gap (she's older), forced proximity, black cat/golden retriever spicy romance.

Falling in love was never on Bridget's to-do list. Having sworn off relationships, she's only interested in temporary flings to avoid getting hurt again. Ethan is a hopeless romantic who loves deeply and wears his heart on his sleeve. When their one-night stand leaves him wanting more, Ethan is determined to get Bridget to take a chance on him. After an unexpected surgery forces her to rely on him, he becomes part of her carefully guarded world. As Ethan pieces together Bridget's shattered trust, she must decide if she's ready to risk everything and let herself fall in love. Can he mend all her broken pieces and show her that love is worth it?

All Our Broken Vows

Becka, Robert, and Bennett's story. An MMF, bi-awakening romance with found family, a single dad, and friends that become so much more.

From the first moment I saw my wife, I vowed to do anything to make her happy. Maybe it's the rule-abiding teacher in me, but I love my wife, and I take my vows seriously.

Lately, though, it feels like something is missing in our marriage. What started as a rut quickly escalates into a night of sexual exploration at Club Pulse.

And when a friend of ours needs a place to stay, I can't say no. Nor can I stop the fantasies in my head, envisioning a life with the three of us together.

Will the world embrace our love? Can our families accept our polyamorous relationship? When our relationship looks nothing like we once envisioned, can I come to terms with all our broken vows?

All His Broken Rules

Maybe some rules are meant to be broken.

John

As a dom at club Pulse, I know rules are important to keep a submissive safe. As a professor at Faith Union College, I know rules keep order in my classroom.

I don't sleep with submissives and I don't get involved with students.

But all my rules go out the window when I see my new sub walk into my classroom. Everyone has secrets, including me, but mine are the only thing keeping me from truly claiming her as my own.

Emma

Being around men is hard for me given my past, but when a friend recommends someone who can help with my aversion to touch, I don't expect my new dom to be so good at it.

I especially don't expect to fall for him so completely.

Even though he always wears a mask, I see who he is at his core. With so many obstacles standing in our way, can I convince him that I'm more important than all his broken rules?

All Their Broken Promises

Coming 2026

The Chestnut Mountain Series

The Santa Rules

Sometimes, the best gift isn't under the tree, it's finding someone who makes you believe again.

Hardy

Last Christmas, I messed up so badly my daughter asked Santa to be her new dad. This year, I'm determined to make it right—except I